TAMUNA NADIRADZE
Cape Cod
July 3, 2005 year.

COOL
REPENTANCE

Antonia
FRASER

CRIME LINE ™

BANTAM BOOKS
New York · Toronto · London · Sydney · Auckland

*This edition contains the complete text
of the original hardcover edition.*
NOT ONE WORD HAS BEEN OMITTED.

COOL REPENTANCE

A BANTAM CRIME LINE BOOK / PUBLISHED BY ARRANGEMENT WITH
W. W. NORTON & COMPANY, INC.

PRINTING HISTORY

W. W. Norton edition published 1985

Bantam edition / May 1991

All rights reserved.

*CRIME LINE and the portrayal of a boxed "cl"
are trademarks of Bantam Books, a division of
Bantam Doubleday Dell Publishing Group, Inc.*

Copyright © 1982 by Antonia Fraser.

Cover art copyright © 1991 by Tom Hallman.

Library of Congress Catalog Number: 82-8300.

ISBN 0-553-28072-4

PUBLISHED SIMULTANEOUSLY IN THE UNITED STATES AND CANADA

Bantam Books are published by Bantam Books, a division of Bantam Doubleday Dell Publishing
Group, Inc. Its trademark, consisting of the words "Bantam Books" and the portrayal of a
rooster, is Registered in U.S. Patent and Trademark Office and in other countries. Marca
Registrada. Bantam Books, 666 Fifth Avenue, New York, New York 10103.

PRINTED IN THE UNITED STATES OF AMERICA

RAD   0 9 8 7 6 5 4 3 2 1

For Fred and Simone
and Laverstock where
Jemima Shore was born

'And with the morning cool repentance came.'

SIR WALTER SCOTT

CONTENTS

ONE

Spring Flowers

'Glad to be back?'

The questioner sounded urgent but the woman putting spring flowers carefully into a low vase merely smiled in reply, said nothing. The deep window to her left was open and from time to time the wind stirred her hair gently as she worked — hair the same colour as the daffodils at her feet. The flowers too stirred in their glass container, when the breeze touched them. The newspaper on the floor held white narcissi with bright red perianths, as well as trumpet-shaped daffodils, whose colour ranged from pale yellow to ochre, and other delicate flowers of the spring; sometimes the newspaper rustled. Everything was bright. Nothing was still.

The curtains of the drawing-room at Lark Manor also appeared to have been chosen with spring in mind. Hanging thickly to the floor, lined and interlined, they were made of yellow and white chintz, while twin gold mirrors, with brackets containing fresh white candles on either side, further reflected the lightness of the sunshine outside. The carpet, patterned and Victorian-looking, was grass green: it matched the colour of the grass exactly, just as the daffodils, blowing and rippling on either side of the drive to the hills beyond, were perfectly co-ordinated with the yellow and white chintz. Where the hills drew back like curtains to reveal a small but distinct patch of sea, that colour was pale azure. But the sea was not forgotten in the Lark Manor drawing-room: small bright-blue cushions, piped in white, reposed on the big yellow sofas by the fireplace, reminding you pleasantly but inexorably of its part in the view.

'Glad to be back?' the person repeated. 'You must be glad to be back.'

Christabel Cartwright gave another smile, not quite as marked as the first, and lifted her eyebrows. She picked up the garden scissors and shortened the stem of a jonquil. There were spring posies and pots of clear blue hyacinths everywhere in the large drawing-room. The flowers which Christabel was arranging stood on a highly polished Sheraton table and would form a centrepiece of the room when they were finished.

'Those are pretty, aren't they? A new variety. Or new to Lark. You were surprised to find them out there by the woods when you went picking, weren't you?'

Christabel Cartwright, a jonquil in her hand, hesitated and then put it down. She continued to inspect the glass vase with concentration.

'Perhaps you wouldn't have planted them? Or if you had planted them, perhaps you wouldn't have planted them just there. By the wood, I mean.'

'I think they're beautiful,' Christabel said at last. Her tone was surprisingly deep for a woman, without being at all husky; it had a charming melodious timbre. 'I noticed them at once.'

'It's just the sort of thing you do notice, isn't it? Flowers, and dogs.' The voice sounded increasingly pressing about it all. 'Didn't you go to the corner of the wood, where they buried Mango, at once? Immediately, I mean. Straightaway? Dreadful smelly old dog.' The person questioning Christabel gave a sudden violent shudder of disgust and the person's tone grew rougher. 'I wasn't a bit sorry at what happened to him.' Perhaps there were tears, one tear, in Christabel's eyes. The person continued in a more satisfied calmer tone: 'Didn't you notice that the trug was waiting for you, and the scissors, your special scissors, all bright and clean?'

Christabel, who had picked up the scissors again, put them down. She did so fastidiously. But then all her movements tended to be precise, as well as graceful. With the modulated beauty of her voice, and her careful management of all gestures, however small, it was easy to believe that she was — or had once been — a famous actress. The tear — if indeed it had been a tear — had vanished.

'What was the first thing you did when you came back?' went on the voice, as though Christabel had given it some sort of answer. 'Do you remember? Can you think back? Oh, do try.' There was a pause.

Christabel looked at the floor. The pile of flowers, with their long thick pale-green stems ranged on the newspaper, had diminished. Out of the glass vase their white and yellow heads were now springing airily like the quills of an ornamental hedgehog. Christabel bent her soft golden head which gave the impression of a kind of halo; in her bright-blue clothes, contrasting with the grass-green carpet, with the white flowers in her hand, she might have been part of an Annunciation scene by Rossetti. Then she picked up the corner of her blue skirt and rubbed the half-moon table on which the vase stood; despite all the care taken, the paper laid down, a drop of water had fallen on the polished wood. Christabel eliminated it.

'Did you take a photograph of Lark with you when you went, by the way? Do cast your mind back. You're getting so forgetful these days. I don't want to sound horrible, but perhaps it's your age, your time of life. You would have taken a special one, your favourite angle perhaps, the corner of the wood, Mango's grave, taken it with your own camera. No, wait.'

There was a sharp intake of breath and another laugh. But the roughness had also come back into the voice: the person talking to Christabel looked heated, either in anger or triumph.

'No, wait, it wasn't Mango's grave then, was it? You would hardly have known that corner of the wood was going to be Mango's grave. Seeing as that awful old Mango was still alive when you left him, left him to die. Still, you always did love that corner . . .' The voice trailed away and there was quite a long pause.

'Otherwise,' it resumed briskly, 'there were always the photographs in the press. Newspaper photographs. There were plenty of those.'

Christabel was picking up the last flower from the newspaper. It was a narcissus. She touched her cheek with the fluttery white petal and smelt it. Then she inserted the narcissus deftly into the vase like a bullfighter inserting a banderilla. She stepped back and gazed at her work.

'No one can arrange flowers like you,' said the person thickly: the voice now sounded admiring, almost gloating. 'I've always said that. It's been my firm contention all along.' There was another long pause.

'What a pity it is, a great pity, that you have to die.'

For the first time in the conversation — if such it could be called — Christabel Cartwright gazed directly at her interlocutor. Her eyes were enormous, blue like the distant sea, just a little less vivid than the cushions on the sofas. Round her eyes a network of tiny but distinctly visible lines radiated outwards so regularly that they might have been drawn on to her face; the effect was not unbecoming. Her strongest feature, an indisputably Roman nose, scarcely noticed beneath the radiance of the big eyes.

Otherwise there were no hard lines or planes on her face; everything was soft, some of it a little too soft perhaps — her small chin was almost lost in the folds of the blue and white chiffon scarf which ruffled at her neck. Together the frills and the daffodil hair, waving lightly back from her forehead, gave a slightly eighteenth-century effect: the powdered head of a Gainsborough portrait perhaps. The light powder and delicate patches of pink on her cheeks contributed to this illusion.

Christabel Cartwright, in the sunlight of the Lark Manor drawing-room, no longer looked young: but she did still look oddly girlish. With her pink and white complexion and the pronounced lines on forehead and chin as well as round her eyes, she gave the impression of a much younger woman made up to look old.

Even her figure — although she was quite plump in her soft blue cashmere jersey and skirt — was not exactly middle-aged. For her legs remained excellent, really quite astonishingly pretty legs, and in their patterned navy-blue stockings, they commanded attention from the slight heaviness of the hips and bosom which the years had brought.

'No, really,' the voice went on, 'you didn't expect to get away with it, did you? Surely not that. Just to say you were sorry, just to *repent*.' The voice put a very nasty emphasis on the word repent as if describing a most unpleasant activity. 'Was it going to be like the song then, *his* song, cool, oh so coo-ool repentance?' The person picked up a long-stemmed flower and pretended to use it as a microphone: then the voice crooned the last four words slowly, mockingly, gloatingly. 'Was that what you thought — that you would come back, come back here to beautiful Lark, and *get away with it*, did you expect that? I can hardly believe it, even of you . . .

'So you see, one of these days I shall really have to kill you. Just to teach you a lesson. A lesson you'll never forget: that you can't just get away with things. I shall probably kill you before the spring flowers are over. Then we needn't have all those ghastly wreaths at the funeral. Just cut flowers only. Just what you would have wanted.'

Christabel continued to stare with her lovely eyes wide

open; they were pools of pure colour: there was no expression in them at all.

'We need some more flowers, don't we — for the study?' Christabel said at length in her low musical voice; she sounded perfectly normal. 'I should have thought of it before. I'll go out and pick some more. There's plenty of time before lunch.'

She picked up the tray and walked in her careful graceful way towards the french windows. At the steps she paused and said with the air of one delivering lines at the end of an act: 'Yes, darling, in answer to your original question, I am glad to be back. Of course I'm glad to be back. I've come back to look after everybody. Everybody — including you.'

Then she walked away into the garden.

The person who had been questioning Christabel Cartwright decided to leave her alone for the time being. Let her vanish alone into the greenness, through the trees, before reappearing on the verge of the drive where the daffodils grew. The person realized that Christabel had forgotten her scissors. It was not too late to do something about that. The person decided to think hard about the scissors and what they might do to Christabel when she came back to fetch them.

TWO

Back to Normal

The enormous bedroom upstairs was still quite dark, although everywhere in the garden at Lark Manor the sunlight was seeking out the grass beneath the tall trees.

Regina Cartwright, guiding her white horse down the path from the stables to the drive, careful of the surrounding flowers, could see that the bedroom curtains were still drawn. She patted the horse's neck, pulled his head up where he had decided to chomp the grass, and said, rather self-consciously: 'You see, Lancelot, everything's back to normal.'

The remark was caught by her sister Blanche, emerging or rather slouching out of the open french windows of the kitchen. Blanche was dressed in tight white cotton trousers and a sun-top. She wore one sandal, and held the other, which seemed to be broken, in her hand.

'Really, Rina, you are a baby. Still talking to that horse at your age. And does he answer back, then?'

'I may be a year younger than you,' retorted Regina, 'but I used to be in the same form at school, don't forget, so who was the baby then? And by the way Blanche you're far too fat for that sun-top,' she went on more automatically than scornfully. Then her voice changed. 'Those are my trousers, my white trousers, give them back you thieving little bitch, you've swiped them.'

Blanche starting to scream back in her turn at one and the same time turned and fled in the direction of the kitchen windows. Regina on Lancelot thundered after her, now careless of the paths. The shrubs shivered, and shed flowers as the big white horse passed. A host of fallen red camellias lay to mark his tracks.

Even when she reached the kitchen where Blanche had taken refuge, Regina did not dismount from Lancelot but simply urged the horse in through the french windows. Uneasily he stepped on to the cork floor, placing his hooves carefully on the surface as if aware of the heinous nature of the gesture. The animal's enormous shoulders filled the opening making the large airy room, with all its polished wood surfaces, seem quite dark.

It was at this moment that Julian Cartwright, yawning slightly, entered the kitchen by its inner louvred swing doors. He wore a navy-blue silk dressing-gown, piped in white, over blue pyjamas. His dressing-gown was firmly belted in the centre. His dark hair — the same thick dark straight hair which Regina had inherited, but flecked with grey — was neatly combed and his feet shod in dark-red leather slippers. He looked gentlemanly and rather relaxed, despite the early hour, and gave the impression that he would probably always bear himself with similar distinction, whatever the hour of the day.

His words, however, were not relaxed.

'Oh really girls, really Rina, really Blanche, haven't you any consideration at all? You know how Mummy likes to sleep on in the mornings. That noise would wake them in the church at Larminster.'

He did not seem to have noticed the presence of the horse.

'They're awake in the church at Larminster,' pointed out Blanche from her position of advantage behind the polished wood kitchen bar; her tone was extremely reasonable. 'It's Easter Sunday morning. Are you and Mummy going to church?'

'Don't be so silly, Blanche,' Julian Cartwright sounded even more irritated, although whether at the idea of going to church himself or at the idea of anyone going at all, was not quite clear.

'I expect Daddy meant: wake the *dead* at Larminster Church,' suggested Regina from her station on Lancelot at the window. 'Wake Grannie Cartwright and old Mr Nixon and Cynthia Meadows's little sister — that's all the most recently dead we know, and the ancient dead are probably more difficult to rouse. But there could be others from the village —'

'Regina!' Julian Cartwright suddenly shouted in a very loud voice indeed. 'Get that horse out of the kitchen!'

Regina hastily backed Lancelot out of the french windows; he trotted off in the direction of the drive. She shouted something over her shoulder which sounded like 'my trousers', but could not be heard clearly.

It was a few minutes later that Christabel Cartwright appeared at the entrance to the kitchen, swinging the doors open with both hands so that she stood for a moment as if framed. She wore silver mules edged with swansdown and a thin wool kaftan of a very pale blue, embroidered in white. Her hair, which stood up becomingly round her head, looked as if it might have been blown in the wind, rather than combed. She wore no make-up at all and her face had a slight shine on it. Without concealment of powder, she looked very beautiful, if haggard, and slightly dazed.

Blanche's plump face, with its lack of contours, and mass of fine hair surrounding it, as well as its too-strong nose, showed what Christabel had perhaps looked like long ago —

but Christabel must always have had beauty. Blanche at the present time had none.

'What a frightful row!' Christabel began. 'You woke me up.'

'It was all Rina's fault,' said Blanche in a voice which suggested sobs might be on the way if its owner were harshly treated.

'No, not you darling, though by the way Blanche, it's far too cold for those kind of clothes today. It's only April, you know. As for that top — well, we'll talk about that later. No, Daddy woke me up. Yes you did, darling. I was having a beautiful sleep at the time. I know I was. I didn't even need to take a second pill. Seriously, I thought the bull had escaped from the top field.' Christabel, who had sounded rather faint when she first spoke, was now coming back quite strongly. She went on: 'Well, as I am awake, shall we all have breakfast together? Blanche darling? Julian?'

Her eyes fell on a breakfast tray already laid on the bar. The service was of bone china, ornamented by sprigs of lily of the valley, with the exception of the coffee pot, which had a dark-green and white ivy pattern. The voile tray-cloth and single napkin were embroidered with lilies of the valley.

'Whatever happened to the coffee pot belonging to this set?' Christabel demanded quite sharply. There was a silence.

'It got broken,' said Blanche. 'I think Mrs Blagge broke it.'

'Then I think I'll have the ivy-leaf set for the time being,' Christabel broke off and gave a little laugh. 'Sorry, darling — I'm being quite ridiculous. I know I am. But you know how I feel about things that don't match. I just can't help it.'

Julian put his arm round his wife's shoulders and kissed her cheek.

'Goodness, you do look pretty this morning,' he said. 'Doesn't she, Blanche? Eighteen, going on nineteen. Blanche's age exactly. And Blanche is looking pretty good this morning too.'

'She isn't eighteen though', said Blanche in a sulky voice.

'She's forty-seven. At least that's what it says in *Who's Who in the Theatre* and Ketty says actresses always lie about their age. You're only forty-three, Daddy. You're nearer to eighteen than Mummy is.'

'If you're going to be in that kind of mood, I shall feel nearer a hundred,' said Julian. 'Cut it out, Blanche, will you.'

'I really am forty-seven, darling.' In contrast to Julian, Christabel spoke in a pleasant rather amused voice. 'Exactly four years and five days older than Daddy, if you want absolute accuracy.'

'Look darling,' Julian gave Christabel another hug, 'don't worry about the lily-of-the-valley coffee pot. I'll order another one from Goode's or wherever it came from. I should have thought about it before.'

'We did think about it!' exclaimed Blanche, sulkiness suddenly abandoned. 'Ketty and I thought about it. We discussed it for hours. Whether you would want your own tray without the proper coffee pot or another set, all matching, and Ketty thought —'

'A silver coffee pot might have been the answer.' But Christabel's attention had manifestly wandered. 'Where *is* Ketty?' she enquired, that sharper note returning to her voice. 'Isn't she supposed to look after breakfast on Sunday mornings when the Blagges are off? What's wrong with her?'

'Easter Sunday. That's what's wrong with her. Ketty's at her own church in Larminster praying for us all. Especially for *you*, Mummy. She says God never loses sight of any one of us sinners, just like the newspapers. Those were her exact words. She's terribly religious these days; I think it's something to do with the new Pope and the fact he was once an actor. She made something called a novena for you, Mummy. To be forgiven.'

'Are we or are we not going to have breakfast?' Julian Cartwright took the clean folded white handkerchief out of the breast pocket of his dressing-gown and blew his nose loudly.

'And if so, is there the faintest chance of a man having a cup of coffee and perhaps even some decent bacon and eggs before it's time for lunch? Are you, Blanche, going to make it, or am I?'

'I'll make it, darling,' cried Christabel, smoothing her hair back with one long-fingered hand. The nails were long, too, and unpainted, but her hands in general, unlike her face, were the hands of a middle-aged woman. 'Besides, Blanche is going to change into something warmer and more suitable. Yes you are, poppet, this minute and no argument.'

Christabel was already opening the fridge and getting out eggs and limp rashers of raw bacon. She certainly gave the air of knowing where everything was. Even the three attempts she made to find the jar of coffee were done so purposefully that she might have been performing some agreed ritual of opening and shutting cupboard doors.

'This reminds me of Sunday mornings in London,' she said over her shoulder to Julian. 'We just need some Mozart.' Her voice was tender. 'When I was in that long season at the Gray Theatre. We never used to come down to Lark on Sundays then; too exhausting. The girls had to go to school on Monday morning. Ketty went to church: my contribution to church-going was playing the Coronation Mass, and cooking us brunch. Do you remember?'

'I rather think that I used to cook it more often than not.' But Julian's voice too was tender. 'You used to sleep so late, the girls and I would have starved if we had waited for you to put one dainty toe out of bed — and shall I put some Mozart on for you now? Have it wafted in from the drawing-room?'

Christabel set down the frying-pan and faced him: in her high-heeled mules she still looked up at him.

'Happy?' she asked in her low musical voice. 'Happy now?' Her wide blue unblinking eyes met his; he had the illusion that there was moisture in them or perhaps it was in his own.

He could smell the strong lily-of-the-valley scent she always used.

'There's no one like you, Christabel.' His voice, unlike hers, was husky. 'You know that.' With one hand Julian grasped the back of his wife's head and pressed his lips hard to hers. His other hand went down towards her breast beneath its thin wool covering.

Christabel stayed quite still for an instant without responding or resisting. Then she gave a minute but quite unmistakable shudder of disgust.

'I'm sorry,' she said very low. This time there were definitely tears. Their eyes met again. They were both breathing quite heavily.

'Back to normal then,' Julian continued to hold her by her head. After a moment Christabel kissed him on the cheek.

'Hello, young lovers!' said a voice from the french windows. 'Happy Easter anyway to the two of you — but you look happy enough already. I've brought some eggs for the girls by the way — we've been having an Easter egg hunt here for the last few years, Christabel, and I thought you wouldn't mind if we continued the tradition.' An extremely tall man, at least six foot five or six, stood there, bending his head much as the horse had done.

'Gregory!' exclaimed Christabel, patting her hair. 'What an unearthly hour to come calling.' The gesture was not coquettish; and she made no attempt to sound pleased. 'And aren't the girls getting a little old for Easter eggs?' she added.

'Unearthly? I've just dropped Mrs Blagge back at the cottage after Mass. Miss Kettering drove herself but refused to drop Mrs B., so I suppose they've had one of their religious rows about the new doctrines again. Now to the Easter egg hunt, and then I'll be away back to the woods — no one is too old for Easter eggs by the way, not me, not Julian, not even you, Christabel.'

Christabel raised her eyebrows and smiled; she resumed her attention to the frying-pan.

'Look, old man, why don't you stay to lunch?' said Julian after a pause. 'After the hunt. You'd be a great help to us, as a matter of fact. You see we've got some people from television coming down; strange as it may seem, they're coming all this way for lunch. And frankly we're dreading it. But if you were here, with all your experience of television —'

'Yes, why don't you, Gregory darling?' added Christabel sweetly from the stove. 'Quite apart from television, you're so good at talking to everyone about everything, and finding out things —'

Gregory Rowan sounded, for the first time since his arrival, uncertain. 'I thought you'd said goodbye to all that kind of thing for good, Christabel. Or is it a retrospective? "Christabel Herrick Remembers?" "My Twenty Years a Star?" "No Regrets Herrick?" Something along those lines perhaps?'

'Don't be ridiculous, Gregory.' This time Julian was definitely cross. 'This is nothing to do with Christabel. It's the Larminster Festival. Surely I don't need to remind you of the existence of the Larminster Festival?'

'Hardly. Yes, thank you, Christabel, I will have an egg. No toast. Yes, I know I should look after myself more and I'm too thin. Both sides please.'

'I know your tastes, darling.'

'Hardly can I forget it,' continued Gregory, easing himself down on to the polished bench, with its bright check cushions, by the kitchen table. 'It's rapidly turning into the Gregory Rowan Festival, I fear. Since that touring company is bringing down one of my plays — their idea, nothing to do with me. I would have so much preferred to write a moving piece specially for the Festival about the night King Charles II spent at Larminster escaping after Worcester. Good rousing local stuff: the village inn, the village maiden, lots of them, a rib-tickling mistress of the tavern, a Mistress Quickly part — would have been a good part for you there, Christabel, if you're really making a come-back — exciting new departure style —'

'The Larminster Festival,' said Julian, pointedly interrupting, 'has been chosen by some television company —'

'Megalith,' put in Christabel. 'Cy Fredericks runs it. That's the point. He's a darling. Or rather, he used to be a darling. That sort of thing doesn't change.'

'Larminster has been chosen to feature in a coming series about British arts festivals. From the highest to the lowest.' Julian smiled, more at ease. 'I imagine Larminster comes somewhere near the bottom of the latter category. If not *the* bottom. The presenter, or whatever you call it, is that woman with reddish hair everybody goes on about for being so beautiful and so brilliant, what is she called? She generally concentrates on social causes like housing and unmarried mothers and that sort of thing. She did that huge series last year called "The Poor and their Place". The arts, we gather, are a new line. What *is* she called, darling?'

But it was Gregory Rowan who supplied the name.

'Jemima Shore,' he said in a thoroughly disconcerted voice. 'Jemima Shore Investigator, as she is laughingly known. General busybody might be a better name. You have to be referring to Jemima Shore. Is *she* coming here? To the Larminster Festival?'

'*She* is coming to Lark Manor,' responded Christabel, placing a perfectly fried egg in a ramekin in front of Gregory; she gave the impression of performing the action in front of a larger audience. 'There you are, just as you like it. Eat up. Never say I don't look after you, darling.'

THREE

Sea-Shells

On the way to Sunday lunch at Lark Manor, Jemima Shore took a détour which brought her down to the sea. She took along her assistant, the lovely Cherry; Flowering Cherry as she was known at Megalithic House. The famous curves which were the toast of that establishment were on this occasion delineated by a tightly belted mackintosh; it covered Cherry's traditional outfit of white silk pearl-buttoned blouse, buttons hardly adequate to the task imposed upon them, and short tight skirt (Cherry was one of those girls who never noticed the temporary disappearances of the mini-skirt from the ranks of high fashion).

Cherry, who both admired and loved Jemima Shore with all the enthusiasm of her passionate nature, nevertheless felt able to disapprove her inordinate taste for the sea without disloyalty.

'At least she can't plunge in, this time,' thought Cherry, huddling her shoulders as she stood among the pebbles; she looked like a plump little bird, fluffing out its feathers.

Jemima Shore, immaculate as usual in a red suede jacket and dark-blue trousers with long boots — 'That jacket must have cost a *fortune*,' thought Cherry reverently — stood at the edge of the water watching it hiss towards her feet. She looked, Cherry reflected with less reverence, as though she expected a message from Megalith Television to arrive in a bottle.

But when the message came, it was not from Megalith Television and it was not in a bottle. Jemima and Cherry appeared to be alone on the sea-shore. The stretch of shingly beach was not in itself very extensive: the centre of it was a river — the river Lar no doubt, for according to the one signpost Jemima had suddenly spotted on their route to the manor, they had passed through Larmouth. The river was surrounded by groups of trees on either side of its banks where it flowed onto the beach, making a shallow course among the pebbles. The village itself appeared to consist of one pub called The King's Escape (jolly picture of a black-moustached Charles II swinging in the breeze above, empty plastic tables outside), a telephone kiosk and a row of cottages. But the beach was quite hidden from the view of the houses by a turn of the cliff; this made it an unexpectedly secluded and charming place.

Jemima's fast Mercedes sports car, a recent acquisition, was parked on the crunchy pebbles where the grassland gave way to the sea-scape beneath the lee of the cliffs. It was a new crunch which attracted Cherry's attention, although Jemima — 'mooning as though she'd never seen the sea before' in Cherry's words — did not turn her head.

The crunch was caused by a very large, not particularly well-kept, estate car; it was black and with its long body bore a certain resemblance to a hearse. The man who got out of it was however so long in himself that Cherry got the feeling that he might have needed the hearse to house his legs. Like Jemima, he wore very tight trousers, although his — pale cords — were as worn as hers were pristine. Standing together by the sea-shore, with their height and slimness, they resembled two birds, two herons perhaps, visiting the sea.

Cherry was one who, however preoccupied, never failed to assess a male face; she had rather liked the look of this one as he passed. The worn countenance in particular appealed. Cherry was, as she put it, currently into older and worn men (it was fortunate too for her enthusiasm that the two categories so often coincided). Cherry was a great watcher of late-night thirties movies on television, a way of life which had probably started the craze. Of this particular worn face, she had noted as he passed, with satisfaction: 'Like Bogart. On stilts.'

Cherry, watching them at a distance, thought sentimentally that they made a nice couple — 'Both so tall. Though Jem always seems to fancy more the short and powerful type. Is he some dishy country squire, I wonder? Would Jem like that — the lady of the manor? Probably not. Never mind Jemima. Would I like it?' Thus Cherry's mind made its accustomed moves towards local romance and its fulfilment, particularly as she had lately decided that a Substantial Older Man (face, but not bank account, well worn) was the kind of interesting new development her life-style needed.

The actual words which were being exchanged while Cherry indulged in these agreeable reveries were rather less romantic.

Jemima Shore had not thought that Gregory Rowan looked in the slightest bit like Humphrey Bogart, although she did have time to notice in a rather more oblique fashion than Cherry that he was quite attractive. And then something happened immediately which made her decide that Gregory Rowan was quite one of the most aggressive over-bearing — and thus unattractive — men she had encountered in recent years.

Gregory Rowan began bluntly enough:

'I hardly think the Larminster Festival is in need of your kind of publicity, Miss Shore,' he said, dragging quite violently on his cigarette as though it was in some danger of extinction.

'And what might my kind of publicity be?' enquired Jemima in her coldest voice, the one she used to freeze unruly — or socially undesirable — interviewees, tycoons wrecking the environment or bland cabinet ministers determined to be jocular rather than truthful.

But Gregory found himself well able to answer the question. To Jemima's considerable surprise she found herself being described as a cultural busybody, a parasite on the body of the arts, and a few other choice terms of abuse — all whilst standing on a cool sea-shore, with the wind whipping her fair hair in her eyes, but hardly disturbing Gregory's own, which was so bushy as to be apparently impregnable to the wind's attacks.

'Why don't you just chuck this programme, Miss Shore? Go away? Go back to London where you belong, and sort out a whole new generation of unmarried mothers who weren't old enough to watch your programme on "The Pill — For and Against" —'

'I'm glad at least you're a fan of my work,' interposed Jemima sweetly.

'Fan! You may take this as you wish, but it's the sort of programme you make, the sort of woman you are — oh, all right, before you speak, *person* if you like — which drove me away from jolly old London to live in the woods of Lark! "Gregory Rowan, the Happy Hermit." A good television title? I read your mind. But that is one title you will never see flashing up on your screen. Which is just one reason, having made my choice, why I don't want my retreat polluted by the mating cries of television.'

'Aren't you taking all this rather too personally, Mr Rowan? After all —' This time Jemima was valiantly maintaining her sweetness of manner, as much to annoy as to placate, when suddenly a swoosh of icy water covered her boot and caused her to jump sharply backwards. To her surprise, Gregory Rowan paid no attention whatsoever, either to her jump or to the ingression of the sea. The swirling wave covered his feet in their gym shoes, sought out his ankles, and he did not even move.

Jemima Shore, retreating, continued her sentence, trying to match his own composure. The tide was coming in quite fast, and even Jemima, dedicated bather in a more salubrious climate, did not propose to be involuntarily immersed in the English seas in April.

'After all, Megalith Television is not trying to mate with you, Mr Rowan, merely cover the Larminster Festival as part of a nation-wide series — not at all the same thing —'as for your dislike of London —' The waters were softly receding but Jemima kept a watchful eye for the next insurgence —'it doesn't seem to extend to the West End theatre, I notice? Or to the production of your plays in London television studios? So that while *you* expect to be sacrosanct, West End money —'

Whatever Gregory Rowan would have replied to that was swallowed up by Jemima's hasty and crunchy retreat up the shore at the next wave.

Gregory Rowan watched her. Once again he made no move either to retreat himself or assist her on the pebbles. He merely smiled. His smile gave an unexpectedly pleasant cast to his countenance — that countenance Cherry had aptly characterized as 'worn' — but his words were if anything even more ungracious.

'I suppose you expect me to cry out penitently *touché* and fall at your feet in worship? You've got me quite wrong. It's not London productions of my plays I object to, the more the merrier so far as I'm concerned. Hello, Shaftesbury Avenue, hail to the National! I'll even consider something warm, human and musical at the RSC. Failing that, a permanent rotating series of my plays at the Round House, or if Chalk Farm sounds too pastoral, the Royal Court. And all that goes for television too. How is Megalith's drama by the way?'

'Exquisite,' Jemima put in swiftly. Gregory proceeded as if she had not spoken.

'No, its Larminster I want to preserve from your ghastly grip. Larminster and its inhabitants.'

'Principally yourself?'

Gregory looked at her as if measuring her. His gaze, if speculative, remained cold. Whatever he was measuring her for, was not she felt, likely to appeal.

'Oddly enough, not,' he said after a while. 'As you've pointed out, I at least have considerable experience of television. And,' he paused, 'I've nothing to hide. But have you thought of the effects a television programme, the sheer making of a television programme, has on ordinary people?'

He lit another cigarette. The water was swirling round his shoes again; Jemima remained out of danger.

'People who do have something to hide? Bruised people? Vulnerable people? There are such people in the world, Miss Shore, even if you, with a toss of your golden head, have no cognizance of them. Let me come to the point. Hasn't Christabel suffered enough from you people? Haven't we all suffered enough on her behalf and through her? Her husband? Her children? Everyone who is or was close to her, some of them very humble people by your standards, Miss Shore, but still people by mine. Vulnerable, bruised people, people who have — forgive my old-fashioned language, so unlike the language no doubt to which you're used — people who have repented what they did. What might television do to them? You might even try thinking sometimes of the meek, Miss Shore — after all it's not Megalith Television that's going to inherit the earth.'

Jemima wondered whether there was any point in reminding this odious man that her name in television as Jemima Shore Investigator had been made by calling attention exactly to the meek — the inarticulate, the oppressed and the helpless. The arrival of Cherry, brightly extending one plump little paw on which lay a small pinkish cockleshell, decided her against it.

'Look, Jem, for you,' she cried. 'For your shell bathroom in London. To join the world-wide collection.' Cherry, goggling huge eyes at Gregory Rowan, was clearly demanding an introduction. Jemima, thinking that Flowering Cherry was welcome to the disagreeable Gregory Rowan, duly made it.

'Jemima brings back sea-shells from all round the world,' Cherry confided. 'And I help her.' Cherry (one of the stauncher characters Jemima knew) was one of those people who managed to look nubile and in need of protection, even in a mackintosh. Possibly for this reason, Gregory Rowan addressed her in quite a different tone, both lighter and warmer.

'You sell sea-shells to Jemima Shore. Hence the name. It's an alias, I suppose. Foolishly, I had always supposed she was born with it. However I'm not sure these particular Larmouth shells are going to qualify. You see, my dear young lady, I've been trying to persuade your boss to cancel her programme. Leave Larminster and its Festival to its own devices.'

Cherry looked quite astonished: she could no more envisage cancelling a scheduled programme without reason than she could envisage anyone not actually pining for that programme to happen, not jumping at the chance to be featured in it.

Gregory Rowan said in his newly pleasant voice: 'Amazed, are you? I see you are. Your eyes remind me of the dog in the fairy story, eyes as big as saucers. Clearly *you* have nothing to hide. Get your boss to explain that remark by the way.'

He swung round. 'Look, there it is. There they both are, as a matter of fact. Have you got good eyesight?'

He was addressing Cherry again but it was Jemima who replied in her cool voice: 'I can see most things pretty clearly, I fancy.'

'Look then. Two gaps in the hills, like bites. Or gaps between huge teeth. The Giant's Teeth we call them round here.

You can see the theatre quite clearly: that black turret effect. More like a watchtower than a theatre at this distance. Hence its name. It was supposed to be called the Royal like the old one, but Watchtower just stuck. Lark Manor is more difficult to spot: the light local stone.'

'So close to the sea! The theatre, I mean,' exclaimed Cherry; it was apparent at least to Jemima that Cherry's agile mind had rushed ahead to picnic-time, to time between shooting, to light evenings, to young actors, perhaps, or those not so young, all far from home. Jemima said:

'It's an excellent view. Thank you for showing it to us. An opening shot, perhaps?' she addressed the last remark, at least in principle, to Cherry.

'Locals round here don't like the way the theatre dominates the landscape. So harsh and modern. Unlike Lark Manor which melds into the background. That's why I showed them both to you. It clashes with our quiet rural life, they think with unpleasant results. Like television. Think about it, Miss Jemima Shore, and take your sea-shells home after lunch.'

On this note, Gregory Rowan walked rapidly away. But not, to Cherry's surprise, in the direction of his long black hearse car. He simply walked a little further along the pebbly beach to where a ridge of large stones indicated the high-water mark.

And there, under the stunned gaze of the two ladies from Megalith Television, he proceeded to take off first his thick dark-blue fisherman's jersey and then his battered corduroy trousers. He did not appear to have been wearing anything under these clothes at all; or if he had, he had removed all his garments at the same time. Clad then merely in a pair of old white gym shoes, Gregory Rowan strode back purposefully in the direction of the sea.

Jemima and Cherry could not tear their mesmerized gaze away, and comparing notes afterwards, agreed that they had still expected him to stop on reaching the sea's edge. But

Gregory did not check his progress. At first the sea was shallow and merely splashed round his ankles. Then there must have been some shelf and a drop, for he suddenly struck out strongly, swimming along the line of the shore.

The two women watched him silently for a moment, still mesmerized, and then by unspoken agreement turned back in the direction of their own car.

'We-e-ell!' Cherry could hold no silence for very long. To Jemima's irritation her tone was definitely admiring. 'Nothing to hide indeed. What about that? And he didn't even have a towel. Did you notice?'

'I noticed what I was intended to notice,' replied Jemima crossly.

'It must have been freezing,' pursued Cherry. 'And he didn't even pause as he went in. I must say he's quite —'

'I dare say we were supposed to notice that too. Come on, Cherry, stop thinking about old Triton, and find me the route back to Lark Manor. I've got something extremely important to ask you.'

'Triton?'

'Shelley at Lerici, then.'

'But Shelley *drowned* at Lerici!' cried Cherry eagerly; as Jemima was well aware, Cherry had once worked on that notorious series 'The Magnificent Shelleys' and could be relied on to get the reference. Unfortunately the literary reference did not have the desired effect of distracting her from the subject of Gregory Rowan. Instead Cherry stopped and began to look back anxiously. He was still swimming strongly and quite fast along the line of the shore; soon he would reach the cliff and the line of jagged black rocks which closed the end of the small bay.

'Jem, you're such a strong swimmer, do you think you should —'

'He won't drown. Of that I can assure you! Come *on*, Cherry, now the thing I want to ask you is this —'

But it was not until they were both back in the Mercedes, sitting, untangling the hair (Jemima), spraying on new forces of *Charlie* (Cherry), that Jemima could thoroughly distract her friend from the black head in the sea.

'Something that man said. Something that puzzled me. He made this very firm reference to Christabel. Christabel and the Festival. Cherry, who is Christabel? Who or what is she? And what connection has Christabel, any Christabel, with the Larminster Festival?'

'Christabel,' repeated Cherry. 'I can't think of any Christabel connected with it at all. Hang on, I've got the actresses' names here. Anna Maria Packe, Filumena Lennox . . . And most of the other Larminster Festival names. The Committee.' She scuffled in her large ethnically-inclined tote bag. 'No wait, my God, what am I saying? *Christabel*. Christabel Herrick. *The* Christabel Herrick. The actress. She used to be married to Julian Cartwright, Julian Cartwright, he of Lark Manor, with the lovely deep voice on the telephone, the man we're going to see. Don't you remember? Then she ran off. Oh years ago. There was all that frightful scandal.'

'Scandal? What scandal?'

'Oh, Jem, you're so *ungossip-minded*!' On Cherry's lips this was definitely a reproach. 'But this you *have* to remember. The newspapers wrote screeds about it. It was all so frightfully juicy. And then tragic. But of course that's years ago. I mean, I shouldn't think Christabel Herrick has shown her face down here for years. She wouldn't dare. Certainly not at the Larminster Festival, I mean that would be a *real* scandal.'

'I'm sure you're right, Cherry,' said Jemima slowly.

Behind their backs, the dark head and arms of Gregory Rowan could now be seen heading for the shore, as a shark might be seen cutting through water.

FOUR

Watching Christabel

The person who thought Christabel was getting away with altogether too much these days was really quite disgusted by the scene at Lark Manor that Easter Sunday: with Christabel presiding so airily over the large lunch table.

'Or rather her husband's lunch table,' the person threw in as an afterthought. But the person knew better than to put this kind of sentiment, however justifiable, into words: it was better to hug these feelings to oneself — until absolutely the right moment presented itself. Events this morning had rather proved that, hadn't they? So the person continued to mask both anger and repulsion under an impassive front.

All the same, the person knew that Christabel was really rather frightened by now. Under all that make-up Christabel wished after all she hadn't come back to Lark Manor.

Maybe it would have been better to have stayed in London and been poor and sick and sad and lonely. In spite of having no rewarding work. No marvellous lover. And getting older and uglier and not having beauty creams and hair dyes and perfumes (the smell of her lily-of-the-valley scent filled the house all over again now she was back) and people to wait on her and her lovely dresses such as that soft hyacinth-blue just the colour of her eyes, and *jewels*. How many kinds of blue jewel Christabel was wearing today! A long string of turquoise mixed with *the* pearls with the sapphire clasp, the Cartwright pearls, she'd got them out of the bank pretty quickly, hadn't she? The aquamarine ring, on the other hand, the one she always wore, she'd taken with her when she went. At lunch, of course, she was wearing it on her left hand. Her white hand, creamy and be-creamed, caressing and now once more caressed.

In spite of all this Christabel was going to die and the warm soft round body under the yielding cashmere would grow cold and be put in the dank rich mouldy earth of Larminster Churchyard. So all the creams and lotions and perfumes were not going to save her, and the blue jewels, all of them, all of them save the aquamarine and perhaps that would be buried with her, would go back into the bank.

Christabel had this knowledge now: Christabel was frightened under that sweet sorrowing manner of hers.

'Please don't torture me,' she had said.

Admiring the arrangement of spring flowers in the centre of the dining-room table — scillas and narcissi, blue and white like the china — the person decided not to be in such a hurry to end the game after all. Christabel's torture should not be ended too quickly. The prospect would make up for the fact that there might not after all be spring flowers on her grave, not even tulips, but something full blown like roses, the first big fat creamy roses, the Gloire de Dijon, which grew on the sheltered wall in the courtyard garden of Lark Manor in May. Roses, full-blown roses, were finally much more appropriate to Christabel, the person decided regretfully, than spring flowers. You had to admit that, Christabel's spring was long past.

The person revelled in Christabel's discomfiture and Christabel's secret fear grew.

Jemima Shore, on the other hand, thought that her hostess's aplomb was really quite remarkable. Under the circumstances. The circumstances which Cherry had hastily but vividly outlined to her on the road from Larmouth to the manor. Had the prodigal son been quite so urbane at the feast given in his honour by his father? Certainly this prodigal wife radiated confidence, and even blitheness in her return.

'Of course she is an actress — *was* an actress.' But Jemima, numbering a good many actors and actresses among her friends, knew that emotional control in private life was not necessarily allied to talent on the stage — even with a woman who had once been as celebrated as Christabel Herrick.

Lunch was being handed round by a manservant, an elderly and distinguished-looking man in a very clean white jacket; he was assisted by a woman with tightly set auburn hair, wearing a neat dark dress, who alternately stood at the sideboard and darted out to marshal in fresh supplies of food. From time to time Julian Cartwright issued orders to the manservant in quite a loud voice — he had called him Blagge but the woman Mrs Blagge — as a result of which both Blagges stopped doing whatever they were engaged in and still more wine was poured into the array of bevelled glasses. Christabel Cartwright's precise words could on the other hand hardly be distinguished, but it was noticeable that things moved much faster whenever she did speak; dishes, a delicate egg mousse for example in a blue and white soufflé dish, were whisked round the table again and again; plates were removed, fresh plates were substituted; it all happened so fast and so deftly whenever Christabel murmured that she might have been whispering some magic password which made the table itself start spinning.

Meat was carved. Spring lamb appeared, presto, on the latest wave of blue and white plates. Mrs Blagge proffered mint sauce and gravy in matching dishes, first to Jemima Shore.

'Madam —'

The hand with which she extended the sauce-boat was quite blotched and claw-like, the hand of an old woman; the striking auburn hair must be dyed.

If only Jemima could be quite sure that Cherry wasn't drinking too much (such efficient service of wine, she felt, plus the presence of such an indubitably glamorous older man as Julian Cartwright presented an irresistible combination of temptations to Flowering Cherry) she, Jemima, could have concentrated totally on Christabel Herrick's, no, Christabel *Cartwright*'s, dazzling performance.

Even the white bandage which Christabel wore on her right hand had an air of elegance: a white kid glove or mitten perhaps. Although at one point Christabel did wince at some inadvertent gesture: had one of her daughters, the sulky little fat one in the unsuitable sun-dress, touched the hand by mistake?

Immediately on hearing the slight cry, Julian Cartwright broke off his conversation with Cherry, perhaps to the ultimate advantage of the latter; since Cherry was leaning forward dangerously in her tight white pearl-buttoned blouse, while her large eyes bore an expression which Jemima for one found it all too easy to interpret.

'All right, darling?' Julian Cartwright called out down the table. The sound of his voice, so redolent of authority that it made a question sound like a command, drew other conversations to a close. 'Christabel, poor sweet, did herself some fearful injury on a pair of garden scissors this morning,' he explained. 'Stabbed herself in one hand in some quite remarkable way, while cutting flowers after breakfast. Darling, do you know, you've never had time to tell me properly how it happened?'

Jemima, professionally trained interviewer, became suddenly and acutely aware that some special tension had been brought into the room by Julian's question. She could not say exactly where this tension was located. After all, everyone in the room gave the polite appearance of listening for Christabel's explanation. Nor could she say further what had stirred her instinct; she only knew that curiosity, Jemima Shore's dominant emotion, had been aroused — curiosity and a strange feeling of apprehension.

Jemima looked down the table and inspected the guests.

The dexterity with which the two servants were handling the meal was made the more remarkable by the fact that it was a large lunch party. Jemima as presenter and Cherry as production assistant were the only two official guests from Megalith since the director, Jemima's old friend and former assistant Guthrie Carlyle, was still in Greece — shooting the Parthenon for what he assured Jemima was a wholly uncontroversial programme on the Elgin Marbles sub-titled 'Ours or Theirs?'

Then there were the two Cartwright girls, who sat together at their mother's end of the table, on either side of a woman whom Jemima assumed to be some kind of governess (although they were surely rather too old for that kind of thing?). This lady was familiarly addressed by the Cartwrights as Ketty, but introduced to Jemima as Miss Katherine Kettering — 'the two names have somehow got combined over the years.' She was certainly much at her ease; the girls chattered to her, rather than to their other neighbours, throughout the meal. Fat little Blanche's sulky face lit up talking to Ketty in a way that it never did, Jemima noticed, when Blanche addressed her mother.

'But, Ketty, you remember: the Easter Sunday we all went to the beach and Daddy did press-ups and got sand all over his cricketing trousers —'

The pretty dark-haired daughter Regina, who chose at one point to recite a good deal of Christina Rossetti in the overloud voice she had inherited from her father, addressed those words also to Ketty. 'When I am dead, my dearest, sing no sad songs for me . . .' and so on and so on. Ketty listened intently and then said: 'Well done, Rina,' as if she had been hearing a lesson.

'Regina,' she informed Jemima across the table, 'has been making a study of Christina Rossetti. She knows most of her work by heart.' 'How delightful,' murmured Jemima, hoping that no one had any plans for recitations of the works of Christina Rossetti by Miss Regina Cartwright aged seventeen in the course of her television programme. As usual, it was Cherry who saved the situation:

'Oh, I adore Christina Rossetti,' she cried happily. 'And Dante — Dante Gabriel, I mean, not the other Dante.' Cherry proceeded to quote at length, by virtue of her past involvement in 'Christina and Company — a Rose among the Rossettis'. The series might have been one of Megalith's most noted failures, reflected Jemima, but at least Cherry's education had benefited; and Ketty and Regina were temporarily routed.

Like Mrs Blagge, Miss Kettering had very dark red hair, of a hue which was so bizarre as to be surely dyed; in Ketty's case the hair was strained back into a large thick bun, revealing a pair of dangling green earrings set in big powerfully lobed ears. It was while pondering on the coincidence of two women with the same strange taste in hair dye being in the same room that Jemima realized how much Ketty and Mrs Blagge also resembled each other in other ways. They had the same long thin finely chiselled noses and small firm mouths. Ketty however wore a violent scarlet lipstick; Mrs Blagge none.

Sisters? If so, one sat at the table and drank, Jemima observed, at least her due share of wine. The other served.

On Christabel's right, sat Gregory Rowan. He had arrived rather late, with a scant air of apology, into the charming sun-filled conservatory adorned with orange trees in large dark green wooden tubs where the Cartwrights had doled out pre-lunch drinks. His hair was still conspicuously damp, its thickness temporarily restrained, and Jemima had seen Christabel give him a slightly sardonic look on arrival.

'Did you go for a quick one, darling? Quick cooling off?' she enquired. She handed him a silver goblet.

'Had to wash off the taste of chocolate,' replied Gregory. 'Next year *you* can organize the Easter egg hunt. If you're still with us, that is. To the return and the stay of the prodigal.' He lifted the goblet on whose silver surface the chilly contents — champagne and orange juice — had already left white clouds.

It was the only conceivable reference, Jemima noted, throughout the meal and its prelude, to Christabel's past. Christabel merely gave one of her low musical laughs.

Jemima, who was on Julian Cartwright's right, had the Director of the Larminster Festival on her other side. This seemed rather a grand title for the pleasant-faced boy, scarcely older than the Cartwright girls, who introduced himself to her as Nat Fitzwilliam, told her that he was Bridset born, and confided that he had been running the theatre since he left Oxford 'because no one else much wanted to do it.'

The Boy Director was deputed to escort Jemima and Cherry over to the Watchtower after lunch. Jemima observed that whenever he was not coping rather frenziedly with the knives, forks and glasses by his side, as well as the persistent attentions of the Blagges — he hardly touched his wine — Nat Fitzwilliam gazed almost literally open-mouthed at Christabel Cartwright. Jemima could well imagine the effect of the return of such a dazzling creature on a stage-struck youth. How old had he been when she left?

At this point, Jemima discovered with a slight jolt to her interviewer's complacency that Nat Fitzwilliam was not quite the naive amateur of her imagination. It was not so much the list of his credits at Oxford which impressed her — indeed she had a nasty feeling that she might have caught his Chinese

(Sung Dynasty) *Hamlet* while at Edinburgh and found it wanting. No, it was the discovery that Nat Fitzwilliam had already directed a play for television, an opera in Holland, and part of a series for the BBC on English poets and their private lives, which Jemima had much admired. All this, while also residing in Bridset and as Nat engagingly put it, 'trying to keep the Watchtower upstanding'. It all went to show that Nat was not only older but also more energetic than he looked.

Next to Cherry sat Julian's uncle, introduced as Major Edgar Cartwright. At first Jemima assumed that the old boy had merely been wheeled into action in order to even up the sexes a little. But Major Cartwright also revealed himself as the Chairman of the Larminster Festival Committee. Jemima expected this information to be followed up by some hard discussion of the subject. Major Cartwright, however, merely leant forward and asked Jemima one question in a very fierce voice:

'This television business: do you pay us or do we pay you?' Having received a roughly reassuring reply — no money need necessarily change hands — he relapsed into a morose silence. This left him free to contemplate Cherry's décolletage with apparent outrage, while every now and then casting a look which Jemima interpreted as acute dislike towards his nephew's wife.

Surprisingly, it was the Major who chose to answer Julian's open question to Christabel about her accident. She had given her little laugh and taken a sip of wine before answering — Jemima noticed that throughout the lunch Christabel's drinking, like that of Miss Kettering (and Cherry), had kept well up with the pace of the Blagges' refilling. Before Christabel could speak, the Major butted in, making his second remark of the luncheon, so far as Jemima was concerned. His voice, like that of his nephew, was commandingly loud.

'The woman's not used to gardening any more, living in some basement in London. That's all there is to be said on the subject.' The Major took a deep swig of his red wine; Christabel drank further of her own glass. At which the Major added something like: 'Damn it', and proceeded to glare round until Mr Blagge refilled his glass. Further draughts of red wine silenced him once more completely. Christabel's fair powdered skin looked rather pink, but perhaps that was the effect of the wine.

It was left to Nat Fitzwilliam, riding with Jemima in her Mercedes after lunch to inspect the Watchtower, to voice the obvious about the very odd social occasion they had just attended. He was able to curl himself confidently into the front seat since Cherry, attempting to hitch a lift from Julian Cartwright, had found herself palmed off with the Major as her chauffeur.

'I always ride with the girls on Sunday,' had been Julian Cartwright's excuse. 'Otherwise the horses wouldn't know it was the Sabbath.' He elected not to hear Cherry's valiant offer of mounting a steed herself — or perhaps a glance at her tight skirt discouraged him from taking her offer seriously.

'Wowee,' breathed Nat Fitzwilliam. Then as if that were not sufficient, he whistled and passed his hand over his brow. 'Wow,' he added. 'What about that? Christabel *Herrick* back at Lark Manor. Why on earth do you suppose she came back? After all these years?'

'Perhaps she repented her wicked ways. Alternatively perhaps she missed the very comfortable gilded cage.' Jemima spoke lightly. As far as she was concerned, the events which had overtaken Christabel Cartwright, or had been provoked by her, lay in the past.

While Jemima admitted to a healthy curiosity on the subject of Christabel's reappearance and the strange combination of graciousness and tensity which the atmosphere at Lark Manor presented, her main concern was with Megalith's seventy-five minute programme on the Larminster Festival. Jemima could see in Christabel's dramatic return a possible obstacle to the successful execution of her endeavour. Already Gregory Rowan, one of the most prominent local residents and one who should certainly feature in the programme, had issued his appeal for cancellation. Now if everyone at Larminster was going to spend the summer discussing the concerns of Christabel Cartwright, it might be very difficult to film the Festival in a relaxed and spontaneous manner.

Nat Fitzwilliam's next remark made her heart sink.

'Do you suppose, since she *is* back, I could persuade her to take part in the Festival? Smashing television for you, of course, and smashing publicity for us. Absolutely transform the programme.' He paused. 'Wowee,' he exclaimed. 'I think *The Sunday Times* might take a piece from me now . . . they've turned me down once . . . now that I've got Christabel Herrick, the return of Christabel Herrick, to offer . . .'

As Nat Fitzwilliam expatiated on these daydreams, Jemima took another look at his cherub's face, its look of candour and sweetness enhanced by the broad brow and wide-set trusting eyes. She realized with some alarm that the cherub's exterior only partially hid the ruthless and empire-building ambitions. Did he cultivate the look of youth to trap the unwary? But Nat had already passed on to the subject of the visit of the touring company, named after its famous theatre of origin, the King Charles at Bridesbury.

'*The Seagull* and that hoary old favourite of Gregory's about Marie Antoinette in prison, showing how she came over all noble at the end,' he was muttering. 'Repertory companies always trot it out if they've got a talented leading actress. Two wonderful parts for *her*, anyway. I believe I could get Anna Maria to step down, she owes me a favour, or if she won't, the bitch, there's always blackmail isn't there. Then I'll tell Boy Greville that he can't direct the second episode in my series unless he steps down —'

The cherub's eyes were gleaming.

'Look here,' Jemima interrupted strongly, wrenching his

attention away from the King Charles Company to his present situation. 'My dear boy, this is all moonshine. What on earth makes you think that Christabel Herrick *wants* to return to the stage? Isn't it rather the point that she's returned to her family and abandoned the stage? And I should add that Megalith Television is concentrating on Larminster as its typical homespun English festival, not as a major *pièce de scandale*.' Jemima made her words as cold as possible, hoping to punctuate Nat Fitzwilliam's wishful thinking.

'Oh right, right, absolutely. Sorry I got carried away. You're absolutely right. Look, here we are. Park on the left. Then you get a good view of the sea *and* the Watchtower, right in line. As it was meant to be seen.'

Jemima gazed dutifully up at the extremely modern pentagonal building, constructed of blackish stone and darkened glass which loomed above them. Her appreciation was just turning to admiration — at first sight it was one of the most successful modern buildings she had seen — when she received an unpleasant inkling that Nat Fitzwilliam was one of those people who never wasted time in argument, merely proceeded with their plans underground when checked.

'To think, *she's* never even been here!' he was exclaiming fervently as he unlocked the front doors. Jemima could see the empty interior of the foyer through the transparent cinnamon-coloured glass.

'I want you to see it this way,' Nat continued. 'Our little modern masterpiece. Featured in the *Architectural Review* twice. All built with Cartwright money when the dry rot made the old theatre a public hazard. *She* must have had the idea; and then she never saw it finished.'

They crossed the foyer. Jemima did not like empty theatres. She found something creepy about them; even the locked box office, also made of cinnamon glass, did not please her. She made a mental note not to allow the architectural properties of the Watchtower to dominate her programme: this was to tell the story of the Festival, not a little modern masterpiece. Even so she had to admit that the stage and surrounding seats — on four of the five sides — were so well constructed as to give the interior of the theatre an appeal in its own right. All the same, all Guthrie Carlyle's shots would show people, lots of people, or would if Jemima had anything to do with it . . .

Nat Fitzwilliam fumbled for another switch and flooded the theatre with more light.

'Can't you just imagine it?' he said gloatingly. For a moment Jemima actually thought he was referring to the television programme she would make, they would make together. But Nat was once more in the grip of his vision.

'Christabel Herrick makes her come-back, directed by Nat Fitzwilliam. Oh, I know she'll do it for me,' he added quickly and joyously, to quell Jemima's objections. 'You see, I was a great friend of Barry's.'

'Barry?' queried Jemima.

'Barry! Barry Blagge! The infamous or famous boyfriend, depending on your point of view. Me for the latter, of course. Barry Blagge! Better known as Iron Boy! Don't you remember: "Coo-ool Repentance"?' He crooned the words as though clutching a mike.

'Iron Boy!' exclaimed Cherry, coming through the doors behind them. 'And that was my favourite of them all, that and "Daring Darling". I told you, Jem. Listen, very quickly, while the old boy parks his car, do you know what he told me on the way here? The solitary remark he made as a matter of fact. That couple, serving that Buckingham Palace of a lunch. Can you believe it? *They're his parents* — Iron Boy's parents.' Cherry's eyes were now as round as mill-stones.

'She runs off à la Lady Chatterley, well, that sort of thing, with the handsome stable lad. That's all he was — Iron Boy was — in those days. And his old parents are still there working at the Manor. They just keep on working. And they're *still* there when she returns . . . Talk about Cool Repentance.

Under all that quietness and graciousness, they must absolutely *loathe* her.

'What a weird set-up,' pronounced Cherry, with much satisfaction, adding with that talent for stating the obvious which never deserted her even in moments of greatest crisis: 'I mean, it would never happen in London.'

FIVE

'I'll Be Safe'

During May a great many things happened both in London (Megalithic House) and Larminster (the Watchtower Theatre) to advance the planning of Jemima Shore's Festival programme. Most of these things happened more or less on schedule. Even the things which did not happen on schedule, like Guthrie Carlyle and his cameraman Spike Thompson going to the wrong restaurant in Larminster when they were on a reccy — not the one in the *Good Food Guide* — did not in the end impede the development of the programme overmuch. It was an error incidentally for which they most unfairly blamed Cherry: but Cherry was quick to point out that she had booked them into absolutely the right restaurant in the first place; it was pure male chauvinism which had led them to prefer Christopher's Diner (unlisted) to Flora's Kitchen (highly recommended) once on the spot in Larminster.

One of the unscheduled things which was felt to be a hindrance was the constant presence of Nat Fitzwilliam in London. As Director of the Festival being put together in

Larminster, rather than the programme being worked out in London, it might have been supposed that Nat Fitzwilliam would have concentrated on the rustic side of things. But this would have been to under-estimate the cheerful cherub's capacity to be in both places at once, or at any rate to commute on his motor-bike all too regularly between them.

'That young man will be the death of me,' grumbled Guthrie Carlyle after one of Nat's unsolicited calls at Megalithic House. ('I was supposed to see both Peter *and* Trevor this morning — they're interested in my Sung *Hamlet* at the National — no, no, it's Trevor who's talking musicals and *Middlemarch* at the RSC — but luckily Peter chuckled, so that I thought that on my way to see Jonathan at the BBC, I'd just pop in —') 'Correction. This Festival will be the death of me,' continued Guthrie. 'Or if not me, the death of someone probably in the contracts department, in view of Spike Thompson's latest *coup* over his expenses.'

'Wouldn't it be lovely if it was the death of Nat Fitzwilliam?' Jemima spoke wistfully. 'I speak purely professionally, you understand. Just his reputation. I don't want his youthful corpse on my hands, looking all pathetic, appealing to the mother in me. But this morning he gave me most cogently *his* views on *Jonathan Miller*'s views on Shakespeare and I'm not sure that I can take —'

'Have you heard the latest?' Cherry tripped in. 'Our Nat is going to direct *The Seagull* himself. Boy Greville has withdrawn. Personal reasons, *he* says. And that is not all, my friends. *What* about this?' She paused for effect, and who could deny the effect was ravishing — pale-pink T-shirt perilously scoop-necked and pale-pink skirt slit up both sides to reveal plump smooth olive-skinned thighs.

Guthrie whistled appreciatively. 'Wowee, as Nat Fitzwilliam would say. And has Spike Thompson taken time off from his expenses to have the pleasure?' But Cherry for once was not in a mood for tribute.

'Believe or not, she's agreed! Our Nat has fixed it. Christabel Herrick stars! *The Seagull*. And that lovely weepy piece of Gregory Rowan's everyone does at school, *Widow Capet*. You know, Marie Antoinette in prison, thinking about the diamond necklace etc. etc. She'll be Marie Antoinette, yes? Très, très revolutionary France. And *The Seagull*.' Cherry's voice dropped. 'Very, very nineteenth-century Russia.'

'Knowing Nat Fitzwilliam, I wouldn't be a bit surprised if it was exactly the other way round,' observed Jemima tartly. But she was more concerned to digest the surprising and not particularly welcome news of Nat Fitzwilliam's successful recasting. She had no doubt already that the return to the stage of Christabel Herrick — even to the stage of the Watchtower, Bridset, would attract a great deal of interest not all of it purely theatrical in origin. Was this quite what Cy Fredericks had in mind when he had spoken to Jemima of including in her series 'one really superbly insignificant country festival'?

Cy had warmed to his theme: 'Significant in its very insignificance, my dear Jem. A repertory company of the greatest integrity; local worthies, each more respectable than the last, whose wives have never even raised their eyes above another man's feet, sleeping in their seats, the sleep of the just after a long day's work like characters in Hardy, the whole lot preferably in dinner jackets, the worthies of course, not their wives. The wives should be wearing gowns of classical inextravagance in keeping with the plays presented, eternal values kept decently in check. This festival, through the medium of Megalith Television, should symbolize of itself all that makes English cultural country life what it is today.'

Cy had leant back in satisfied contemplation of his own eloquence. 'In short, my dear Jem, the sort of thing that you and I would run a mile rather than attend.' Remembering rather too late that he was in fact recommending Jemima to spend several weeks at such a festival, Cy had added quickly: 'Except in the line of duty, that is.'

Was this new improved version of the Larminster Festival quite what Cy Fredericks had in mind as the significantly insignificant? At the same time Jemima was uneasily aware that Cy Fredericks was hardly going to back out from televising the return of Christabel Herrick to the stage; something to which it would appear that he had inadvertently secured the exclusive rights. Under the circumstances she hardly thought that Cy would stick by his original notion of decent cultural obscurity. Her instinct told her that her own programme was due to undergo roughly the same transformation as the Larminster Festival itself in the immediate future.

And so indeed it proved. Over the next few days Cy Fredericks abandoned the whole concept of the insignificant festival with suspicious alacrity. Larminster and its Festival now became infinitely more central in the whole Fredericks scheme of things and that in turn reflected on the lives of all those concerned with the original programme.

Guthrie Carlyle, swearing outwardly over the damage to schedules, comforted himself inwardly with dreams of prime-time television. Cherry took the opportunity to end — most regretfully — a romance with a craggy forty-year-old producer in another department on the grounds of pressure of work; her secret dreams were of Julian Cartwright's handsomely greying head on her pillow in some Larminster hostelry while Christabel busied herself with her career. Even Spike Thompson, saturnine as ever in his legendary battered black leather jacket, with looks which made his claim to descend from a family of Italian ice-cream manufacturers named Tommaso at least plausible, spared time from the possible financial implications of such a change to murmur: 'Christabel Herrick, she looks pretty good in her photographs and some of these older women are fantastic.'

'Christabel Herrick, isn't she absolutely into younger men?' enquired a passing secretary innocently. 'I mean, didn't she run off with a randy teenager?'

'Yes, Spike, you'd better keep an eye on your Focus Puller,' concurred Guthrie in a bland voice which was not at all innocent; leaving the secretary to wonder why the great — and greatly fancied — Spike Thompson gave her a wide berth in the Megalith canteen thereafter, despite a series of very straightforward propositions made there on previous occasions.

Jemima Shore for her part found herself with two new tasks. The first was to get to know Christabel Herrick, the distinguished actress who had dominated a generation before abandoning the stage, through the medium of the Megalith cuttings library. The second was to get to know Christabel Cartwright, the lady of Lark Manor, in person.

She was half-way through the first task, when she was interrupted by a telephone call from the object of her researches. Already Jemima had become torn between morbid curiosity and personal disgust as sensational headline followed headline. Listening to Christabel Cartwright's delightful low voice on the telephone, she found it very difficult to equate the two images.

Christabel's call fortuitously set the second task under way, for she had rung up to propose lunch together. She suggested Larminster — Flora's Kitchen — rather than her own house on the rather vaguely expressed grounds that 'there's so much always going on at Lark'.

A few days later at the restaurant Christabel was more explicit: 'We're redesigning the courtyard garden to make it less *doleful*, there are no flowers there in the summer, except climbers, which is ridiculous, lots and lots of peonies I thought, Julian says they take years to establish, but I said, we've *got* years darling, years and years, at least speaking for myself . . .'

Yes, thought Jemima, it was certainly very difficult to reconcile the romantic heroine — or villainess — of the newspaper with this pleasant pretty well-dressed woman sitting opposite her, rattling on about her garden planning. Jemima watched Christabel pouring herself a large vodka from a half-bottle produced somewhat surprisingly from her Gucci handbag, and thought that was about the only eccentric note she struck. And even that proved susceptible to explanation.

'No vodka here,' cried Christabel, 'and I can't have lunch without a voddy, can I? So Poll doesn't mind if I bring my own.'

Poll was a girl with very long very straight hair who served them in virtual silence, except for occasional low-voiced suggestions. She moved mysteriously and gracefully, vanishing from time to time into the kitchen at the back with a swish of her long skirts. Whereupon from the kitchen much louder noises of furious expostulation usually issued.

'That's Moll,' confided Christabel during one of these bouts. 'She cooks. And yells at Poll. They're a devoted couple except when Moll gets one of her jealous fits about Poll and the male customers. They met as art students. In Florence, you will not be totally surprised to hear.'

The menu featured Botticelli Salad, Boeuf Primavera and Syllabub Uffizi. Impressionistic figures, roughly based on those of Botticelli, had been painted all over the walls of the dark little restaurant, giving a pleasantly cavernous effect. The table-cloths and napkins were made of Botticelli-printed linen: Jemima found herself staring down at Venus's left breast, the nipple centrally placed between her knife and fork. All the food was absolutely delicious, and except for its name, there was nothing Italianate about it at all.

The house wine was also very good. Poll, unasked, brought a bottle of red and placed it before Christabel. Since Jemima then gently enquired for some white, Christabel was left alone with the red; the level, Jemima noticed, went down quite rapidly, as Poll filled and refilled Christabel's glass silently and deftly.

In the far corner of Flora's Kitchen, appropriately enough in the shadow of the Three Graces, Jemima noticed Spike Thompson having lunch with Nat Fitzwilliam. Poll's long hair drooped and dipped tenderly over Spike Thompson's plate in a way that Jemima thought would not greatly please Moll were she to witness it. Spike, in a scarlet polo-necked jersey under his black leather jacket, was the only truly Italian-looking thing in the restaurant; in contrast to the schoolboy appearance of Nat Fitzwilliam, he looked quite aggressively masculine.

Jemima removed her gaze, banished some unprofessional thoughts on the subject of her cameraman, and concentrated on Christabel. Christabel's fluffy hair was framed rather than covered in the halo of a blue chiffon scarf. A ruffled white blouse under a pale-blue jacket on which a full-blown creamy rose was held by a jewelled pin made her look as ostentatiously feminine as Spike looked masculine. The jewelled pin which held the spray was in the shape of a lily of the valley simulated in pearls and jade. Yet Jemima did not feel that she had dressed with any special care for this occasion; merely that her appearance in general was the result of constant cherishing. The right word for Christabel was glamorous. In that respect she resembled royalty — or an actress.

THE ACTRESS AND THE PLOUGHBOY — that was one glaring headline which came back into Jemima's mind. All that side of Christabel Cartwright seemed quite incomprehensible, looking at her now — unless of course one was inclined to explain the whole history of the world in terms of sex. And that, Jemima, despite being most amiably disposed towards the subject herself, had always supposed to be an error. Perhaps Christabel's history had something to teach her.

According to the newspapers, Christabel Cartwright's torrid romance with Barry Blagge, the handsome red-haired only child of the married couple who worked at Lark Manor, had begun when he was about twenty-one. It was of course nonsense — pure headlinese — to describe him as a ploughboy. Even the columns beneath the headlines themselves contradicted the notion. Barry Blagge, leaving aside his remarkable looks, revealed even at that stage in fuzzy newspaper photographs, had been bright, very bright. He had secured first O-levels and then A-levels at Larminster Royal, hardly a universal occurrence at that quiet school in the early 1970s.

His bent however had not been academic, as various obliging friends had pointed out to various interested newspapers. No, a pop star was what Barry Blagge had decided that he intended to be. There was nothing in his background to explain such an ambition. Mr Blagge was a former soldier who had been Major Cartwright's batman while Mrs Blagge had been lady's maid to Julian Cartwright's mother, Lady May — two sober people. The trouble was that Barry had been born to them late in life. As a result, observers agreed, there had been far too much indulgence there, which they gleefully blamed for what followed: 'Mrs Blagge always spoiled young Barry rotten, gave him everything he wanted, motor-bike when he was sixteen, and then he wore silver bracelets! I ask you, a boy of seventeen in silver bracelets like a duchess. And that ridiculous clown's costume he paraded in about the place. And as for his hair, why didn't his father just make him cut it, cut it himself if needs be, he was in the army Jim Blagge, he knew the score, oh yes, they always gave him everything he wanted . . .' And so forth and so on went the happy prurient chorus.

But the Blagges had not been able to give Barry everything he wanted. They had not been able to make him into a pop star overnight for example. The opportunities in Larminster for singing, even with the most humble group, being naturally somewhat limited, Barry's career had languished. Even so there were those who were sufficiently struck by his remarkable physical appearance — the features of Michelangelo's David set in a halo of profuse auburn curls which gyrated fiercely as he sang — combined with the weird sensuality of his singing, to remember and recount later the odd amateur performances. On the whole however Larminster regarded young Barry Blagge on or off his motor-bike, in silver bracelets, pierrot costumes, singing or silent, with distaste or disapproval.

What the Blagges with their manorial connections could do for Barry was to get him a job, a job of sorts. Hence the ploughboy epithet, although Barry was actually helping to bring in the harvest at Lark.

It was during the long hot summer of 1976, when the Bridset fields were whitening in the sun, that the romance of Christabel Cartwright and Barry Blagge flamed, much as the rest of England flamed in the dry intensity of that legendary weather. Christabel had planned to spend a quiet summer holiday with her daughters, then thirteen and fourteen, after a long season at the Gray Theatre. Instead she fell passionately in love with Barry Blagge. When autumn came she returned to London and the theatre — taking Barry with her.

The whole scandal might still have been contained since Julian Cartwright maintained a front of total reserve. He continued to refer in public to his wife's absence, even their separation, as purely temporary, something to do with the alien world of the theatre, no concern of Julian Cartwright's, the ever-courteous lord of the manor of Lark. In this way he even managed to countenance the undeniable fact that Barry Blagge was living in Christabel's apartment in Eaton Place. 'Being helped with his music,' said Mrs Blagge, caught on the telephone at Lark Manor, and Julian Cartwright went along with that too. So there the story might well have rested, for lack of further developments. Had it not been for Barry Blagge himself.

Jemima had to admit that Barry Blagge's first exclusive interview with *Sunday Sink* — headline MY FIRST LADY OF PASSION — made compellingly lurid reading even five years later. There was even a kind of black humour, a bizarre turn of phrase about some of his utterances — if indeed he and not a newspaper ghost-writer was personally responsible for them. With hindsight it was possible to see that it was not out of character for Barry Blagge, an unknown young man in his early twenties, to seek out a Sunday newspaper and insist on delivering his intimate memoirs of a famous actress. At the time the sensation caused both by the revelations and by the flagrancy of the deed itself was enormous.

Would Barry Blagge's career have taken off without this bold stroke of treachery? Probably. The ambition which had caused him to contact the *Sunday Sink* in the first place would surely have enabled him to win through sooner or later — even if you discounted his astonishing looks, reinforcing his voice and lyrics. Within four months of the *Sunday Sink* story, Barry Blagge's first record 'Iron Boy' — a suitable title — got high into the charts. A few months later 'Daring Darling' — another suitable title — reached No. 1. Six months later Iron Boy himself, as Barry Blagge was now mainly known in public, promoting his new record 'Cool Repentance', conquered not only Britain and the United States but most of the rest of the world.

And what of Christabel? At first she continued to work as she had always done, occupying that prominent role on the English stage so ably described by Barry Blagge when he had called her the 'First lady of passion' — if the passion as delineated by Ibsen and Chekhov was of a rather different nature from that envisaged by the *Sunday Sink*'s readers. At first, too, there were small gossipy pictures of Barry Blagge attending her opening nights. Later these were replaced by very large pictures of Iron Boy at her opening nights, in a series of his remarkable costumes. As he grew more famous, he made some remarkable statements too on the subject of the theatrical scene. Some of his comments on Christabel's fellow-actors were really rather funny (Jemima guessed by now that the black humour was his own) as well as quite insupportably impudent. Then he discussed Christabel herself — in simpler and more laudatory terms: 'Christabel rules OK.' It all read rather oddly put side by side with the theatrical reviews of the piece in question: her rather subdued Hedda Gabler for example.

As Iron Boy's comments on the person described by some newspapers as his paramour grew more outrageous, the critics, as though not to be outdone, became rather more strident too. Christabel Herrick, their darling for so many years, began to falter in their estimation. Her Hedda Gabler was merely received coldly — but that could have been the fault of an innately poor production. It was more sinister when the word 'emotional' began to creep into the papers. The reviews became more barbed, with unpleasant undertones. One critic, describing her Portia, spoke of 'liberties with the text on the first night, of the sort we do not associate with Miss Herrick'.

There were no photographs of Christabel Herrick at Iron Boy's concerts, although her face, looking sad and very distinguished, like a French marquise at an eve-of-guillotine feast, occasionally stared out of photographs taken at restaurants afterwards.

Six months after records such as 'Iron Boy' and 'Cool Repentance' had ensured their progenitor world-wide acclaim (that amazing Far Eastern tour, for example, which even Jemima, no connoisseur of the genre, remembered), Christabel left the cast of a new play just before it opened in the West End. Her agent, apparently taken by surprise, spoke gallantly of the need for a complete rest. It did not help therefore when Christabel was subsequently photographed at London Airport on her way to the United States, where Barry was enjoying a further triumphal progress. Her agent's second statement was even more embarrassed than the first. Christabel in this particular photograph looked haggard and much older than what Jemima reckoned roughly to have been her forty-five years. The scarf she wore on her head did not suit her; her eyes looked huge and scared, her nose too prominent. It was as though she knew in advance of the humiliations which awaited her on the other side of the Atlantic.

That was the last picture of Christabel Herrick in the Megalith cuttings library. There were plenty more cuttings of Iron

Boy, of course — during the four months he had left to live. Jemima leafed through them with a horrid sensation of nemesis, knowing the grisly end to the story. But there was no picture of the scene when Christabel discovered that Barry had moved into the apartment of a famous black model, six foot tall, nineteen years old and very beautiful — nicknamed Tiny Georgianne. It seemed that he never even met Christabel when she arrived in New York, but relied on his usual mode of expression, the press statement, to convey to her the news. But of that Jemima could not be sure.

Even the cuttings about Christabel diminished now. Somehow she had obviously struggled back to London, eluding the press at Heathrow, since there was no picture of her arrival. She had been in London, living alone, when the last pictures of Iron Boy were careened all over the newspapers — the day after his beautiful sinuous arrogant body had been cut roughly in half by a lorry, as he rode his motor-bike down the freeway in the Los Angeles dawn, pierrot clothes flying, surrounded by his followers, going from the dawn to oblivion.

Christabel Herrick's statement on Iron Boy's death — no new picture available, just the old distraught one at London Airport — was short and dignified. It spoke with regret of the loss — and that was all. She did not, of course, attend the funeral, which took place in Los Angeles and was marked by hysterical scenes of grief from Iron Boy's fans. Nor, so far as Jemima could make out, did Mr and Mrs Blagge, still of Lark Manor. Nor was any statement from them printed on the subject of Barry's death.

In the cuttings library, Jemima Shore pondered on Christabel's use of the word loss. There was the loss of life, of course — Barry's. Then there was the loss of love — Barry's too — assuming he had ever loved her. And what of the other losses which surrounded this squalid little story? The loss of reputation and dignity to Christabel herself? The loss of security and privacy to her children? The loss of everything to her husband?

Sitting now in Flora's Kitchen, Jemima gazed with something like awe at the smoothly powdered brow before her, the large turquoise eyes eyeing her seductively over a glass of wine, held in a white hand on which a huge aquamarine shone with a shallow blue light. Was it really possible to return, as Christabel Cartwright had evidently done, and bury the past, as securely as Barry Blagge had buried himself in Iron Boy, and Iron Boy was now buried in some Californian cemetery?

She could not help wondering whether Christabel herself felt any regrets for what she had done. Back in the lap of the manor with her rich husband and adoring children, did she ever think back to the events of her lurid past? Jemima sighed. She knew that her Puritan streak, inherited from generations of stubbornly Nonconformist ancestors, shrank away from the spectacle of Christabel's uncomplicated equanimity.

She did not exactly want Christabel to be *punished* for her sins . . . that was a ridiculous notion for Jemima Shore, the famously tolerant liberated lady of the eighties, professionally engaged in comprehending and thus pardoning all around her. Perhaps she just wanted her to feel something, to show something of her past in her manner, in some way to repent.

Jemima pulled herself up sharply. Now that really was a ridiculous word for Jemima Shore to use, straight out of a Puritan past. She would be advocating the stocks for adultery on television next! Jemima was never quite sure whether or not she believed in sin, but she was quite sure she did not believe in public repentance. Jemima set herself firmly to carry out the real task before her. This was not only to get to know Christabel Herrick but also to actually like her — much the best preparation for a successful programme.

Oddly enough it proved remarkably easy to like Christabel: as well as genuine warmth, she had an excellent racy sense of humour which appealed to Jemima. It was not so easy to get to know her. Throughout lunch, Jemima sensed some reserve, some nervousness which made Christabel's original invitation to her seem rather puzzling in retrospect. Had Christabel really asked her to Flora's Kitchen merely to swap amusing stories of theatrical acquaintances and devour Syllabub Uffizi with mutual cries of dietary guilt?

It was at the end of the meal, when Christabel was powdering her nose and looking in the mirror of her gold compact with its jewelled clasp — Cartier no doubt — that she made the first revealing remark of the lunch.

'I'm so frightened about all this, you know,' she said suddenly.

Jemima gave a tactful murmur: 'You mean the stage after so long.'

'That — and other things.' There was a silence while Poll placed the bill between them, her long hair brushing the paper. Jemima, used to entertaining in the way of business, made an instinctive gesture towards it. Christabel swept her hand away: 'On my account.' Without looking at the bill, she thrust a very large tip on top of it and signed to Poll to take it away. Poll, like a witch in *Macbeth*, departed as silently as she had come. The distant shouts of Moll greeted her return to the kitchen.

The restaurant was now empty, Nat Fitzwilliam and Spike Thompson having presumably returned to the theatre.

Jemima's murmur grew still more tactful. 'You mean — also so much public attention — after' — how should she put it? — 'quite a gap. You mean — the loss of privacy. The publicity.'

'No, no,' Christabel leant forward and clutched Jemima's hand across the nymph-strewn tablecloth. Jemima could smell the lily-of-the-valley perfume which wafted from her like a sharp sweet cloud. 'Don't you see, darling, I *want* publicity. That's just why I'm doing it.'

'Well, of course, I do see —' began Jemima. Although nothing surprised her about the general avidity for publicity,

Christabel Herrick might under the circumstances have been an exception to that rule.

'I don't think you do. When Nat asked me, I jumped at the chance. He thought he had to persuade me. He didn't. I jumped at it. Even his ludicrous underwater *Seagull* and that maudlin play of Gregory's about Marie Antoinette, never one of my favourites, though it's a good part. I suddenly saw it was the way, the only way.'

'To get back onto the stage?'

'No, to be *safe*.' Christabel's voice was low and very thrilling as she pronounced the words. 'You see, darling, I know I'll feel secure with the eyes of the world upon me. The eyes of television. I'll be safe. Safe at last. Back on the stage. Your programme will be the saving of me.' Her voice grew lower and more tremulous. 'Oh, Jemima, I've been so terribly, terribly frightened, you can't imagine. Locked away at Lark. It's so dangerous . . .'

She broke off. The low door of the restaurant opened. Gregory Rowan, stooping, entered. He was accompanied by the red-haired woman known as Ketty, and the two Cartwright girls, one tall, one short, who stood rather awkwardly at the door.

'Here we are, my dear,' said Gregory with the utmost geniality. 'Your jolly old chauffeur, all present and correct, come to fetch you. I brought Ketty too, partly to do some shopping, partly because she wanted to go to confession.'

'Oh darling, what a shame,' Christabel sounded completely calm. 'I brought my own car. All this way for nothing.'

'Ah, but what you don't know is that Julian has already driven your car back after the County Council meeting. He thought driving might be rather a mistake after your lunch with Miss World Investigator here — you know. Better come quietly, hadn't you?' he added jocularly.

Christabel obediently followed him out of the restaurant. Miss Kettering with Regina and Blanche brought up the rear.

SIX

'Mummy, Mummy, Mummy'

No one could remember afterwards with any certainty who first suggested having the Festival picnic by the sea. Or rather, when it was discussed in the light of what happened later, everyone seemed to have a different version of how the idea arose.

The Megalith contingent — Jemima, Cherry, Guthrie Carlyle as well as Spike Thompson — received their invitations from Nat Fitzwilliam. This left Jemima with the distinct impression, confirmed by Guthrie, that the initiative had come from Nat in the first place. Unquestionably Nat regarded the occasion as yet another opportunity for exercising his directorial powers. He confided to Jemima that his ideas for *The Seagull* (that production scoffingly described by Christabel as 'underwater') derived their inspiration from boyhood experiences on the Larmouth sea-shore.

'By enclosing the whole production in fishermen's nets, and grounding it in sand, using rocks covered in sea-weed for furniture where necessary instead of that predictably dreary nineteenth-century Russian stuff, I think I'm groping for the symbolism *under* the symbolism of *The Seagull*. But of course I'm not forgetting Chekhov's outward intentions as well, not for a minute. I utterly despise the kind of director who simply forgets about the author altogether. I just want to fuse the two — the inner Chekhov then, the outer Chekhov now. By creating this kind of Russian picnic of us all, the whole Larminster Festival society, I think I shall strike some kind of blow towards that.'

'It all begins to make sense,' said Jemima solemnly.

'It needed doing,' echoed Guthrie with equal gravity. These two phrases had served them well in tight corners before now.

Nat looked pleased. Then a look of slight uncertainty — a rare expression — crossed his face. 'Of course I meant the other way round. The outer Chekhov then, the inner Chekhov now. But you realized that.'

'Of course,' said Jemima and Guthrie together.

At breakfast at Lark Manor on the other hand, Julian Cartwright was busy blaming his daughter Regina for the whole thing.

'For God's sake, Rina.' He spoke in a distinctly testy voice, 'Poor Mummy's already getting absolutely exhausted. You know how tired she gets when she's working. You don't remember? Well you know now. And then this bloody picnic.' He pulled himself up with the air of one who had been sufficiently sorely tried to desert a principle. 'I apologize. This disastrous picnic. We could have had a peaceful Sunday lunch. Whatever induced you, Rina, to suggest it?'

'We always used to have lovely picnics at the sea on Sundays in the summer.' Regina for once sounded as sulky as Blanche. 'Besides, I want to ride Lancelot down to the sea and let the wind flow through my hair.' She shook back her thick black tresses ostentatiously before adding: 'Anyway it was Blanche's idea, not mine.'

'As a matter of fact, Daddy, the picnic was probably Ketty's idea in the first place.' Blanche, in contrast, was in unusually high spirits. 'She wants to meet all the actors in the Festival. She keeps droning on about the old days at the Gray Theatre. And since the Blagges do all the work I don't see it's such a terrible problem for Mummy.'

'Sand in the sandwiches! Tepid coffee, empty lemonade bottles.' Julian Cartwright's handsome face flushed with irritation as he too cried 'Ugh' in his turn. He was so unreasonably bad-tempered that both girls burst out laughing.

'Oh Daddy,' cried Blanche, 'as if Lark Manor picnics were ever like that! No, we shall have our usual sumptuous food, served in our usual sumptuous style, and the actors are going to cook theirs on a huge fire —'

'Which means,' chimed in Regina, 'they will eat up all ours and be rather embarrassed and we will eat up all theirs and not be embarrassed at all. Then footing it featly, we'll all rush into the sea together, all taking hands, chanting "Come unto these yellow sands . . . curtsied when you have and kiss'd — the wild waves whist." '

'Talking of wild waves, you will not be swimming today, Regina. Nor you, Blanche.' Ketty had come into the kitchen, surprisingly quietly, through the louvred doors. There was no expression in her voice. She stood surveying the little breakfast party with her narrow lips slightly pursed. She was wearing a dark-green dress with a full skirt, rather too long for fashion, and two rows of enormous amber beads. Her thick knot of hair was skewered with a tortoise-shell pin. Without her garish lipstick and green eyeshadow, thought Julian, Ketty would really be quite a good-looking woman: but who could imagine Ketty without her war-paint?

'Jim Blagge says there's quite a sharp breeze at the point,' continued Ketty. 'He went fishing this morning. The tide will be going out at lunch-time. The river makes odd currents at low tide. It's far too dangerous. You could be carried out round the point.'

'It's very hot here, Ketty, no breeze at all,' Julian spoke mildly. 'Very hot night altogether. Mrs Cartwright couldn't sleep at all. In fact I must speak to Blagge about her shutters.' He paused and said in an even more diplomatic voice: 'She was thinking of swimming herself. I think she wants Mrs Blagge to help her find her old bathing-costumes, and there should be some old bathing-caps somewhere too.'

'I'll tell my sister, sir.' Ketty stalked out.

'Of course we're going to swim!' exclaimed Blanche before the doors had swung shut. 'All the actors will swim. I've been talking to some of them. It just makes the day quite perfect if Mummy swims too.'

Julian thought that with her flushed cheeks his elder daughter looked really quite attractive: it remained a pity that she would never be so pretty as Regina (nor for that matter as glamorous as her mother) and additionally unfair that Regina had also turned out to be more intelligent. If only Blanche could discover some real interest in life as Regina had turned to poetry. Not the theatre however. He shuddered.

'Lancelot and I are *definitely* going to swim,' said Regina in a loud obstinate voice.

In the pantry of Lark Manor — a kind of inner kitchen lit by a circular window looking onto the courtyard garden — Mr Blagge counted out rows of bamboo-handled knives and forks, considered suitable for picnics. Mrs Blagge folded a cotton table-coth printed with a pattern of shells and other artistic forms of marine life; then she began to sort out its matching napkins. Her husband shot her a sideways glance.

'How many does that make, then?'

'Enough,' said Mrs Blagge sharply, setting her lips firmly together much as Ketty had just done. 'The Lark Manor party, including the Major. Mr Rowan of course, as usual. And the television people, as instructed by Mr Julian. I am not catering for the actors. Mr Julian did not mention them. They must make their own arrangements. It makes too much work.'

Mr Blagge fetched down a row of tumblers painted with shells from a shelf — as pretty as plastic tumblers could be. 'I thought I heard you suggesting the picnic to Mr Julian the other day as making less work in the house at lunch-time.'

'What's the difference?' countered Mrs Blagge even more sharply. 'Lunch on the shore, lunch in the dining-room. It's all work, isn't it? But I didn't suggest it. I have no doubt it was Katherine's idea. She's more pleased with herself than ever these days, despite the return of' — Mrs Blagge paused before pronouncing disdainfully, 'Her. You must have heard the high and mighty Miss Katherine Kettering suggesting it.'

'People do say your voices are very similar,' was Mr Blagge's only comment.

Upstairs in her cool bedroom, Christabel Cartwright lay between white linen sheets edged with tiny scallops of lace. The vast bed was left unstirred by her slumbers: she might have been a corpse lying there for all the signs of occupation the bed showed. Her eyes were closed.

Christabel knew exactly who it was who wanted the picnic to take place. She put off as long as possible the moment when she would have to leave the safe and silent bedroom and face the day. She drew the white sheet over her head and thought about what might happen at the picnic on the sea-shore. She thought about swimming in the sea, whether it would be safe to swim in the sea.

A few hours later, on the Larmouth beach, it was a very different Christabel Cartwright who emerged. She was now officially Christabel Herrick — perhaps that was the difference. It was Christabel Herrick who was beguiling the whole King Charles Theatre Company as well as enslaving the more susceptible representatives of Megalith Television — Guthrie Carlyle, for example, and Cherry. (Spike Thompson on the other hand showed no particular signs of joining her court as yet, but remained beside Jemima.)

Christabel even clowned for all their delectation in one of the extraordinary bathing-caps which had been rooted out of some cupboard by Mrs Blagge. She ignored a plainer-looking one beside it. Op Art? Pop Art? With its black and white rubber rosettes springing up all over the scalp, the cap she chose certainly belonged to some vanished era of garish fashion.

'I look like a mad magpie especially with this ghastly vulgar bathing-dress,' exclaimed Christabel. 'All the same, I think I should go the whole hog and wear the turquoise one, don't you? You'll certainly all be able to keep an eye on me in the briny. Make sure I don't sink without trace.'

'Are you really going to swim, Mummy?' enquired Blanche solicitously. Regina, who had ridden down to the shore on Lancelot, kicked her heels into the horse and trotted away down the beach. Jemima noticed Julian Cartwright frowning.

'We'll have to build a monster fire in honour of our leading lady's dip,' said a young actor in striped bathing-shorts and rugger shirt, in whose direction Jemima noticed that Blanche Cartwright had been casting yearning glances. He was called something like Ollie or Obbie Summertown and Jemima vaguely recognized him from various small parts in television: junior detectives, young policemen, and other budding representatives of law and order. He had already been tearing about the beach gathering driftwood; but Jemima had imagined it was for the benefit of Filly Lennox rather than Blanche Cartwright.

The fame of Filumena Lennox, like that of Jemima Shore, sprang from television. In 'Country Kate' Filly's ingenious depiction of a disaster-prone city girl trying to run the farm left to her by an unknown admirer had left a deep impression on the public. She was much less experienced on the stage, a state of affairs she was at present trying to remedy by working with the King Charles Company. It seemed that, unlike some famous television stars, Filly Lennox was able to make the switch effectively. Provincial reviewers — and the odd visiting critic from London — had admired her during the previous season.

Jemima, appraising her with interest (she had to admit to a secret fascination with 'Country Kate'), thought that Filly Lennox was a good deal less pretty in real life than on the screen. Her floppy fair hair — presumably she had worn a curly wig in the series — made Filly's nose look rather unexpectedly beaky in a small pointed face. In a way she was not unlike a much younger version of Christabel Herrick, although neither lady would probably have relished the comparison. Only Filly's wonderful eyes, large, hazel, fringed by what were clearly naturally long and black eyelashes, remained to startle.

That — and her figure. Gazing speculatively at what could be seen of it already in white cotton trousers and white T-shirt printed with heart and arrow, Jemima thought that for once Flowering Cherry, the toast of Megalithic House, might have to look to her laurels. She need not have worried. The moment when Cherry threw off her fringed purple poncho, edged with jingling bells, was dramatically superb; and what was revealed beneath more than justified her performance of disrobing.

After that Ollie Summertown decided to stop gathering driftwood quite so energetically and strip off his own rugger shirt 'to get some decent sun before lunch'. As if by chance, he lay at Cherry's feet, and was thus conveniently able to share the sun-oil with which she rubbed her gleaming olive legs and shoulders. Blanche looked wistful. Cherry hoped that Julian Cartwright would feel jealous and oiled Ollie's back.

Filly Lennox, unfazed by Ollie's defection, started to flirt quite blatantly with Gregory Rowan: 'Oh, you should have seen my Baroness Anne in your *Tower*! Well anyway the dress. You see, we had this designer — Knocky Pallett — don't ever work with him — if you'd seen what he did to your lovely play . . . somehow he insisted the period was entirely top-less . . .'

To Jemima's surprise, Gregory Rowan seemed to take to this dialogue with enthusiasm.

'Nonsense, my dear, perfectly historically correct. The part shall never be played any other way in my lifetime. Now can we get down to discussing your costume in *Widow Capet*? No false modesty here, I hope. The girl's a brazen hussy, you realize that. What's Knocky Pallett doing these days, I wonder? We might get hold of him for some last-minute liberating sugges-tions. Nat, what do you think?'

But Nat Fitzwilliam was sitting literally at Christabel's feet, recapitulating for her benefit the triumph of his Sung Dynasty *Hamlet*. Despite the heat he was wearing an anorak and his habitual long scarf which completed the schoolboy look. An expression of outrage crossed his face at the mention of the name Knocky Pallett, but whether at the mere idea of someone else's liberating influence on his own production or at Knocky Pallett's in particular, was not clear. Nevertheless he did not pause in the flow of his disquisition.

Jemima thought that the whole set of Christabel's face looked rather melancholy now that it was in repose. The lines round her mouth were more obvious and there was a sad downward curve to her lips. Perhaps she did not care for the attention Gregory was paying to the flirtatious Filly Lennox: Jemima thought there might have been a gleam of jealousy there. Christabel was certainly a woman accustomed to being the centre of attention as of right. But it was impossible to tell the true expression in her eyes, behind her dark glasses, as she contemplated Nat. She looked beautiful of course — in her own style. A couple of gold chains strung with real shells set in gold hung to her waist. A leopard-skin printed scarf protected her daffodil hair from the sun. Her long diaph-anous robe of the same leopard-skin printed material, worn over a matching sun-top and shorts, made the young things' display of·nudity look rather odd — or vice versa, thought Jemima, depending on your taste.

As yet Christabel showed no signs of taking to the sea; although the bathing-costumes and caps discovered by Mrs Blagge — including the despised turquoise ruched number and magpie cap — remained by her side. 'Safe at last' — among a company of actors — she had told Jemima. She did not give the impression of one who felt safe.

A group of the other actors — male — were sitting by the fire discussing the Test Match with great earnestness; such was their absorption that the flames would have died down altogether had it not been for the work of Mr Blagge who ended by coping with both the grand Lark Manor picnic and the actors' barbecue. The actors' voices rose and fell, making soothing patterns, no two phrases absolutely the same, but all phrases remarkably similar, like Bach variations played at a distance.

Victor Marcovich, who would play Trigorin in *The Seagull* and the jailer in *Widow Capet*, looked heavily distinguished on the beach with his fine bald dome and fleshy Roman features. He also looked much older than another actor generally addressed as Tobs, who would play the ageing Dr Dorn in *The Seagull* as well as mopping up a number of revolutionary and aristocratic parts in *Widow Capet*. Tobs told Jemima that in the latter production he had to alternate between wearing a Jacobin cap and a powdered wig; as a result he had a recurrent nightmare of getting the order wrong and going finally to the guillotine wearing a Jacobin cap.

'But at least whatever scene you shoot, you can't miss me. No need to worry,' he told Jemima engagingly. 'I should say my best moment is when I come to hoik *her*' — he indicated Christabel — 'off to the guillotine. You can forget Dr Dorn: there's nothing in it for me, particularly in our Nat's seaside version. In my sou'wester and oilskins I'm probably quite unrecognizable.'

'I'll remember,' Jemima promised.

The most ancient member of the company — and indeed of any company likely to be formed — was Nicola Wain. 'Old Nicola', as she generally termed herself, had survived her legendary amount of years as an actress by dint of an outwardly placid nature which concealed something altogether more ruthless beneath.

'I hear you have a part for Old Nicola in your latest,' she would murmur in the ear of unsuspecting directors — and even, when times were very bad, playwrights. 'Oh you naughty boy, nothing for Old Nicola? That's not what I hear. Trying to pull the wool over my eyes, are you, you naughty boy? Waiting for Sybil Thorndike to rise from the dead, eh? Oh, he is a naughty boy.'

Certain roles however Nicola considered to be her own. The jailer's mother in *Widow Capet* — a fearful old revolutionary crone armed with knitting needles — being one of them, she had resolutely imposed herself on the Larminster Festival. Even Nat Fitzwilliam had proved incapable of dislodging her. When it was pointed out that there was nothing remotely suitable for her in *The Seagull* — Tobs as a youthful Dr Dorn hardly needed a geriatric Polena — Nicola had the effrontery to suggest that they should play *The Three Sisters* instead, where audiences always loved to see her in the part of the old nanny. Hastily, Nat had settled for giving her the single role of the jailer's mother, as being the lesser of two evils. He had not reckoned on the fact that being in one production only afforded Nicola an excellent opportunity for 'observing all you naughty boys and girls' as she put it, in the other.

Now Nicola sat on the shore holding forth to Major Cartwright on the subject of Anglo-Indian politics, based on a theatrical tour of the Raj in the early twenties when she had played Juliet. Something about the Major's correct but ancient white summer suit and a straw hat with faded ribbon had obviously excited her. Pointedly, the Major denied ever having been East of Suez: he failed to stop the flow.

Ketty had cornered Emily Jones, the rather sweet-looking girl who would play Masha to Filly Lennox's Nina; Ketty, like Old Nicola, was indulging in theatrical reminiscences, although hers were vicariously based on Christabel's career, not her own. Emily Jones looked younger than Filly Lennox in real life, much as the unknown Tobs looked younger than Vic Marcovich; she was beginning to have a rather desperate air as Ketty's amber beads dangled closer and closer to her face, when Mrs Blagge acidly recalled Ketty to her duties.

'If you would be so kind, Katherine, there are certain tasks for you as well as Jim and myself.'

If you looked backwards, the tall harsh shape of the Watchtower Theatre could be seen in the distance, looking down from its great height on the sylvan shore, the dark glass of its structure giving the air of enormous eyes keeping an eye on events. But no one did look back — none of the actors, or the other participants in the Festival picnic. Much as Regina Cartwright had predicted, the actors concentrated mainly on the Lark Manor food — asparagus quiches, smoked-salmon cornets filled with prawns, and cold chicken pie cut in slices. They also drank Julian Cartwright's claret which he dispensed personally with a lavish hand. He used the same formula to everyone as he poured.

'A good light Beaujolais Brouilly '76. Sorry about the plastic tumblers but we can't have broken-glass tragedies on the beach. All the same I think you'll enjoy it.'

He was quite right. The actors certainly did enjoy it.

Filly Lennox, who had definitely drunk too much — a great deal too much — became quite pink and giggly. It was in fact Filly who was responsible for one of the few awkward moments of the picnic. After announcing that she was absolutely pie-eyed, she added that she was bound to regret it. Then she started to hum a popular song, filling in a word here and there.

It took those present several instants to realise that Filly was happily intoning 'Coo-ool, oh so cool repentance', and several more instants to shut her up, since Filly was quite impervious to winks and frowns. On the contrary, she seemed more than likely to plough right on through Iron Boy's repertory, one song leading to another — until Gregory Rowan saved the day by pulling her back down beside him. Then there was some much safer talk of an expedition to France when the Festival was over — 'I'd love to show you what's left of pre-revolutionary Paris', he was heard to say eagerly.

'I suppose that's France over there, isn't it?' Filly cried, waving a hand towards what was in fact the next Bridset headland. 'Take me to it.'

Emily Jones drank a little too much and, freed of Ketty's attentions, moved closer to Spike Thompson; who nevertheless showed no signs of leaving the side of Jemima Shore. Ollie Summertown drank enough to do some startling gymnastics on the beach, for the particular edification of Cherry and the general edification of anyone else who cared to watch.

'Do you fancy that sort of thing?' Spike spoke quite casually in Jemima's direction. Jemima, who was alone in drinking white wine, took first a sip and then a look. Ollie was currently indulging in a prolonged hand-stand.

'It's rather difficult to tell when he's upside down, isn't it?'

Blanche and Regina Cartwright were both poured half-tumblers of wine by their father. But it was impossible to tell how much he, as host, had drunk. Julian continued to look urbane if slightly flushed. He accepted the frequent compliments of the cast on the quality of the wine with every sign of pleasure. Nat Fitzwilliam alone lifted his glass spasmodically without any sign of noticing what he was imbibing; when Blanche, after colloquy with Tobs, tested this theory by pouring Coca-Cola into his claret, he took a sip quite happily.

Christabel definitely drank a great deal: Jemima watched her. Her hands as she held her shell-painted tumbler trembled.

It was possible that her large straw bag also contained a small bottle of solacing vodka.

Vic Marcovich drank the most but without any sign of inebriation at all; until the moment when he threw off his shirt and marched straight off in the direction of the sea, uttering the single superbly articulated word: 'Forward!' The picnic party watched him go. The tide was now very low. His figure, with its fine bull-like shoulders and short muscley legs — it could have been the figure of a wrestler — could be seen for a long while proceeding out across the rippled sands left by the sea.

Suddenly it was as though an emergency warning had been given for the whole party to abandon the site of the picnic as fast as possible. Blanche Cartwright grabbed Ollie's hand as he finished a somersault and before he could object — or cast an eye round for Cherry — pulled him off towards the distant sea. Regina too re-mounted Lancelot, and galloped off in the direction of the sea: she was reciting Shelley at full tilt as she went. The horse's hooves splashed Blanche and Ollie as Regina passed them. Riding bareback in her scarlet costume, with her black hair flying, Regina looked, thought Jemima, like an advertisement for something — not necessarily something as young and innocent as Regina herself.

Her protests about the tide, wind and water ignored, Ketty proceeded to don a severe but not unbecoming black costume and stalked after her charges in the direction of the sea.

Cherry, distinctly flown with wine and free of Ollie's chaperonage, saw her chance with Julian Cartwright.

'Sware for a swim?' was how the words actually came out. But it did not seem to matter since he evidently looked on the proposition favourably. 'What about you, darling?' he enquired briefly of Christabel. 'Are you going to have a dip?'

Christabel was in the throes of hearing from Nat about his encounter with J. S. Grand, editor of the powerful and prestigious *Literature*, at some elegant First Night supper party in Connaught Square, at which Nat by his own account had reduced the mighty editor to silence with his ideas on Chekhov.

'Jamie Grand is such a darling, isn't he?' broke in Christabel. 'And so amusing. I remember he once said to me that the thing about Chekhov and sex — or was it Turgenev and sex — anyway . . .' Her voice trailed away. She was obviously relieved by Julian's interruption. 'Definitely I shall swim!' she cried with a great deal more energy. 'Definitely. But I make no promise as to exactly where and when. In the meantime why don't you join the lady?'

Nat Fitzwilliam looked a good deal less pleased by Julian's sudden appearance. He announced his intention of going back to the Watchtower to get further inspiration for *The Seagull* from its vantage point 'by seeing the shore as an empty hole' — or perhaps he meant whole, it was not immediately clear.

He was also promising darkly to rethink various Chekhovian characters by viewing them at a great distance. Arkadina, for example.

'Not Arkadina, darling, if you don't mind,' said Christabel sweetly. 'You've thought about her quite enough for one production. Give the others a turn. Why don't you keep an eye on Blanche and our Konstantin instead. Or Gregory and the lovely Miss Lennox? There might be insights into Trigorin and Nina there. Or even Julian and Miss —' she paused and gazed speculatively at Cherry in her gravity-defying costume — 'Miss Cherry. So much more rewarding.'

The roar of Nat's motor-bike was heard as he left. Jemima saw Christabel's graceful figure drifting in the direction of the trees at the head of the beach in order to change. She bore a very large straw basket on her arm, containing the despised costumes and caps unearthed by Mrs Blagge. Despite picnic conditions, vodka and Beaujolais consumed in large quantities and her cumbersome burden, Christabel still managed to look immeasurably elegant: she conveyed the impression of a star leaving the stage to the minor characters — purely for the time being.

Filly Lennox now seemed loath to take to the water, even escorted by Gregory Rowan, and murmured or rather giggled a series of rather thin excuses. There was some rather prolonged and playful discussion on the subject of swimming with or without costumes which Jemima found increasingly irritating: why could not Gregory and Filly simply strip off and plunge in and be done with it? But in the end the matter was resolved differently. Filly was not so loath to adjourning with Gregory to the shade of the trees on the far side of the river bank to discuss the matter further: she confessed to the need to lie down. Their figures also vanished. Jemima felt meanly pleased that Christabel had also meandered off in that direction, a fact of which they were evidently unaware.

Jemima found herself alone with Spike Thompson at the now deserted picnic scene — alone except for the Blagges, that is. It was the polite but embarrassing presence of the Blagges which decided her. Taking off her own shirt and trousers, to reveal a new white bikini which she was not at all averse to displaying, she cast an inviting smile in the direction of Spike.

'Our turn,' said Jemima. Spike looked distinctly disappointed when she tugged him off in the direction of the sea, much as Cherry had pulled away Julian Cartwright.

'So many swimmers. Even Her —' Mrs Blagge gestured back to the group of trees to which Christabel had retreated. 'You'd better get the boat, Jim. If you meant what you said this morning about the breeze at the point.' So Mr Blagge departed in the direction of the boat pulled up on a steep bank of pebbles near the river bed. After a bit Mrs Blagge vanished too.

The fire smoked and went out. Only the seagulls still whirled round the deserted picnic site for a while; then they too flew away. The breeze at the point did blow up a little, making a few white crests on the waves outside the bay. The tide started to come in, very fast over the level sands. There was still no one present where the picnic had once been.

Jemima Shore had just changed back into her clothes in the group of trees near the cars, and was busy towelling her thick hair, dripping with sea-water, when the screaming began.

It seemed to come from a little knot of bathers — all men — advancing together through the shallow waters to the edge of the beach. They were moving curiously slowly, staggering slightly. That was because they were carrying something, something heavy. With a sick feeling Jemima recognized the ridiculous black and white bathing-cap Christabel Cartwright had been mocking only a few hours before, and the turquoise bathing-costume.

The person who was screaming was Blanche Cartwright. She was facing the advancing party and their burden.

Blanche Cartwright was screaming: 'Mummy, Mummy, Mummy.'

SEVEN

Her Last Hour

In death Christabel Cartwright's face looked quite young and vulnerable. Even her body appeared slighter and more childish than the full middle-aged figure Jemima remembered.

Julian Cartwright and Victor Marcovich were taking it in turns to kneel over her urgently trying to breathe some movement back into that sodden body, or knead some beat from its still heart. For how long? — it seemed like hours. Now Julian was kneeling back on his haunches with a look of despair on his face. Vic Marcovich bent forward again. Ollie Summertown had rushed past Jemima, still in his striped bathing-shorts, to get help; she heard the angry whirr of his motor-bike ascending the track from the beach to the village.

Christabel's eyes were closed. A strand of fair hair escaped the black and white cap and lay along the pale cheek: the sight of that, no longer fluffy, no longer the bright colour of a daffodil, was unbearably touching.

It was at that moment that Jemima realized that she was

looking into the dead face of Filumena Lennox, Filly Lennox with her pretty full youthful body, in Christabel Cartwright's vivid turquoise costume. Filly Lennox with her fair hair escaping from Christabel Cartwright's magpie cap. She realized it a split second before she heard the characteristic melodious voice of Christabel herself calling from a distance.

'I'm here. What is it? What's the matter, Blanche? Do stop screaming "Mummy, Mummy" like that, darling.'

But Blanche did not stop screaming. She merely transferred her renewed cries in the direction of her mother, who was now advancing rapidly towards the little group at the edge of the sea, and the body of Filly Lennox where the men had laid her. In contrast to the bathers, Christabel still looked inappropriately smart in her diaphanous leopard-skin printed robe. Her hair stood up from her head like a golden aureole.

'Oh Mummy, Mummy, it's not you, it's not you. I thought it was you.' Blanche's voice rose hysterically and then she burst into tears just as Christabel reached them.

The men who had carried Filly Lennox's body included Gregory Rowan as well as two of the actors. He stood slightly apart from the group round the body. It was to Gregory that Christabel turned, rather distractedly, as though she could not quite take in what had happened, did not quite believe it even now, thought it was all a delusion, a joke perhaps, in spite of the manifest presence of poor Filly's drowned body, lying there on the shore, with Victor Marcovich kneeling beside her, still rather hopelessly massaging her chest.

'Darling, what's she doing in my costume?' she asked. 'And that's my funny magpie hat — I was looking for it. Why did she take it?' Christabel put her hand on Gregory's arm. 'Why is she dressed —'

'Christabel, be quiet, the girl is dead.' It was Julian Cartwright who interrupted his wife as though determined to put an end to these frantic and embarrassing enquiries. He moved and put his arm protectively round her. For a moment Christabel stood thus between Julian and Gregory. Then Gregory moved away.

Like Julian, he spoke heavily, almost wearily: 'She must have changed her mind and swum after me. I teased her about not daring to take a dip. But she wouldn't come. And so I left her. Oh my God, the poor, poor child.'

'That was because she couldn't swim really, or at least not very well.' Tobs sounded pathetically eager as though an explanation of her behaviour might actually bring Filly back to life.

'Yes, she told me this morning she definitely wasn't going to swim. We're sharing digs in Larminster. And then Filly washed her hair specially to look nice at the picnic, so I suppose she took the cap —' Emily Jones began to cry, but quietly, not like Blanche, leaning her head on Tobs's shoulder. 'She was so excited at meeting *you*,' Emily sobbed, nodding her head in the direction of Gregory. 'Properly. Not in the theatre.'

'You see, darling, I fell asleep under the cliffs in my old nook.' Christabel was rattling on, although it was not quite clear whom she was addressing. 'I left my things under the trees in the old place where I always used to change, and then, it was so hot, and I felt so sleepy — all that claret I suppose — we should really serve white wine at picnics in future, darling —'

'Christabel, stop,' said Julian Cartwright in an urgent voice. Jemima realized that Christabel was trembling so hard that her long gold necklaces with their pendent sea-shells shook together.

'When I came back from my nap under the cliff,' she finished more calmly, 'the costume and hat were both gone. I was desperate to swim after my nap. I was livid. I lay down again under the cliff and tried to cool off.'

The arrival of Regina, leading Lancelot through the shallow splashing surf from the opposite direction of the eastern cliff, created a diversion. Still in her red costume, with her wet black hair hanging down her back, Regina looked slightly threatening as though she might carry away Filly's body on her horse's crupper like some modern Valkyrie. When told the news of Filly's death, she turned quite white, and stammered something which was probably a quotation from Webster since it sounded like 'She died young', before lapsing into silence.

Even more bizarre was the appearance of Mr Blagge, rowing his boat towards the shore, up the channel of the river. If Regina had fleetingly resembled a Valkyrie, Mr Blagge had the uncomfortable air of a Charon come to row the dead girl away to some oceanic Hades.

His words, when he heard the news, were spoken in a voice rough and cracked with emotion: 'This is at your door,' he cried turning in the direction of Christabel, adding after a pause with terrible polite incongruity: 'Madam. Our boy, this girl —' he continued wildly, looking round at Jemima and Spike Thompson, then at the still weeping Emily Jones, as though appealing for confirmation. He was wearing a khaki waterproof jacket and trousers which presumably concealed the neat suit in which he had served lunch: the outfit gave him a vaguely military air.

'Jim.' The voice of Mrs Blagge, coming from behind them, sounded very sharp indeed. She had joined them from somewhere in the direction of the cars. At the same time Julian Cartwright with equal authority and a good deal of anger, exclaimed: 'That's enough, Blagge. We must all be careful not to upset poor Miss Lennox's friends further.' He emphasized the word 'all'.

Gregory put a comforting arm round Christabel again. It wasn't clear from her expression whether Christabel had taken in the extent of Mr Blagge's venom: she merely looked rather dazed. Then the arrival of Major Cartwright, still immaculate in his white suit and straw hat, meant that the news of Filly Lennox's death had to be broken all over again. Afterwards he kept repeating angrily: 'But what was the girl doing in *your* bathing-suit, Christabel?', thus making it clear where he thought the responsibility for the tragedy lay.

By the time the ambulance arrived, bringing with it rapid professional — but equally unsuccessful — attempts at resuscitation, the picnic party had been transformed into a very different kind of gathering. The story of the last hour in Filumena Lennox's life had also been pieced together — more or less. Rather less than more, thought Jemima. But that thought she kept to herself for the time being, along with some other thoughts on the subject of the untimely death of a young woman, not totally unlike Christabel Cartwright in type and colouring, wearing Christabel Cartwright's conspicuous turquoise bathing-costume and magpie hat.

Gregory Rowan was the last person who had actually spoken to Filly Lennox — on the shore among the trees — but he was by no means the last person to have seen her. Several people had caught sight of her in the sea·or at any rate of the striking black and white hat bobbing about in the water; but of course everyone had assumed they were looking at Christabel.

After Gregory Rowan had left Filly, he had waded into the sea in his favourite place, under the western cliff, on the other side of the river which divided the shore in half; he had deliberately swum away from the merry gathering on the other side of the little bay. 'For peace,' he said. Jemima guessed that he had also privately decided to dispense with a bathing-costume, in his preferred fashion, and had not wished to advertise the fact. So that when Filly decided, literally, to take the plunge, she had gone to look for him in quite the wrong direction.

Ketty volunteered that a figure in a black and white cap had passed her, striking out rather slowly, in view of the waves, in the general direction of the point: 'I *did* think it was rather unwise.'

Ketty, in her tight-lipped way, was obviously very shaken by the incident, and evidently blamed herself for not warning the girl about the tide and the currents. 'Believing it however to be Mrs Cartwright and believing she would remember — she couldn't have forgotten that — she used to swim there all the time — once — believing it was my duty to look after the girls . . . Besides, Jim Blagge was out there somewhere with the boat. He should have helped her.'

But Jim Blagge was one of the few people who had apparently not seen Filly in her magpie cap, Julian Cartwright being another.

Blanche confirmed that she had seen Filly swimming — 'But it was Mummy, I knew it was Mummy, that was the whole point.' Blanche was on the verge of howling again before Julian Cartwright curtly indicated to Ketty that she should put an end to these hysterics.

Regina's contribution was briefer: 'I swam alone and saw no one and nothing.' Then she added illogically: 'I thought it was Mummy anyway,' and burst into tears. But unlike her sister, she cried quietly.

All the actors had swum in the end, or at least paddled, with the exception of Old Nicola and Major Cartwright. After lunch, at which she had drunk at least her fair share of claret, Nicola had adjourned to the upper shore. Here she had plonked herself down on a comfortable chair unwillingly abstracted by Mrs Blagge from the Cartwright Land-Rover. Robbed of the company of the Major — who rapidly backed away from the prospect of a further tête-à-tête on the subject of the British Raj — Nicola settled down to a little post-prandial sport with the triumphant words: 'Time to watch you naughty boys and girls.' Out of a dark-grey plastic bag which had itself seen better days, she had produced a shapeless mass of knitting of roughly the same colour. (It was part of their power struggle that Nat Fitzwilliam was quite determined Old Nicola should not produce her own knitting on stage during *Widow Capet*:

but she had by no means conceded the point.) And then Old Nicola had noticed Filly Lennox staggering towards the sea.

'Staggering, my dears. I'm afraid there's no other word for it. The poor girl was quite — well, you know. She was laughing too, and singing. That Iron Boy song you wouldn't let her sing before, "Cool Repentance". Not that she had anything much to repent about, the poor little duck. And some of the other Iron Boy songs. She looked very happy. I dare say it was a very happy death. We should all try to look at it like that.'

This picture of Filly Lennox, weaving and laughing her way towards the sea, Ophelia-like, singing snatches of songs — worst of all the banned songs of Iron Boy — upset everyone anew. Jemima saw that Tobs's eyes were wet.

'Of course I knew it wasn't Christabel!' continued Nicola. 'I wasn't fooled for a moment. Much smaller bottom. We all spread out as the years pass, don't we, my dear?' The old woman turned to Christabel with a well-delivered conspiratorial look. 'And you really have lived well over the past few years, haven't you? Which is funny, because my friend Susan Merlin told me you were absolutely starving in a garret —'

Some of the members of the company remembered amid the general embarrassment that Christabel for one had been strongly opposed to the introduction of Old Nicola into the Larminster Festival. 'She's a positive croaking raven; give me Susan Merlin any time even if she can't remember more than one line in three . . . at least that line comes from the right play . . .' Old Nicola had evidently nosed out Christabel's hostility.

Now feeling that she had created enough trouble for one day, Nicola finished her account of Filly's passage to the sea by timing it precisely, 'Four o'clock. On the dot. I looked at my watch. No, I never make that kind of mistake.' In a lower voice, she added: 'And wasn't one of you naughty boys giving her a bit of a cuddle in the sea? Or was it just a girl giving her a helping hand? I've got eyes in my head, you know. At least it wasn't you, Major, do you remember, you went for a walk on to the cliffs, spying on all the pretty girls where they were changing, I saw you, you old rascal.'

Major Cartwright, curtly denying the motive, did admit the walk. And since Old Nicola did not name the cuddler — or the helper — and nobody had mentioned encountering her in the sea, that parting shot was not thought to be particularly important by the company in general: merely part of Old Nicola's general propensity towards malice. Jemima Shore, who did note it vaguely, pushed the remark to the back of her mind for the time being.

After Nicola lost sight of Filly Lennox, the girl had been alone.

Alone with no one to warn or help her, she had taken the treacherous route to exactly where the currents made by the river debouching its subterranean waters were most dangerous. Somewhere out there a sudden freak wave breaking — not an uncommon occurrence — must have taken her by surprise, filled her mouth with water, then her lungs . . . No one of course had seen her getting into difficulty or waving for help or heard her shouting — if she had been able to shout. No one said it aloud but everyone remembered how much Filly had drunk in the course of the picnic. Perhaps she never knew quite what was happening to her. Or perhaps Filly Lennox had waved, waved and struggled desperately for survival, and everyone near her had merely interpreted it as a cheerful salutation from Christabel Cartwright.

That had been Victor Marcovich's experience: and he, like Ketty, blamed himself passionately for the mistake, convinced that he might have done something to save Filly had he known.

'The trouble was I was pissed,' he groaned.

'We were all pissed,' Ollie corrected him. 'I lost the little girl altogether, she vanished. Which one was it? Blanche, the fat one —' He seemed unaware of Blanche's continued pres-

ence, standing beside Ketty. 'I dived off in search of you —'
He looked towards Cherry, standing in her once-gay purple
poncho, which now had the air of a funeral garment.

'It's all rocks out there, and little bays and inlets at low
tide. You do lose sight of people.'

'Yes, I lost sight of you altogether', put in Cherry rather
plaintively. 'Where were you? Where did you go?'

Julian ignored her. Then his calm air of authority suddenly
broke and he too groaned: 'Oh my God, the poor girl, why
did we swim at all? Why didn't I stop you?'

It was Tobs who was in the worst state of all: for it was
Tobs who had found Filly's body floating on the surface of the
sea, the face half-covered with water; the waves were propel-
ling it inexorably towards the shore.

One of the ambulance men said, before Filly's body was
rushed away to hospital, still in the vain hope of resuscitating
it: 'It is very dangerous swimming out at the point at low tide.
Someone was drowned here I believe a couple of years ago.
Also from London.' There was a very faint note of reproach
in his voice.

After that no one had much to say. Breaking the news to
the world in general and Filly's family in particular was obviously the next painful task to be faced. And breaking the
news to the world at any rate — wasn't that at least in part
the concern of Nat Fitzwilliam as Festival Director? It was also
the concern of the Festival Chairman. Major Cartwright departed in his Bentley to inform such bodies as his Festival
Board, with a view to preparing a statement on the whole
distressing episode.

'As Chairman, it was my duty to come to this festivity,' he
commented gruffly to no one in particular. His gruffness appeared to hide some strong emotion, presumably disapproval
of the whole Bacchanalian nature of the picnic. In the meantime, what of the Festival Director?

Nat Fitzwilliam — oddly enough, no one had thought of

him in the course of the crisis. He had last been seen, still in his scarf and anorak, heading for the Watchtower Theatre where he had intended to view the shore from on high and seek further inspiration . . . first of all, someone had to tell *him*.

Guthrie Carlyle, as representative of Megalith, volunteered for this disagreeable duty. Jemima Shore, in exchange, agreed to shoulder the burden of breaking to Cy Fredericks, head of Megalith Television, the news of the tragedy which had just struck at his Larminster Festival programme. Cy Fredericks was certainly the right person to handle the whole public mourning which would follow the lamentable decease not only of Filumena Lennox, but of 'Country Kate'.

But it rapidly transpired that Guthrie Carlyle had the best of the bargain. There was the noise of another motor-bike arriving, and Nat Fitzwilliam appeared in person at the head of the beach.

'I passed an ambulance,' he began. 'And then you were all standing there on the beach for so long after the swimming stopped. I saw you. I was watching you all the time. From the top of the theatre.' Jemima suddenly noticed the large pair of binoculars slung round his neck, half-hidden by his scarf.

The person who hated Christabel also noticed the binoculars. The person thought it would be a pity if it turned out that Nat Fitzwillian had witnessed certain things through those binoculars. The person was really very sorry indeed about the death of Filumena Lennox, which had been a stupid mistake, and just showed the foolishness of giving way to impulse after so long. The person thought: you could certainly lay that death at the door of Christabel; if she had not come back to Larminster in the first place, none of this would have happened.

EIGHT

Late at Night

'What are *you* doing, flapping round here?' The question was directed at Nicola Wain — with no pretence of grace — by Christabel Cartwright. Indeed, the old woman did have something of the air of a bird, if not a vulture or a raven, still something vaguely ominous, a rook perhaps; with her bright little black eyes, and her long nose which gave the effect of a beak.

It was very hot in the conservatory at Lark Manor, although the glass windows were all flung open. Nicola was wearing no stockings. Her legs, beneath her dark print dress, looked aggressively white and at the same time gnarled, patched with veins and other bumps. Christabel's beautiful shapely legs were also bare but beneath her pristine pleated white cotton skirt, worn with a pale-blue silk shirt, they looked smooth, tanned, expensive — legs which were caressed daily by lotions and creams, things which, even in her hey-day, would never have come within reach of the old actress's purse.

The emphasis on Old Nicola's legs was due to the fact that

she had stretched them out on one of the comfortable chaise-longues in the conservatory. The rich foxy scent of the regale lilies, standing everywhere in pots, filled the air. The summer cushions had lilies printed on them: just as in winter the cushions had a pattern of ferns.

'It was your sweet little girl invited me up,' confided Nicola. Christabel's eyes fell on a silver tray, placed on a low stool beside the chaise-longue; plates still bore the remnants of a delicate yet tasty meal. 'She knows I'm not very comfortable in my room at the Spring Guest House. Old Nicola does like to be comfortable at her age, well *you*'d understand that, and the little duck suggested Mr Blagge should collect me in Larminster along with the shopping and just give Old Nicola a little, just a little taste of honey. Then she's talked to Mrs Tennant the manageress at the Royal Stag. Tonight that nice Mrs Tennant is going to squeeze me into a room, just a *wee* room, at a price an old lady can afford —'

'Then where *is* Blanche, since she has so kindly made herself your hostess?' Christabel had recovered her composure, but it was noticeable she still made no pretence of welcoming Nicola. For that matter the old woman remained stretched out on the liliaceous cushions without any attempt at moving.

'Little Blanche? Oh, I imagine *she*'s still at the audition.' At which point Old Nicola helped herself to the remaining sandwich, popping it neatly into her mouth like a seal swallowing a fish. 'Nat is reading for the new Nina this morning. Poor little Filumena. But still, the show must go on, mustn't it? And so say all of us.' Old Nicola polished off the last macaroon with equal delicacy and even greater relish. 'As you know, my dear, I'm not in *The Seagull*, but I should have thought you at least might have wanted to be there. To see how the little duck makes out. And she *is* a little duck, too, I think it's a lovely idea to have your own real-life daughter playing Nina, even if she has absolutely no experience.

'I said so to Vic Marcovich only this morning, who didn't

quite see it that way, I must admit, but then he wouldn't, would he?' Old Nicola somehow managed to munch and speak at the same time. 'Bloody unprofessional were the words he used — if you'll pardon the expression. Shall we say he's been just a *wee* bit disappointed all along that our dear Anna Maria never got to play Madame Arkadina after all? You came along at such *very* short notice, and you were *such* a big star. So we needn't pay any attention to that naughty old Vic, need we, after all he and Anna Maria are just like two kittens in a basket —'

Then Nicola went on to demolish the last two tiny creamy éclairs.

'*What* are you saying?' *Blanche* as Nina? It was at that moment exactly, almost as though Christabel's anguished cry had given him his cue, that Julian Cartwright strode into the conservatory. He was accompanied by Ketty and Mr Blagge.

'Blanche as *Nina*?' He hurled the words at his wife. Ketty looked extremely nervous, Mr Blagge wore a slightly sardonic expression, and Julian Cartwright looked plainly furious. 'Is this *your* doing?' he added.

'Over my dead body!' Christabel answered, in a voice approaching a scream. 'She can't *act*. At school Blanche couldn't even play the Gentlewoman in the Lady Macbeth sleep-walking scene, and God knows that's no test of ability. Never ever have I been so embarrassed in the whole of my life sitting there. She even got her lines wrong: "It is an accustomed action with her to seem thus washing her hair . . ." and then the whole school burst into roars of laughter. And *then* she went and gave her name on the programme as Blanche Herrick Cartwright, when her middle name is actually May after your ghastly mother.' In her hysteria Christabel did not seem to have grasped that she and her husband were actually on the same side.

Only Old Nicola, finding a sponge finger she had previously

overlooked, continued to bear an expression of placid happiness.

About the same time, telephoning from a rather less elegantly furnished room in a Larminster hotel, Jemima Shore was trying to explain to Cy Fredericks just why the casting of Blanche Cartwright as Nina in *The Seagull*, would be a total disaster. From the point of view of Megalith Television, that is. It would also, in Jemima's opinion, be a disaster from the point of view of the Larminster Festival, the King Charles Theatre Company, the present production of *The Seagull*, and last and possibly least, the future of Miss Blanche Herrick Cartwright on the stage. But since Cy Fredericks notoriously did not recognize any point of view other than that of Megalith, it was hardly worth mentioning these further considerations.

'As it happens, Blanche Cartwright is not a dish and she's not a doll either,' Jemima was explaining as patiently as possible. She kept her voice down. Cy Fredericks, like Julian Cartwright, had a tendency to shout when aroused and she did not wish to encourage him: the conversation had already lasted twenty minutes. 'But that's nothing to do with the case. You see, Cy, while you *don't* have to be a dish or a doll or a fruit or a chick to play Nina, you *do* have to be able to —'

But the word 'act' was quite drowned by Cy Frederick's amiable roar down the line:

'It helps, my dear Jem, it helps,' he boomed. 'Think of us old men leaning forward glassy-eyed in front of our sets, all passion spent, and then suddenly — what do we see? We see a lovely young woman, daughter of our greatest British actress — yes, yes, I know, she's been retired for ages, but *we* are old, don't forget, we remember her — and this lovely young woman is making her début. And where is she making her début, I am asking you? Why, on Megalith Television! Jem, already, I tell you *already*, I am reaching for my handkerchief.'

Jemima prayed for patience. Her voice grew lower still. 'To begin with, as I told you from the beginning Blanche Cartwright is *not* a lovely young woman. She's a stocky, rather plump, teenager, who, when she's fined down in a year or two, will be lucky if she's half as good-looking as her mother is now —' Jemima ignored an interruption which sounded like 'the first fresh dawn breaking' and ploughed on relentlessly: 'She's stagestruck and she's sulky and she's jealous of her mother, and Cy, listen to me for a minute, just listen, none of these things matter in the least compared to the fact that SHE CAN'T ACT FOR TOFFEE! I was there at the audition. It was PAINFUL.' Jemima allowed herself at last a higher register on the final words.

Satisfied she had secured if only for a moment Cy's attention, Jemima moved in for the kill: 'Listen to me, Cy. Something is going on here. Something I don't understand. Something unpleasant. Someone has set this girl up, or rather set up the production and Christabel Herrick along with it. You see, *someone* suggested Blanche should read for Nina in the first place, and now everyone denies it.

'It certainly wasn't her mother, let alone her father, who hates all things theatrical for obvious reasons, and the girl herself says she simply got a telephone message from the Director telling her to turn up for the audition. The Director — Our Nat — utterly denies having sent the message, and I must say I very much doubt whether he would take any step quite so liable to ruin his precious production. The death of Filly Lennox was trouble enough, with all the publicity it caused: the post-mortem showing death by drowning, and the coroner's inquest — accidental death, but still most unpleasant, with all those revelations about wine drunk at the picnic. Then the funeral and then back to the rehearsals and no Nina. But *he* thought it was Christabel's own personal request to include Blanche; he got a tip-off that she was on the point of withdrawing from the production altogether, because of Filly's death and all the newspaper coverage, unless Blanche got the part.'

Jemima paused. It was time to use her trump card: 'There's some kind of plot here, Cy, a conspiracy and I don't want Megalith to get mixed up in it.'

'A plot!' There were two words Cy Fredericks recognized in any language; one was 'plot' and the other was 'conspiracy'. Associated with the name of Megalith, these were a lethal combination. After that double invocation, it was not really too difficult for Jemima to get her way. Was that not indeed one of the reasons why Cy Fredericks employed her? Trumpet, cajole, bluster — and on occasion break down and weep as he might, he could rely on Jemima Shore not to give in to him, if she believed that by so doing a programme would be ruined.

On this occasion Cy Fredericks ended by giving Jemima *carte blanche* to deal with Nat Fitzwilliam. Megalith would finally withdraw from the filming of the Larminster Festival — having honourably weathered the death of Filly Lennox — if Blanche Cartwright was allowed to play Nina.

Under these circumstances the footage of film already taken would be consigned to that special limbo reserved for fragments of Megalith programmes which had been scrapped. This included rehearsals of *The Seagull* which was well advanced and early rehearsals of *Widow Capet*. The same would go for the long interview already filmed with Nat Fitzwilliam and the short interview with Major Cartwright as Chairman of the Festival (so short it scarcely amounted to more than two questions and three hostile looks). Even some of Spike Thompson's fine work on Larminster sunsets illuminating the Watchtower Theatre in Blakean fashion would similarly be scrapped.

Jemima apprised Spike Thompson of Cy Fredericks's decision. They were sitting in the bar of the Royal Escape at the time. Spike was drinking Scotch. He offered Jemima a drink. 'Come on, my lovely love, what shall it be? You can't be serious with all that white wine you keep knocking back, no better than cat's piss in a pub like this. Come on then, what's your heart's desire?'

'Truthfully, champagne. But at the moment, nothing. I have to go back to the Watchtower to have a little talk with Our Nat which *may* be awkward, then on to Lark Manor for a talk with Little Blanche which *will* be. Champagne wouldn't help.'

'You don't mean she got the part? Guth and I had an idea of covering the audition, but Jesus when she came on — the poor kid — it was pathetic. Look, darling, if you're worried, I could drop a word in Equity's ear —'

But in the event Jemima found her interview with Nat Fitzwilliam unexpectedly easy. While her interview with Blanche she decided to postpone to another day, to let at least one night pass before crushing the poor kid's ambitions.

Nat Fitzwilliam was sitting in the third row of the stalls, gazing raptly at the stage, on which for once nothing whatsoever was to be seen. He did not hear Jemima approach: the theatre was thickly carpeted in cinnamon-colour which extended all over the seats and walls, making it in some ways more like a cinema than a theatre.

Jemima had found the dark-glass front doors unlocked. A girl with long straight hair was sitting in the little glass booth which served as a box office. For a moment Jemima had the impression that all girls in Larminster had the same drifting hairstyle and were attired in the same pre-Raphaelite patterned muslin. Then she realized she was gazing not at Poll's double, but at Poll, she of Flora's Kitchen, herself.

Poll, away from Moll, was surprisingly chatty, to the point of being effusive. She confided to Jemima that bookings for the Festival were brisk and that the death of Filly Lennox had not affected them, despite her popularity as a television star; newspaper reports of the drowning had simply called further public attention to the event itself. Above all, declared Poll, the general public wanted to be on telly.

'It's perfectly super!' she exclaimed. 'They all want to be there the nights you're filming. No problem with a full house at all. I've explained everything just as they said. Reduced visibility, cameras in front of their noses, bright lights. It doesn't seem to put them off one bit. They're all interested in just one thing — will they see us? The audience, that is. Nat's a bit depressed about it all, to tell you the truth. For a moment he thought they were more interested in television than in Chekhov, his Chekhov that is. Which would be absurd.'

'Absurd,' echoed Jemima.

'Anyway he's in the theatre,' Poll added, 'seeking inspiration.' Was she serious? It was impossible to tell. Jemima headed for the auditorium.

'Oh, by the way,' Poll called after Jemima, 'see you later?' For a moment Jemima was disconcerted. Then she remembered a tentative rendezvous with Spike Thompson — and Guthrie Carlyle of course — at Flora's Kitchen to discuss the latest developments in l'affaire Nina. She supposed that either Guthrie or Spike must have booked a table — probably the latter who, since the original mistake which had taken him to the inferior cuisine of Christopher's Diner, had proved a regular customer at Flora's Kitchen. Since food at Flora's Kitchen, although delicious, was not served at rustic prices, Jemima had a momentary loyal pang for Megalith's bank balance. Then she reminded herself that the regular eating place of Cy Fredericks, representing management, was the Connaught, arguably the most expensive restaurant in London. Why should Spike Thompson representing the workers — and after all Spike was nothing if not a worker — fare any worse?

'See you later,' she echoed to Poll.

'Not a word to Moll then.' A grin which was quite roguish lit up Poll's pale elfin features. 'I'm moonlighting here. Helping

Nat out of a hole. We're mates. We lived together for a couple of years, one way and another. Moll can't take that. She's —' As Poll indicated the cutting of the throat, Jemima hastily promised silence.

So into the soft dark cinnamon-coloured world she passed. Nat started up when she touched him on the shoulder.

'Oh, Jemima.' He looked for a moment slightly surprised, then he looked delighted.

'Poll told me you were communing —' she began.

'I wanted to see you anyway,' he exclaimed, jumping up from his seat which folded silently upwards. 'There's something I'd rather like to talk to you about.'

'Nina, I suppose? Blanche Cartwright — look, I'm afraid, Nat, that Cy Fredericks won't wear that at all. And I agree.' Even as she spoke Jemima realized that for once Nat was not thinking about Megalith Television. The tone — almost cajoling — with which he addressed her showed that it was she, Jemima, not Megalith, who was the object of his attentions. Now Nat twisted the fringes of his white scarf, in what he seemed to imagine was a beguilingly youthful manner, as he addressed her.

'No, no, not about Blanche as Nina. Whose idea was that anyway? Someone who wanted to ruin the whole production, I'll bet. Blanche was absolutely hopeless of course. Emily Jones is our Nina, that's for sure, which leaves Masha — I see a kind of severe sailor-suit here, by the way, in contrast to Nina's mermaid costume — the sea-creatures and the creatures of the land. And wonder of wonders Anna Maria Packe will do it, despite being chucked as Arkadina: says she adores the part, always has, which means she really adores Vic Marcovich. Boy Greville's coming too. That's the only flaw. He should have directed it, but under the circumstances I felt I must —'

'What will Boy Greville do here?' demanded Jemima desperately, wondering where all this was leading.

'Oh nothing. Fuss. Take pills.' Nat sounded quite unconcerned about it all. 'He's married to Anna Maria you see and a frightful hypochondriac. He won't do anything. Just look on. He'll like that, I can assure you. He likes being an on-looker, it doesn't tax his health.' Nat sighed. Then he began to plait the fringe of his white scarf as he resumed: 'It was about something quite different I wanted to talk to you, Je-mima. Something much more personal. You're such a calm person. Yes you are. *Calme, volupté et luxe . . .*' Nat let his voice trail away as though *calme* was the operative word here, *volupté* and *luxe* merely bonuses which Jemima could take or leave as she wished.

'You have this wonderful outside-inside calm,' he went on. 'And so I'd love to cast you as Volumnia in my green-green *Coriolanus*, the one I'm going to do at Edinburgh.'

'Green-green?' she questioned, momentarily taken aback. But she should have realized that Nat's personal approaches always related in some manner to his career.

'Yes, I'm terribly excited about my discovery: green is ab-solutely the key to *Coriolanus*. All the different greens; from hope to envy — you do see how exciting it will be? Faces, costumes, sets, all green. And you could be my Volumnia.'

'My greenish silence?'

'Oh you're wonderful, you're teasing me,' Nat cried.. 'And don't worry about your age by the way: it's your *inner* age I'm after and that's perfect. No, seriously, I'd love to talk to you properly. Alone. Just you and me. I feel we should get on terribly well away from all this, the narrow artificial world of the theatre.' Nat waved his hand grandly, as though to sweep away all his productions; past, present and to come. 'Could we have, do you think, dinner together?'

But Jemima had other plans for her evening. Dinner plus a full exposition of the green-green *Coriolanus* — possibly even worse than the traditional dissertation on the Sung Dynasty *Hamlet* — was not at all what she had in mind. She said so: that is to say, she said that she had other plans for the evening while indicating placatingly that she might well be free the next night.

This merely meant that Nat returned to his cajolery. 'I could even help you with your investigations, you know.' Jemima began to curse the persistence which was undoubtedly Nat's dominant characteristic. 'I'm quite a good investigator myself,' was his next remark — the tone only barely modest. 'A natural talent for observation, an eye for detail. I'm an onlooker too, although in quite a different way from Boy Greville.'

'Oh, I'm sure of that,' Jemima replied sweetly. 'But you see, I'm not making any investigations at the moment — except into the workings of your production for Megalith. I mean, what else is there to investigate round here?'

A rather curious expression crossed Nat's face: for once he did not rush into the breach. It was as though smugness was struggling with caution — or perhaps some uglier emotion was at work. Smugness, of a limited nature, won.

'I could tell you something about being an onlooker — my sort of an onlooker,' he said after a pause. 'I was an onlooker for example on the afternoon that Filly died. An onlooker through my binoculars. What do you make of that?'

Jemima, from having been exasperated and even bored by Nat's advances, became suddenly alert; she did not necessarily want to betray her interest to Nat.

'I should really ask you what you make of it,' she spoke quite lightly. 'Whatever it is you're referring to.'

'Supposing I saw something through my binoculars, something rather odd, something which didn't seem odd at the time, but in retrospect, thinking it through, right down to the sub-text, which is what I like to do with everything and is I think one of my strengths as a director —' Jemima's heart sank as Nat appeared to be returning to his well-worn theme but she was prepared to hear him out. However just then Nat broke off:

'Oh, come on, Jemima, let's have dinner. And then I'll

talk to you in depth about Volumnia. I know I can persuade you that being in my production will give a further integrity to your career. Think about it. Volumnia *is* Jemima is Volumnia.'

It was the last sentence which was fatal. One thing was quite clear: Jemima was definitely not Volumnia, but Jemima. Nat was obviously trying to lure her with his references to investigations: conversation at dinner would be angled heavily towards the green-green *Coriolanus*.

'Tomorrow,' she said firmly. 'Not tonight. Any other night.'

'Tomorrow then, eight o'clock. It has to be Flora's Kitchen of course. I used to work as a waiter in Christopher's Diner and a close acquaintance with their kitchen. . . .' Nat, to her relief, agreed without further protest to a postponement.

'So what did you see?' Jemima could not resist asking jokingly at the last minute.

'Ah, interested in spite of yourself!' The teasing note had returned to Nat's voice. 'We might discuss it tomorrow — and then we might not. Tell me one thing, do you promise to think very very hard about Volumnia tonight? Think about it all tonight? And then, if you're favourably disposed tomorrow, and I know you will be —'

'I won't have a wink of sleep,' Jemima swore solemnly.

'In that case —' The same odd expression — half-complacent, half-greedy — crossed Nat's open boyish face. 'I will tell you something. You're not the only person interested in this particular piece of information. And yet the funny thing, the hilarious thing, is that I actually saw nothing. My mind was very much on my production, you realize. Using my binoculars, I was conjuring up new images, juxtaposing the reality of the beach and the trees and the sea with Chekhov's inner reality. It was only afterwards, when I tried to make sense of the macabre patterns of that dreadful afternoon, that I noticed it. I saw nothing where I should have seen something, or to put it another way, just a little discrepancy between text and sub-text. Once again part of my director's instinct, I suppose. Now if we worked together on *Coriolanus* —'

'Quite so,' interrupted Jemima hastily. 'We'll talk about all that tomorrow. One last thing though — I don't suppose you've discussed all this with anyone else as yet? Or have you?'

Nat smiled back at her. Now the greedy look was quite apparent on his face. It occurred to Jemima suddenly that what she saw was the look of a predator, the expression of one who had been, or was about to be, preying on someone else.

All Nat said was: 'Haven't I? Let's see about that too tomorrow. Sleep well, Jemima Shore, or rather dine well and then think, think deep about Volumnia. Green. Green-green. It really is the key to everything you know.'

On which mutually unsatisfactory note — Nat having failed to persuade Jemima to have dinner and Jemima having failed to pump Nat — they parted.

After all, Jemima had dinner with Guthrie alone. Spike Thompson, whom she had expected to be present, was busy despatching spools of *Widow Capet* rehearsal and Bridset countryside by rail to London. Cherry, much to her surprise, had been invited to sample the delights of The French Lieutenant in neighboring Dorset by Major Cartwright.

'Totally new place, can't be too careful,' was the rather strange form the invitation took. Cherry wondered if she was supposed to taste the food for the Major and see if it was poisoned. However, under the circumstances — after all the Major was unarguably an older man and a substantial one to boot — she had felt it right to accept.

Poll, serving in Flora's Kitchen, was as deft and silent as before: her conversation with Jemima in the Watchtower might never have taken place. When Nat Fitzwilliam himself came in with Anna Maria Packe and Victor Marcovich (no sign of Boy Greville), Poll scarcely acknowledged his presence beyond depositing the Botticelli menus on the table. Moll in the kitchen remained raucous but unseen.

There was nevertheless some feeling of tension, expectancy in the air.

When the Cartwright party swept in and occupied a large table on the opposite side of the restaurant, Jemima felt she had known all along that they were coming. It turned out to be Blanche's birthday. To celebrate the occasion, she was trying out a new sartorial style: she wore a man's hat, a baggy checked jacket over a shirt and a flowing tie, and what looked like baggy trousers beneath. Hat and all, she was, Jemima feared, imitating Diane Keaton in the film *Annie Hall*. Christabel elegant in contrast, in a mauve linen dress and matching bandeau covering her fair hair, looked relaxed. She kissed Nat Fitzwilliam, then Vic, then Anna Maria warmly and passed on. Julian Cartwright, in spite of the heat in the restaurant, kept on his jacket over the dark silk polo-necked jersey: he did all the ordering. Gregory Rowan made the jokes. Blanche looked happy if hot. Evidently unaware of her dismissal as Nina, she waved ecstatically at Nat. Then she took him over a large chunk of birthday cake and hugged him. Ketty and Regina were on the whole silent.

Jemima Shore, suddenly feeling the whole Larminster scene to be claustrophobic, left as soon as she could. She had a quick drink — more white wine — with Guthrie at the bar of the Royal Stag and decided to retire to her bedroom. The Cartwright party was arriving at the hotel for some final celebration as she mounted the stairs. She heard Julian Cartwright's loud authoritative voice. She wanted to be alone.

But when she opened the door of her suite, she was not alone. There was someone waiting for her. Spike Thompson was sitting there, quite at his ease, in the most comfortable chair in the room, wearing jeans and a blue top which might or might not have been a kind of vest. Through the door, she could see his black leather jacket was laid carefully on the bed — which was very large, a four-poster and advertised as having been occupied by King Charles II on his escape from Worcester. He had not bothered to draw the curtains of the rooms more than half-way.

'I think you said champagne was your heart's desire.' There was a bottle cooling in a silver container beside him. 'I paid for it in cash, by the way.'

'Ah. Cash. Now that *is* serious.'

'Exactly. Now why don't you take off your clothes, and then take off mine, unless you'd prefer it to be the other way round? I want this to be your treat, starting with the champagne.'

'If this is to be my treat,' said Jemima thoughtfully, 'I think one or the other of us should wear your black leather jacket.'

In the end it was Spike Thompson who took off the clothes and Jemima Shore who wore the black leather jacket. Spike Thompson also opened the champagne. Neither of them remembered to close the gap in the curtains.

It was a long time later that Jemima raised her head from Spike's chest, her fingers clutched into the nests of black curly hair.

'Spike?'

'Mmmmm.' He tightened the grasp of his arm, equally hirsute, about her.

'There's a light on in the theatre.'

'Fuck the theatre. This is television.'

Nat Fitzwilliam, when he went back into the Watchtower Theatre, also found someone waiting for him, someone sitting silently in the front row of the stalls.

'Who is it?' he called from the back of the auditorium. But the figure, apparently gazing fixedly at the empty darkened stage, did not answer. It was very dark and still in the theatre: the lights which Nat had switched on did not illuminate the silent figure where it sat and to Nat, suddenly nervous, it had something of the horrid immobile air of a guy, a guy waiting patiently for the drama to begin.

'Who are you?' Nat called again, walking quickly forward.

'And how the hell did you get into the theatre?' His voice sounded sharp, even commanding, but he was twisting the ends of his white scarf as he spoke.

'Oh, I know where the key was left,' said the person suddenly, rising up from the seat, and pulling Nat's white scarf from between his hands. Taking advantage of Nat's surprise, the person most efficiently then placed the scarf round Nat's neck and pulled it tight, tight, till his round eyes began to pop out of his head, and his poor bragging tongue started forth.

The theatre was quite quiet and no one saw the person who had just murdered Nat Fitzwilliam leave by the Stage Door and go away.

Nat Fitzwilliam remained sitting, sightless, on the edge of the seat of the stalls where he had fallen, the white scarf twisted round his neck. After a while his body keeled forward and pitched down on to the floor. His body made no sound, resting on the thick theatre carpet. And when the seat, relieved of its burden, clapped back again upright it made no sound either.

NINE

Forbidden Thoughts

It was Julian Cartwright who broke the news of Nat Fitzwilliam's death to Christabel. He intended to do so with that gentle deference which characterized his treatment of his wife. At the time Christabel was immured alone upstairs in her white bedroom whose windows looked to the sea. She was in that trance-like state half-way between sleep and the anguish of the day in which she might linger for hours if not called by Mrs Blagge.

When rehearsals began, Christabel's orders had been precise: 'My breakfast tray exactly two and a half hours before rehearsal, darling — not a minute earlier, not a minute later. I like to have a bath, find my face again, recover from those wretched but essential pills. And I want the female Blagge to bring it, no, not you, Blanche darling, no Rina, of course not, and above all not Ketty — the female Blagge is the only one of you who won't talk at that time of day. Silent disapproval is ideal at that time in the morning, because it really is *silent*.'

Julian Cartwright had not offered to bring the tray himself and thus ran no risk of being repulsed.

Now he stood beside his wife's large bed, gazing down at her in the semi-darkness. The day was overcast: the sultry night had ended in a small storm and a shower of rain, freshening the heavy green summer garden: so there was no sunlight to eat its way through the chinks in the curtains. All the same Julian could discern the soft contours of his wife's body under the bedclothes; she slept, as she always had, he remembered, well over on the right side of the bed, although there was now no rival occupant to disturb her repose. Had she slept like this too during those years away, those years when — surely her bed then had been all unruly —

These were forbidden thoughts. Putting them from him, Julian touched Christabel's shoulder lightly.

She stirred and muttered something like 'Curtains'. Seeing that her eyes were still tightly shut, Julian suddenly bent down and kissed her naked shoulder where he had touched it, as though to soothe the mark away.

Christabel gave a little cry, opened her eyes, cried out again more strongly, and then stopped. She looked quite frightened as she clutched the white sheet across her breasts, only partly concealed by the white silk nightdress. Julian sat down on the edge of the bed.

'Darling Christabel, listen to me.' He did not attempt to touch her again.

'What time is it?' Christabel sat up more fully, and tried to squint at the little lapis lazuli and gold clock on her bedside table. 'What time is it? Have I overslept? Where's Mrs Blagge?'

'Listen to me, my dearest. The police have telephoned from Larminister. There's been an accident. I want to prepare you.' For once Julian's voice was really low; his tone, as ever, was reasonable.

He was violently interrupted by screams coming from the

landing. The voice was that of Blanche. The cry — 'Mummy, Mummy' — was the same primitive wail which had announced the discovery of Filly Lennox's body on the seashore.

Blanche came running into the bedroom. She was wearing very tight jeans and a T-shirt, with her fair hair pulled tightly into a ponytail. Julian had an automatic reaction: Blanche shouldn't wear jeans or pull her hair back, even last night's baggy outfit had been better. Then Blanche's story came tumbling out at high speed:

'He's dead! Murdered! Vandals came in the night! They killed him — and now —' She began to weep copiously, hurling herself across the silk coverlet embroidered with sprigs of lily of the valley. 'I'll never be an actress now, I know I never will.' As Blanche's weeping turned to howls, Regina's much taller and slimmer figure, also clad in jeans, was seen rather wistfully standing in the bedroom door.

'Come in, Rina, come in, don't hang about there,' he called out impatiently. 'Mummy's awake. You can see that. Ordinary rules don't apply. Besides —'

Regina stepped tentatively into the bedroom. Her eyes were full of tears.

'Oh Daddy,' she began. 'The pity of it —' She stopped as she saw that Julian's arms were struggling with Blanche's prostrate form, half-comforting her, half-trying to lug her off Christabel's bed. Regina too began to cry.

About the time that Julian Cartwright with the help of Blanche was breaking the news of Nat Fitzwilliam's murder to Christabel, Miss Kettering was performing the same office for the Blagges.

Mr and Mrs Blagge were together in the main kitchen; Mrs Blagge was setting Christabel's breakfast tray. Ketty watched her sister for a moment in silence.

'Give over, Katherine,' muttered Mrs Blagge rather irritably. 'Give over watching me, why don't you? Haven't you got any of your own work to do?' Mrs Blagge folded a tiny voile napkin and made it look like a butterfly. 'If I don't call her in good time before rehearsal —'

'No need to hurry yourself, Rose, no need whatsoever. There won't be any rehearsals from this time forward. Not for Her at any rate. For others more worthy, there will be. After all sin will not triumph.' Ketty's tone was solemn but beneath it, something approaching glee could be discerned. Mrs Blagge was bent over the fridge, searching out a minute pat of butter.

'What's that you say, Katherine?'

'Thought better of it, has she then? No rehearsals? Repented her wicked ways?' If Ketty sounded a note of subdued glee, Mr Blagge was positively jovial.

'Nat Fitzwilliam, he's dead. Mrs Nixon and Joan found him this morning when they went to clean the theatre. A terrible sight! Strangled with his own scarf. It's all over Larminster. They got the police of course, but he was quite dead. Must have been dead for hours. Somebody must have broken in. May God Have Mercy on His Soul.' Ketty crossed herself.

Mrs Blagge did likewise. Mr Blagge did not move. Then the jug he was holding crashed to the floor and splintered into fragments as though some unseen force had prised open his fingers. He made no attempt to pick up the pieces.

'Barry! He was just the same age as our Barry — and now they're both dead — well, at least it's fair — when you think —'

'We agreed that we'd never talk about that, Jim,' interrupted Mrs Blagge. 'That's forbidden, Jim, to think about that, about those days.' Mr Blagge subsided.

'Broke in, you said?'

'Well, they must have broken in, mustn't they?' observed Ketty in a pious voice. 'We are not dealing with the supernatural here, Jim, and he was not likely to have let in his own murderer was he? He was a foolish boy, but he was not *that* foolish.'

'So the key wasn't used?' Mr Blagge's voice was hoarse.

The two women looked at each other; their expressions were unwontedly sympathetic.

'What's that, then, Jim?'

Mr Blagge sat down heavily at the kitchen table, the debris of the jug crunching under his feet.

'Last night. While you, Katherine, were having dinner with them in that arty-crafty place they love so much with the mucked-up food and those two hens who run it, Rose went to call on Father O'Brien and Mrs Lang — I stayed in the car. Then *She* asked me to fetch her shawl from her dressing-room. Found a teeny weeny draught in the restaurant' — Mr Blagge cruelly imitated Christabel's beguiling tones — 'and of course Mr Julian had first rushed off to look for it. Came back without it. No key to the theatre — forgot about asking for it, in all his hurry to look after *Her*.

'So then I was called from the car to make the second visit. The key was produced by Master Nat — he was having dinner there too you know — and into the theatre I go. Very cheeky he was too, when I asked him for the key. Gave him a piece of my mind right back, I did. I wasn't standing for that from young Nat. I don't care who heard me.'

'Into the theatre, Jim! Why you might have been killed,' gasped Mrs Blagge ignoring the references to Nat's cheekiness. There was something quite self-righteous about her exaggerated anxiety.

'That is, not into the actual theatre,' Mr Blagge corrected himself carefully, 'through the Stage Door, where I picked up the key of her dressing-room, and ended up with the aforesaid shawl . . . The only thing is . . .' he hesitated. 'When I returned the shawl, Mr Julian told me not to bother to give young Nat back the key. I was very glad not to have to hand it back to that cheeky bastard, I can tell you. He'd left the restaurant by that time with the bald actor, the one who plays Sergeant Bartock on telly, and some woman. I saw them crossing the square to the Royal Stag on my way back.

' "Leave it under the big stone by the dogs' drinking-trough," he said — Mr Julian, that is. "Mr Fitzwilliam will pick it up later. It'll be quite safe." So forth went I out and deposited it, just as he, Mr Julian, had requested.'

Already there was something about Mr Blagge's words which smacked of the prepared statement.

'And so you did, Jim?' Mrs Blagge prompted him.

He nodded.

'Then you've done nothing to reproach yourself with. Even if it wasn't a break-in. You were just obeying orders. Mr Julian's orders.'

'Ah, but, Rose, anyone could have seen him,' Ketty resumed her most pious voice. 'You must bear that in mind. Anyone could have heard you, Jim, come to think of it.'

'Heard me! Heard Mr Julian, more like. It was he what was making the arrangements, don't you forget it. A voice like a bull, as She has so often put it —' Mr Blagge now sounded quite agitated.

'Be that as it may, I prefer to look upon the bright side of things, myself,' Ketty in contrast was all sweetness.

'And what might that be?'

'The end of Her return to the stage. No more attention for Her.' Ketty smacked her lips. The gesture appeared to remind her of the need for bodily sustenance in this difficult time. She helped herself most adroitly to a piece of toast from Christabel's tray and buttered it. Mrs Blagge frowned.

'Let Her sleep,' declared Ketty with confidence as she munched. 'Poor Nat. I remember his mother, Maisie Johnson; I was at school with her. We should have a Mass said for him, Rose, you talk to Father O'Brien about it. Father O'Brien's very interested in everything to do with the theatre — I'm sorry, Jim, I know your opinions, but it's true. They're not all bad people — you should have met some of the ones I met in London — perfect ladies and gentlemen.' Jim Blagge made no comment but looked unconvinced. 'Still, I'd like to see Her face when she hears the news that the production has been cancelled.' Ketty went on cheerfully.

Miss Kettering was however to be denied that satisfaction.

The verdict of the Larminster Festival Committee, as represented by Major Cartwright, on the subject of cancellation was clear enough. Major Cartwright's statement, for him, verged on the eloquent.

'Can't be done. Glad to be shot of the whole business, myself, police crawling all over the place, not as bad as those television johnnies of course, no, nothing could be as bad as that. At least you know where you are with the police, at least the police are doing a job of *work*.'

Major Cartwright glared at Gregory Rowan, to whom these remarks were being addressed, as if he might disagree.

'Oh quite,' responded Gregory earnestly. 'Give me murder and the police over a straightforward television programme any day.'

'Absolutely, my dear boy, absolutely.' The Major was delighted by this unexpected support. 'You know where the police are, and they know where you are. Whereas television! Tripped over a damn camera myself, the other day, and went for a burton. Good as murder any day, show you the bruises if you like. At least the police never trip you up — it's not their job to do that. All the same' — the Major's expression became more melancholy — 'can't be done. Lots of bookings, local interest, *county* interest. Insurance wouldn't play for one thing. Have to get another director I suppose and face the music. Godawful play anyway, even with *this* director, and he was born in Larminster.'

'There are of course *two* plays to be considered,' Gregory suggested.

'That's right. *Two* godawful plays and we need a new director for both of them,' pondered the Major in a voice of exceptional bad temper. Some sense of Gregory's role in the Festival then appeared to penetrate his consciousness. 'Not yours, old boy,' he added graciously. 'No question of that. Always love your plays. Always have. No! It's all this French Revolutionary nonsense. Historical twaddle. Not my phrase, by the way, but Fitzwilliam's own. The last time I saw him he used that very expression to me — historical twaddle, he said, play only saved by his own first-class production.'

Gregory, with an air of unruffled good-humour, suggested that far too much twaddle was seen in Britain, both on the stage and above all on television. He pointed out that Boy Greville, a highly experienced director with a particular knowledge of his, Gregory's, work, and a real ability to hunt and destroy twaddle wherever he found it — notably and most urgently in Nat Fitzwilliam's productions — was actually present in Larminster. Might it not be a good idea to employ him? The Major agreed. They parted on terms of the utmost amiability.

Cy Fredericks, on the telephone to Jemima Shore, began like Major Cartwright by expressing a strong desire to be shot of the whole business — the business in this case being Megalith's involvement in the Larminster Festival.

'My dear Jem,' he roared indignantly down the telephone, 'they can't keep on dying like this.' Anything that seriously impeded a Megalith programme in the making — that is, one with large sums of money already invested in it — was apt to be regarded by Cy as a deliberate campaign against his own personal survival. Clearly the unscheduled demises of Filumena Lennox and Nat Fitzwilliam fell squarely into this unfortunate category. 'They can't keep on like this and not expect Megalith to pull out. We had a special meeting this afternoon to discuss it all — where were you, by the way Jem, canoodling in Bridset, helping the handsome Spike to despatch his film, if what I hear is correct?'

'On the contrary, I was helping the Bridset police with their enquiries,' replied Jemima in her coldest voice. 'And so was Spike. We're expecting to be arrested at any moment. Then you'll have to stand bail for us both for the sake of your programme — and as we shall then naturally elope, it could be a very expensive business.' Why was Cy's information service always so tiresomely up to date? She made a mental note to find out who had betrayed her and if it was Cherry, to condemn her to a lifetime of dating eighteen-year-olds.

'For you, Jem, nothing is too much!' Cy was heavily gallant. 'As for our friend Spike, nothing *has* been too much for him in the past — the sight of his expenses in Capri on that dreadful deep-sea-diving Axel Munthe film still floats before my eyes on sleepless nights — so I suppose his bail would be merely one more colossal down-payment.' His tone changed. 'Anyway, you will be pleased to know, my dear Jem, that we've decided to go ahead with the programme for the time being. Less emphasis on the production itself. More emphasis on Christabel Herrick's return to the stage on the one hand, colourful local pageantry on the other. In short, we've decided that it would look bad if we pulled out now. We are artistic patrons, Jem, never forget, as well as business men. We have hearts as well as pockets, and we are prepared to dip our hands into both.'

'I never do forget, Cy,' murmured Jemima. The image of Cy dipping his hand into his heart was an irresistible one; she hoped Cy might use it in his next application for a television franchise. 'I think you've made the right decision,' she added more strongly. 'Boy Greville's a perfectly competent director and he happens to be already on the spot.'

'Exactly. I made the same point to Guthrie: at least there's no need to fly him here from some expensive Greek island, which is what we had to do with Guthrie himself. But no more deaths, Jem please, no more deaths. The next time you ring me with the bad news that Christabel Herrick has fallen off a cliff or taken an overdose or been shot point-blank in her dressing-room, you and Spike must expect to interrupt your Bridset idyll. Permanently.'

'The next time!' exclaimed Jemima. 'What makes you think there will be a next time?' Her tone suggested she might be referring more to her relationship with Spike Thompson than to future tragedies involving the Larminster Festival. As soon as she rang off, however, Jemima's thoughts turned away from Cy's teasing to the sadder and more sinister topic of Nat's death.

The Bridset police had treated his death as murder from the start. An incident room had been set up at Beauport under the general command of the county's senior detectives at Bridchester: however the driving force behind this particular investigation was destined to be the Beauport-based Detective Inspector Matthew Harwood. The pathologist's post-mortem report was one of the few concrete pieces of evidence available to him. It gave the cause of death as strangulation and when pressed for an opinion — in the nearest pub to the mortuary — the pathologist had placed the time of death between eleven pm and one am.

There were no signs of breaking into the theatre: the key to the Stage Door had therefore presumably been used, since the front doors were locked and the locks had not been forced. Since one key to the Stage Door was also missing from beneath the Lady May Cartwright Memorial stone drinking trough, where Mr Blagge had placed it, the inference was generally made by the public that this was the key which had been used.

Not, however, by the police. In the formidably bulky shape of Detective Inspector Harwood, the police were a great deal more cautious. In questioning his witnesses, Detective Inspector Harwood was very careful to give no opinion whatsoever as to which key might have been used to enter the Watchtower Theatre. There were, he pointed out, several other keys to the Stage Door. Nevertheless local gossip in Larminster continued to concentrate on that particular key placed by Mr Blagge under the stone on the night of the murder.

'Anyone could have seen him' — it was an echo of Miss Kettering's pious cry. 'The types you get about here in the summer . . . Vandals . . . Hippies . . . Layabouts.' It was comforting to be able to blame some casual criminal, drawn from the outside world: the very existence of a theatrical Festival was felt to have some sinister bearing on the crime. Theatre audiences, if not to be totally identified with hippies and layabouts in the local imagination, were not exactly held to exclude this category either. Robbery was widely suggested as the motive, the box office proceeds as the target. Larminster gossip thus ignored the inconvenient detail that no attempt to enter the box office, let alone rob it, had in fact been made. After all, if the murder had not been committed in this random manner for mercenary motives, it must have been deliberately planned. In Larminster. Possibly by a Larminster resident. This was a forbidden thought.

For precisely the same reasons, the distraught members of the King Charles Theatre Company preferred to believe in the notion of a Larminster murder — a local person of known bad character perhaps — whose identity would be uncovered as quickly as possible. Robbery remained an element in the story which the actors told themselves, although they were rather more cynical about the likely proceeds of the theatre box office.

'I mean, it's not exactly Shaftesbury Avenue, darling, is it?' Thus Anna Maria Packe to her husband Boy Greville.

'I hope no one thinks *I* killed him to get the job,' Boy Greville spoke in a voice of acute anxiety. 'Nat was utterly ruthless. Everyone knows that. The way he got rid of us both when the lovely lady Christabel made her unexpected entrance — blackmail — nothing else. Yet in the end one forgave him.'

'Someone didn't,' Anna Maria said lightly: but she sounded reassuring. This was her habitual tone when addressing her husband just as his habitual tone when addressing anyone at all was one of acute anxiety. A mutual interest in the anxieties of Boy Greville was indeed the basis of their long and on the whole not unhappy marriage. From time to time a peculiarly tempestuous love affair — or a peculiarly demanding lover — would withdraw Anna Maria altogether from Boy's side; there had been several separations and even on one occasion (for who could resist Marty Bland?) a projected divorce. Physical separation from Boy did not however free Anna Maria from her responsibility as general consultant on his anxieties, a role he considered she could still carry out to his satisfaction so long as she remained at the end of the telephone.

Boy was not insensitive: all his consultations pertained entirely to his own problems and he was most scrupulous in not referring to Anna Maria's own situation. Nevertheless it was the persistent nature of these calls which had always persuaded Anna Maria so far that it was easier to live with Boy Greville than at the end of his telephone line.

'Someone had it in for him.' Detective Inspector Harwood, had he but known it, agreed with Anna Maria Packe. He made the remark quite casually to Jemima Shore in her sitting-room in the Royal Stag. 'We don't buy the idea of burglary, of course. No evidence for it whatsoever. Not a thing touched. Nor vandalism for that matter. I mean, think what a self-respecting vandal could have done to those seats! The mind boggles. And the glass. Frankly I'm always surprised that a glass theatre in Larminster doesn't suffer more. You sometimes get these young lads streaking up from Beauport on their motor-bikes. Still, it doesn't. One or two incidents, I believe, nothing very much. Quiet little place, Larminster. Even the Festival brings you a quiet sort of visitor. Quiet Americans. Quiet Germans. Quiet Japanese — well, that's only to be expected. Even the occasional quiet Italians. The noisy sort go to Stratford, I suppose.'

Detective Inspector Harwood had already interviewed Jemima officially, as indeed he had interviewed all those present in Flora's Kitchen on the evening of Nat Fitzwilliam's death. The time of Nat's departure from the restaurant was easily established as ten o'clock. He had then had a drink in the bar of the Royal Stag with Anna Maria and Vic Marcovich, before announcing his intention of returning to the theatre. He also mentioned to Vic Marcovich that he would use his own front-of-house key instead of picking up the key deposited by Mr Blagge, since he had forgotten where Julian Cartwright had suggested it should be hidden. He had said this in the full earshot of all those in the bar of the Royal Stag at the time.

Also in the full earshot of those same people in the bar, Vic Marcovich had criticized Christabel Herrick for demanding her shawl so capriciously in the first place: 'Lady of the Manor, First Lady of the Larminster Festival — which is it to be?' But that ungallant remark belonged to the whole area of background material relating to the case.

No one suggested Vic Marcovich had murdered Nat Fitzwilliam. For one thing he had an unimpeachable if slightly disreputable alibi: he had spent most of the night with Anna Maria Packe in his room 'discussing the production'; as if that was not alibi enough, they had received constant calls from Boy Greville on the house telephone throughout the night hours on the subject of Boy Greville's latest allergy, probably aroused by one of the house plants in the lounge of the Stag. For another thing, Vic Marcovich had no motive.

'And the question of motive brings me to you, Miss Shore.'

'Me?'

'Well, you've a reputation for these things, investigations I mean. I know all about you from my little brother Gary in London — not so little these days, two inches taller than me, Gary Harwood, if three stones lighter, the one who looks like Elvis, or so the girls tell me, and works for Pompey of the Yard. Jemima Shore Investigator . . . and not only on the telly. Am I right or am I wrong?'

'Ah.' Over the years it was true that Jemima had enjoyed a pleasant working relationship with Pompey of the Yard, Detective Superintendent Portsmouth as he had become, formerly Detective Chief Inspector John Portsmouth of the Bloomsbury Division; her relationship with his dashing side-kick while in Bloomsbury, Detective Constable Gary Harwood, had had its pleasant moments too. Her connection with Pompey had begun when she had interviewed him on television in connection with an appeal for a missing child. Subsequently there had been investigations — she was not too modest to admit it — where the confidence of the public in the familiar appearance of a telly star, combined with Jemima's own intelligence and curiosity, had enabled her to solve certain cases which had baffled the more conventional workings of the police.

'I spoke to Gary this evening, as a matter of fact. Nothing official. What's happening in the Third Test, you know the sort of thing.' She did. 'And he said "That Jemima Shore, give her enough rope and —" '

'Go on,' Jemima prompted him sweetly.

' "Give her enough rope, Matt," he said, "and you can watch the Test to your heart's content — because she'll solve your case for you." '

'Ah,' said Jemima Shore again.

'What I need to know, Jemima, is this' — after these combined mentions of Pompey, Gary Harwood and cricket, their friendship was clearly progressing. 'Who *wanted* him out of the way? What's going on here? It doesn't make sense. No debts. We've checked that. No obvious clues. No vicious ex-girl-friends for example. We've checked that too. No romances in the cast — not gay either so far as we know. A girl in his flat in London who seemed devoted to him, very upset at his death, anyway she had an alibi although we didn't quite put it like that, at the theatre with her sister. Professional rivalry? That director, the nervous one, who's taken over — he doesn't look a murderer for my money and anyway if his wife's story — *and* her lover's by the way — is to be believed, he was busy telephoning about his asthma all through the night! Theatrical people. I ask you.' Detective Inspector Harwood shook his massive head.

Jemima thought back to a certain conversation with Christabel Cartwright in Flora's Kitchen.

'On the stage, I'll be safe.' And so she was safe — up to the present time. But Filly was dead, and so was Nat Fitzwilliam. These could no longer be forbidden thoughts. She had to talk to someone about Christabel. And that led her to Gregory Rowan, Gregory who had made no secret of his hostility to Megalith Television on her arrival at Larmouth, but was now suspiciously amiable.

'I'd like to help you, Matt —' said Jemima with her angelic smile, the one she kept for ravishing television viewers when she was discussing importantly boring topics like the Common Market. 'Unofficially, of course.'

'My money's on the playwright,' added Matt Harwood suddenly and rather unexpectedly. 'Had a row with Fitzwilliam over his production of his play. Left for home about eleven o'clock to go for a *swim*! Then went straight back to his cottage. *Swimming!* What kind of an alibi is that? Still, I dare say you will tell me that playwrights never do want to kill directors over productions of their plays.'

Jemima saw no reason to tell him any such thing. But since she had no wish to lower his opinion of theatrical people still further, she merely agreed aloud that it would be a wise move for him to talk further with Gregory Rowan. Privately she decided to go and call on Gregory herself in the cottage in the woods. She thought she would go alone. She did not mention this plan to Detective Inspector Harwood.

TEN

A Real Killer

'Let me help.'

Gregory Rowan put out his arm, an arm so darkly tanned and knotted with muscles that it might have belonged to a sailor, and gripped Jemima by the elbow. She trod water desperately. For a moment he supported her altogether.

'It's the current,' she gulped, 'I'd no idea. I'm quite a strong swimmer. And it's very cold.'

He could just as easily have pulled her under: they were alone, far out from the shore; the beach was deserted. But that was a mad thought, produced by panic. He had saved her, not pulled her down.

Afterwards he said: 'You see. Nobody takes this current seriously. That poor girl — you probably see now how easily it can happen. Anyway you're a beautiful swimmer. You just needed a little help. Even you.' Gregory smiled. 'Even Jemima Shore Investigator.'

Jemima smiled too. 'I was out of my depth.' They were back at his cottage and she was smoking a cigarette, which had Gregory but known it, was another sign that she had felt, even for one moment, out of her depth. So far as she could recall, she had not smoked one cigarette that year.

She had first begun to feel out of her depth when Gregory had greeted her unexpected arrival at Old Keeper's Lodge — in fact a cottage — with extraordinary cordiality. Unlike Detective Inspector Harwood, she was not herself inclined to 'put her money on the playwright'. It was to talk about Christabel that Jemima had decided to pay her surprise visit to the cottage — Christabel and her friends, Christabel and her enemies. In order to find out who might have had reason to kill Nat Fitzwilliam — possibly because of what he saw from the Watch-tower concerning the death of Filly — it was necessary to go back to the beginning and find out what was or had been frightening Christabel. Gregory was her best potential source of information about the past at Lark Manor: but she did not expect the interview (she used the word automatically) to go very easily.

On the other hand she did not herself rate Gregory as a suspect. Or if by any chance Gregory had killed Nat, Jemima could hardly believe that it was for the reason that Matt Harwood proposed. Fitzwilliam's contempt for *Widow Capet* had been much discussed; phrases like 'this middle-class, middle-brow and middle-aged hit' had been quoted, the latter being a remark Nat had chosen to make to Old Nicola of all people, with the predictable result that it had received a wide circulation. Nevertheless if Jemima judged Gregory's character right, this kind of behaviour in a young director was more likely to inspire Gregory to verbal attack in public than murder in private; even if the death of Nat had resulted in the restoration of the original director and sympathetic interpreter of Gregory's works, Boy Greville.

As for the death of Filly, Jemima could not of course imagine any reason at all why Gregory should wish to remove her from the Larminster dramatic scene. Filly's death had considerably weakened the cast of *Widow Capet*: Anna Maria Packe was too old to play Paulinot, the jailer's daughter. Emily Jones, who was the right age, was as yet far too weak a stage presence to compete with Christabel as Marie Antoinette in the famous scene between the two women, which even Nat Fitzwilliam had admitted stood most effectively for the Old France versus the New. What might have been memorable theatre with Filly Lennox involved, would now be sadly tame.

And Gregory killing Filly by mistake for Christabel? Ah, there was the rub. There was a great deal about the strange tangled emotional situation at Lark Manor yet to be unravelled. This was one reason why Jemima had not yet shared her suspicions concerning Filly's death with the police, despite the growing warmth of her friendship with Detective Inspector Harwood.

'He wouldn't want to hear it. It's only supposition. After all there's no *proof*,' she told herself, to explain her reluctance, knowing full well that this was not the true explanation. The truth was that Jemima Shore Investigator, tantalized by the strange situation at Lark Manor — above all by the 'cool repentance' of Christabel Cartwright — wanted first crack at solving the mystery herself.

Gregory's cottage was predictably book-furnished, shelves everywhere, and books also in heaps on the floor and resting on sofas like sleeping cats. Jemima noticed a number of books about Restoration Drama and what looked like an eighteenth-century edition of Rochester's erotic poetry (an admirer had once presented her with something similar). A good many of the books looked as if they came into the valuable category of the very old; others fell into the expensive category of the very new.

The books, whether leather-bound or modern, did not however look dusty. And there was nothing dirty or even shabby about the cottage. The thick woods rising behind Lark Manor had parted to reveal this little patch of green order within the luxuriant chaos of the trees, with a cottage — a Hansel and Gretel type of cottage — in the middle of it. Inside the cottage there was the same feeling of order at work within chaos.

As she looked round, Jemima's eye fell on a large framed photograph of the lady of Lark Manor herself. It must have been taken many years ago: the two solemn-eyed girls at Christabel's side, holding up the ends of her wide sash, were mere children. The photograph was not actually on Gregory's desk but facing it. On the desk, however, was another smaller photograph of Christabel in a gold frame. Her hair rippled out of the picture: she smiled into the camera, at Gregory, at Jemima Shore. That photograph too came from some past era. A further quick glance round the room revealed at least one other picture of Christabel, more of a family snapshot than a posed actress's photograph. It included the father of the family, Julian Cartwright.

Jemima thought that the presence of so many large and obvious photographs of Christabel Cartwright ought to make her task of questioning Gregory on the subject rather easy. The fact that none of these photographs was at all recent — all of them must certainly antedate the Iron Boy affair — could also be considered helpful.

At this point Gregory suggested going swimming.

'And then we can talk all you like, Jemima Shore Investigator,' he ended with a slightly ironic smile; but he still showed absolutely no sign of his earlier hostility. 'And you can ask me all the questions you like. Isn't that what you've come for?'

Somehow Gregory's professed willingness to be interrogated, like his friendliness, gave him an advantage. It crossed her mind to wonder which of them was really going to pose the questions and gain the needful information: who, whom? Once they were back in the cottage, after rattling up from the beach in Gregory's large black hearse-like car, she continued to feel out of her depth, and not only because of her recent chilling experience in the water.

The truth was that Gregory exerted some kind of odd influence over her, she had to face that, and had done so since that first abrasive meeting on the beach. Then he had displayed the rare power to rile her — she, Jemima Shore, whose great asset as an interviewer was the fact that she was never riled, no matter what the provocation, using on the contrary her cool composure to rile others where necessary in the cause of her investigations. Now he was persuading her to smoke and drink whisky before lunch, something which was even rarer; many of Jemima's best friends felt that her whole legendary composure could be summed up by the glass of chilled dry white wine she was so fond of drinking.

Spike Thompson, for example, had been able to convert Jemima neither to whisky nor to cigarettes, under far more intimate circumstances: on him she had imposed her own demand of champagne, and, where cigarettes were concerned, had merely watched while Spike had rolled his own choice of smoke; naked and happy she had gazed at the ceiling and smelt the slightly sweet smell of pot drifting by without any inclination to share it.

The thought of Spike suggested to her, irritatingly, that she was possibly rather attracted to Gregory in a tiresome Beatrice and Benedick kind of way, which scarcely fitted her plans for Bridset relaxation. Jemima, being a free woman, made it her practice to do exactly what she pleased in that direction; especially when she was, by her own reckoning, fancy-free — as she was at the present time. Doing what she pleased, she decided, might include an uninhibited Bridset Idyll with an energetic cameraman, but it definitely did not include any kind of involvement with the provoking and doubtless complicated Gregory Rowan.

Nevertheless the ability of Gregory to intrigue and tease

and annoy her suggested to Jemima, from experience, that she was not absolutely indifferent to him in the mysterious sphere of sexual attraction. She therefore made a resolution not to allow these tentative thoughts on the subject of his physical attraction to go any further; she backed it up with a further resolution to keep this resolution. She was here to talk about Christabel.

It was therefore rather a pity from the point of view of both these resolutions that conversation about Christabel led at once to the topics of love, infatuation and even, though it was not explicitly stated as such, sex and Gregory Rowan. None of this exactly helped to quell Jemima's personal interest in the subject.

A further surprise awaited her. Gregory spoke quite simply when she questioned him about Christabel and the past. His irony as well as his hostility were temporarily dropped. There was an air of relief about his confidences as though he positively enjoyed making them. Was it the magic of the trained interviewer at work, even with a man as sophisticated as Gregory? Or was it, as Jemima soon concluded, that Gregory welcomed any opportunity to talk about Christabel Cartwright?

'I loved her madly. I loved her to distraction. Shall I put it like that? When she ran off with that ghastly ginger-haired lout, my heart stopped.'

'Was that really all he was? Iron Boy? Just a ginger-headed lout. No one here will talk about him — for obvious reasons.'

Gregory considered. 'Am I prepared to talk about Iron Boy? Probably not. Am I even prepared to be fair about him? The answer is, once again, probably not. He was ginger-headed and he was a lout; but he did have a kind of mad vitality, at any rate when he was a boy; people, all sorts of people, had a good time in his company. Beyond that, there's really nothing to be said for him at all. Back to my heart, if you don't mind. It really never started again. Not until she came back to Lark. And even then the old ticker is not what it was . . . How about that? Is all that sufficiently dramatic for you? I am a playwright you know, and as such, unlike some of my contemporaries, frequently accused of too much plot and melodrama in my works.' Gregory smiled calmly before continuing: 'Oh, by the way, perhaps I should add that I also love Blanche and Rina Cartwright. Quite as deeply. And Julian. In many ways I love him the most of all. He's much the nicest character in the Cartwright family: the only unselfish member of it, for example.'

'So that's why you stayed here all those years? Why you never married.' It was irresistible; the curiosity of Jemima Shore Investigator would not be stifled.

Gregory looked rather surprised. 'It's why I stayed here, of course. But I was married. To Anna Maria, yes, *the* Anna Maria, Anna Maria Packe of the King Charles Theatre Company. You might say that I've always had a thing about actresses —'

'Natural perhaps in a playwright,' Jemima put in encouragingly.

'Except that's not the real point. Anna Maria was still at Central School when we got married. It's probably the other way round: the kind of woman who attracts me tends to become an actress.'

'And that is?' Jemima supposed she must number quite a few actresses among her friends, although she did not generally think about them in this category; this was because in her experience actresses, like actors, and most other categories of professional person, were infinitely varied in their personalities. But she was interested to hear Gregory's answer.

'Emotional. Insecure. Vulnerable. Above all the latter. Beneath all the emotion, in need of care and protection.'

Jemima had not been notably struck by the emotional vulnerability of Anna Maria Packe while in Larminster, as the actress to-ed and fro-ed contentedly between her director husband and her actor lover, satisfying both no doubt, and herself most of all. She said so, as delicately as possible.

Gregory hastened to agree with her.

'That's really why it broke up. She was far too tough and so was I. Anna Maria's much happier looking after Boy, with all his interesting hypochondria. And I —'

He stopped. 'But this isn't why you've come, surely. To talk about the past, my past with Anna Maria. The facts about Christabel and me can be quickly told. They're public knowledge, after all these years. We had a wonderful flaming romance during the run of Lombardy Summer — my first really successful play — and it was the summer, the long hot summer of 'fifty-nine. It continued on Broadway in the autumn, that extraordinary season for me, Lombardy such a hit, and of course Anna Maria safely tucked away at Stratford, no chance of joining me.

'But,' he stopped again, then plunged on, 'I also wanted to be free. I didn't put it like that to myself of course: I told myself that I was an artist, needed to live alone, all that kind of rot. So — one fine day, when we were all back in London, and my new play had opened, and flopped — the only one that ever did — Tower, it became an instant classic by the way, never stops being revived to loud critical, where-did-we-go-wrong? applause. Nothing like the failures they themselves have caused to turn on the critics, but that didn't help me at the time. Nor poor Christabel, who played Baroness Anne, one of her few failures. And she wasn't going to be able to revive it again and again over the next twenty years, was she? So one fine day, she upped and married Julian Cartwright.'

'But he wasn't part of the theatre?'

'No, no, he was just her devoted admirer, her rich young man, she used to call him. He was always around. Christabel wanted security, she said. I took it to be financial security she was after. I was bitterly hurt. She'd always sworn to me that she couldn't go to bed with Julian, not my type she used to say, not my type, darling. *I* was her type. I thought.'

'But you came here? You came and lived here? So that in the end — she had both.' Jemima felt she must tread with extreme care. But she no longer felt out of her depth. Many things about the household — and its attachments — at Lark Manor were becoming clear to her.

'Yes, she had both. Financial security from Julian, and a good deal of emotional security as well down the years. Emotional security also from me, encouragement, understanding with her career. More parts. Knowing all about the theatre, which Julian couldn't, or didn't care to do. I found, you see,' he said simply, 'that I couldn't live without her. And Julian too, I liked him. He liked me. I made her happy. We both of us possessed her. Julian is an extraordinary man. I don't know if you realize that. Besides, I too was having my cake and eating it. I had my own kind of family life at Lark, especially after the little girls were born. And I had my freedom. It suited me. It suited everyone.'

Until Barry Blagge came along — or rather grew to his precocious manhood, thought Jemima. But this thought she did not put into words. Gregory too left it unspoken.

'I *have* come to talk about Christabel,' she said aloud. 'Now there is a vulnerable person. For many reasons —' She meant to concentrate the conversation on Christabel's elopement with Iron Boy and her surprising cool return. But it was as though Gregory, having once decided to put the character of the younger Christabel in perspective, the Christabel with whom he had fallen in love, was reluctant to let it go.

'You're right! Women never seem to understand that,' he exclaimed. 'Christabel always has been extraordinarily insecure, full of self-doubt, self-dislike even, even at the height of her fame, even before all — well, all of that, when she was one of the best-known actresses on the British stage. Oh the doubts, the agonies! About her looks, the loss of youth —

that was the attraction of Iron Boy, the confidence it gave her, much more than the mad physical infatuation of the gutter press's lurid imagination. I suppose too she had an irresponsible good time in his company, and she could forget she was an ageing actress, forget everything. After she ran off, I used to think about her new life in the watches of the night. I used to imagine Barry was like Comus, surrounded by his crew of unruly midnight revellers. You know — "What hath night to do with sleep?" '

'Wasn't Christabel rather oddly cast as The Lady? With her "virtuous mind, that ever walks attended By a strong siding champion Conscience —" ' Jemima, who had got a First in English at Cambridge, was not averse to quoting Milton herself.

Gregory smiled. 'I should have known better than to bandy quotes with you. It was Barry I was referring to, not Christabel. "Virtuous mind" — I fear not. In any case my Miltonic visions owed a great deal to my stupid insomnia and that's a thing of the past I'm glad to say. Isn't it odd? I've slept like a top ever since Christabel returned. No comment, please. To return to Christabel herself and her insecurity, when he, Iron Boy, ditched her — took Comus's rout somewhere else, if you like — in one way it was the dream of guilt, or self-hatred come true. In another way it totally destroyed her. I believe she was scarcely sane when Julian went and found her and fetched her down here, so he told me.'

Jemima saw her opportunity. (It was time to put aside those tentative thoughts on her own behalf about Gregory: no one who on his own confession specialized in vulnerable women was going to be drawn to Jemima Shore, that golden goddess of television. It was lucky that the Spike Thompsons of this world had a different method of assessing vulnerability.) Murmuring sympathetically, she encouraged Gregory to explain to her the circumstances of Christabel's return: how Christabel had simply telephoned one day, a short desperate call to Julian and asked him to take her back —'to make a fresh start'. And he had just driven up and fetched her, just like that — 'I told you he was a saint.'

'How did everyone here take it? In this secluded place — the return of the prodigal — if one may put it like that. How did you take it for example?' It was her gentle persistent television interviewer's manner.

Gregory paused and then laughed. 'It sounds ridiculous but at first I felt quite violent. When I first saw her, that day, at Lark, the most perfect early spring day, cold wind from the sea but sunshine, the wind blowing the first daffodils in the drive, and her hair — the wind blowing the beautiful hair, still beautiful — and she so charming, little jokes, just the same, I was amazed by her lightheartedness. She only showed one pang of emotion and that's when we had to tell her that her dreadful mangy old spaniel Mango had died. For some reason Julian had kept that news from her. It was Christabel who adored that dog; Julian couldn't bear him; that was another thing Julian and I had in common: we loved Christabel and loathed her spaniel. I was surprised he even kept Mango after Christabel left, but perhaps he had hopes that Mango would lure her back to Lark. Instead Mango ran out on the main road in her absence, nobody looking after him properly I fear, and got killed. She asked to see the grave, the place where we buried him in the woods. Apart from that, nothing, just little jokes.

'So you see,' he paused, 'for one terrible moment, I wanted to do her some frightful physical injury. I almost wanted to kill her for all the suffering she had caused. So stupid. As I told you, I love her. I'll always love her. You can't kill people like Christabel for what they do. You see, somewhere deep down, she does it to herself worst of all.'

Jemima thought of the elegant pampered woman: the woman who had come back to Lark Manor with impunity to find everything just the same — except for the death of an old dog — and wondered privately if that was actually true.

To Gregory, she continued: 'And the children? Regina and Blanche, how did they take it?'

'Resentful at first. Extremely. But they got over it. They'd both seen their mother in London, of course, over the years, although Julian wouldn't let them visit her alone, always sent Ketty along to ward off evil. Evil in the shape of Barry Blagge. Once they grew older, they chose not to meet Barry of their own accord. It was embarrassing for them: the Blagges, you see, they were still there at Lark as servants; I think Rina felt it even worse than Blanche, although it's difficult to tell with a reserved girl like that. Nowadays, I hasten to say, everything's fine with the girls. But you can imagine why I didn't at first want television, in the shape of you, Miss Jemima Shore Investigator, coming down here and upsetting the applecart.' He smiled again.

'And the Blagges?' pursued Jemima. 'To me, that's almost the most amazing part of all. She ran off with their only child and they stayed here. In the same place.'

'Ah, how little you understand of our delightful country ways! This was their home, wasn't it? They looked after it long before Julian married Christabel. There have always been Blagges at Lark, there were Blagges long before there were Cartwrights, for example. Major Cartwright's father, Julian's grandfather, only bought the property some time in the eighties, but there are Blagge graves in the churchyard stretching back into the seventeenth century. Jim Blagge had been through the war with Major Cartwright: excellent brave soldier, by the way. Resourceful and courageous. "A real killer, Blagge was," the Major is fond of saying: strange to think of that distinguished elderly man handing round the meat and two veg behind his chair as he says it. No, it was she who was the interloper, Christabel, the actress, the woman from the outer world.'

He added: 'The Kettering sisters are local too. Two bright farmer's daughters. Only Rose married Jim Blagge and went into service, and Ketty, the younger sister, became first the girls' nannie, then housekeeper and general factotum when she went with them to London and Christabel was working all the time. She was quite stagestruck in those days. Finally, with Christabel's departure, Ketty was queen of the roost at Lark — with only Rose Blagge to keep her in her place.

'Julian never kept her in her place.' Gregory lit yet another cigarette: 'Too grateful to her for sticking around and preserving order. Ketty was a good-looking woman in her day, handsome rather; the frightful Barry Blagge looked rather like her, I always fancied, only those strong straight features and red hair came out better in a man. Ketty's not so old, either. And she always worshipped Julian. Christabel used to tease him about it — in the old days.'

'And then Julian Cartwright took Christabel back,' said Jemima thoughtfully. 'In spite of everything. Didn't he — well, think of the effect on the Blagges and Ketty?'

'They were appalled, of course. It might have been different if Christabel had shown some true signs of repentance — by Ketty's and Rose Blagge's rather narrow Catholic standards, that is. They love sinners — in theory — so long as they acknowledge their sins. A sort of Mary Magdalen act would have been acceptable, perhaps. Hair turned grey, some modern form of sackcloth and ashes. Instead — well, Christabel carried it off with her usual style, her hair looked better than ever and her clothes ran their usual gamut from Zandra Rhodes to Bellville Sassoon with not a touch of sackcloth anywhere.

'I said Julian was a kind of saint,' he went on. 'But haven't you ever noticed how saints can be curiously insensitive to the sufferings of lesser mortals caused by their own sanctity? I wrote rather a good play on the subject once, although I say so myself. *Holy Margaret*. They're reviving it at the National in the autumn: you should try to catch it. No, Christabel was Julian's obsession, just as she was mine. He'd never lost it. He jumped at the chance to succour her. As for the Blagges and

Ketty, he just assumed they'd share his feelings, in so far as he thought about it at all. And he'd been brought up in a certain way, hadn't he? Kind as he is, to him, after all, and this is going to sound ghastly and old-fashioned, but for him finally the Blagges and Ketty were just servants. His servants.'

As you were both her servants: but Jemima left that thought unspoken too. As she drove back through the Lark woods and down the end of the Manor drive, she pondered on a number of things. She pondered on Christabel's enemies: there certainly were plenty of those to be found in and around Lark Manor. In particular she pondered on the whole matter of servants and the extraordinary intimacy which Cartwrights, Ketterings and Blagges had all shared in this beautiful Bridset valley, after Christabel's departure. Until Julian Cartwright, the master, one day shattered the whole thing by casually restoring Christabel to favour.

Mr Blagge, the father of Barry. Jim Blagge: 'a real killer'. *The* real killer? Jemima was still turning over the two phrases in her mind and picturing to herself Jim Blagge rowing his boat like Charon over the Styx — was it Jim Blagge Nat had seen through his binoculars, paying the penalty for it with his life? — when the telephone rang in her hotel suite.

It was Detective Inspector Harwood. He was proposing a cup of tea on his way home.

'Something to report to Jemima Shore Investigator,' he said jovially. 'Blagge, you know, the butler fellow from Lark Manor, the father of the late unlamented pop star, I believe, the one the good lady ran off with. We have a witness who saw him leaving the Watchtower Theatre.'

'To get Christabel Cartwright's shawl —' began Jemima, still rather confused by the way the telephone call had broken right into her own thoughts on the subject.

'No, no a second visit about an hour later,' Detective Inspector Harwood sounded increasingly jolly. 'More like eleven o'clock. While the Cartwright party were still carousing at the hotel. Now why, I wonder, did Mr James Blagge not mention that little fact in his statement to the police?'

Jim Blagge: a real killer? Jemima put the telephone quietly down and awaited the visit of Detective Inspector Harwood with something much closer to melancholy than the policeman's own cheerful mood.

ELEVEN

Arrested Rehearsal

Everyone was in a very tense mood at the rehearsal of *The Seagull* which took place two days later. It was doubly unfortunate that Megalith's tight camera schedule demanded that this particular rehearsal be filmed. Jemima agreed to reason with Cy Fredericks on behalf of Boy Greville but without much hope of success: she was well aware that further postponement would be financially disastrous for Megalith on top of the delays already incurred by what Cy Fredericks termed rather crossly down the telephone 'these wretched deaths'.

It could never be said that the services of Spike Thompson and the rest of the crew all installed — more or less contentedly — at the Royal Stag were to be secured at light cost. Moreover the profits of Flora's Kitchen would, Jemima felt, bear some close relation to the losses incurred by Megalith Television, since none of the crew condescended to eat anywhere else once it was discovered that Flora's Kitchen was listed in the *Good Food Guide* as 'expensive but worth it — if you have the money and decide to lavish it on lavish Bridset food given pseudo-Florentine names and served in pseudo-Florentine surroundings'. Spike Thompson and the rest of the crew found it, on behalf of Megalith, a decision easy to make: so after a bit Moll and Poll, with fine appreciation of the workings of the market, thoughtfully put up their prices.

At least Spike Thompson proved a tower of strength during the filming of the rehearsal. Guthrie and Jemima felt deeply grateful to him for the usual mixture of unflappability and ferocious energy which he displayed — and he cut a reassuringly urban and flamboyant figure as he darted behind the camera and then away, in his scarlet polo-necked jersey beneath the black leather jacket. The sound engineer on the other hand was in a highly neurotic mood — possibly induced by a prolonged diet of over-rich food — causing him to groan over tragic noises of interference from the Larminster traffic, inaudible to anyone else; he also grumbled perversely about the isolation of the theatre and its proximity to the shore. At one point he even complained that he was picking up the cry of a seagull.

'Isn't he rather overdoing it in his appreciation of Emily Jones's performance as Nina?' murmured Guthrie to Jemima. 'Every time she declaims, "I'm a seagull", I suppose he mistakes it for the real thing.'

Everyone — except possibly Spike — was in a tense mood, and everyone had their problems. The Megalith lighting crew, for example, had not formed a notably high opinion of the lighting system at the Watchtower, nor had they exactly sworn brotherhood with the theatre's stagehands. Guthrie Carlyle reminded himself that his problems lighting the Parthenon for his non-controversial programme, 'The Elgin Marbles — Ours or Theirs?' had been worse, the Greek crew getting thoroughly excited over something; possibly the non-controversial subject matter, possibly the length of the lunch-hour, he never dared enquire.

'On the other hand at least the Parthenon itself stayed put,' he reflected gloomily. It was fair to say that within the Watchtower theatre no one very much stayed put, even someone like Old Nicola, who had no part to play in the rehearsal itself. Lacking a role in *The Seagull*, she had nevertheless infiltrated rehearsals early on, accompanied by her ancient grey plastic bag full of knitting. Even Nat Fitzwilliam had lacked the requisite energy to stop her; and under the new regime of Boy Greville, any threat of removal was met by: 'Oh that poor sweet Nat! What a little genius, wasn't he just? He didn't mind Old Nicola being here, but if you feel differently dear, if you don't quite feel the confidence yet dear, never you mind, you just tell Old Nicola first thing and she'll go quietly.'

So Old Nicola knitted on, regaling listeners with anecdotes of bygone *Seagulls*, mainly featuring her own performances. She claimed to have played Nina and Masha on alternate nights in one season at Stratford.

'And I bet she got the two parts mixed up half the time,' Christabel had been heard to comment. 'Fiendish to play with. She always was, even when she just had one part to remember.' She spoke just within earshot of the older woman, whose hearing, where her own interests were concerned, remained quite acute.

Now the presence of the television crew galvanized Old Nicola into fresh activity. Somehow she always managed to be sitting knitting in exactly the path of the camera and had to be moved at the last minute. In moving, she showed an infallible instinct for selecting a seat which would prove to be in the direct path of the next shot.

'Off you go, my old darling. On your way again,' Spike would shout blithely. Guthrie felt less tolerance.

'Can't we lose her?' he muttered desperately. 'Like forever?'

'By putting her head in her own grey plastic bag?' suggested some other member of the crew enthusiastically. Jemima heartily agreed with the sentiments: she was being personally badgered by Old Nicola to interview her for television on 'My

Wonderful Long Years in the British Theatre': 'You could just let the cameras roll and Old Nicola would give it to you; no need for any of your cutting and editing, I can assure you; Old Nicola knows by this time just what interests an audience.' But she declined to join in the jolly discussions about Old Nicola's possible fate; superstitiously, she remembered wishing some dreadful doom to overtake Nat Fitzwilliam. Old Nicola, for all her cunning and trouble making, looked quite physically frail: another 'wretched death', even the natural death of an old lady, was the last thing that Megalith needed.

Boy Greville clearly felt that he had problems enough as director today, without tackling Old Nicola. The extreme agitation which he displayed in private life on matters such as his health, gave way to such a violent nervosity in public when he was working, that Jemima wondered at first how any of his productions ever succeeded in opening. Yet Boy Greville had an excellent reputation as a director over a number of years, and actors were said to like working with him. Jemima could only suppose that they exerted themselves extra frantically on his behalf, in order to try and alleviate at least some of the worst of his sufferings.

'I can't go on with this sort of thing much longer,' he had been heard to groan to Tobs, who at his tender age was having undeniable problems with the character of Dr Dorn: 'The strain on me, personally: you can't imagine —' Tobs straightened up the painful hunched back with which he was attempting to convey Dr Dorn's burden of years, and tried to comfort his director.

Today however the strain was universal. Emily Jones wept a little, and her voice, always a little too high when she was nervous, did take on a kind of bird-like screech in Nina's speech with its reiterated phrase 'I'm a seagull' which gave all too much point to Guthrie's aside.

No doubt the television cameras were adding to the production's troubles by making everyone additionally nervous but it was difficult to believe that anything by Boy Greville, adapted at the last minute from a production by Nat Fitzwilliam, could ever have gone very smoothly. Nat's 'underwater' conception still haunted the production in the shape of certain costumes, as well of course as the set itself, with its unlikely-looking plaster rocks and realistic-looking — because it was real — fisherman's netting. At least Boy had got rid of the sand from the set, which was driving everybody mad, including Mrs Nixon and Joan who were in charge of cleaning the theatre.

There were a number of good reasons why the set could not be replaced. There was the time element: the Larminster Festival was due to open with the production of *The Seagull* at the Watchtower in under a week's time. There was the expense element: the finances of the Watchtower were shaky enough already, despite contributions from friendly local magnates such as the Cartwrights and the work of the Festival Committee, without the expense of scrapping one whole set and building a new one.

'Committee wouldn't stand for it. Nor would the Chairman,' Major Cartwright, who was the Chairman, told Cherry. He had taken a marked fancy to her, choosing to use her as his conduit of information to Megalith as a whole. His passion was expressed in a series of invitations to meals at expensive restaurants rather further afield than Flora's Kitchen. To the Royal Harbour Hotel at Lar Bay, the Queen Mary at Bridchester, Giovanni e Giovanna, improbably to be found just outside the tiny rustic village of Deep Larkin, Major Cartwright drove Cherry at high speed in his Bentley without speaking. The food was always delicious. All this atoned to Cherry, in some measure at least, for the failure of Julian Cartwright to cast any glances at all in her direction.

'Just have to grin and bear it. That's what I always say anyway about a night at the theatre.' So the Major closed the subject of any possible further expense on the Larminster production of *The Seagull*.

Leaving aside the humorous properties of the play itself — and Nat Fitzwilliam had given the company several interesting lectures on 'Chekhov and the harmonious laughter of the Future' — Cherry thought the Major would probably find a good deal to grin about in *The Seagull* production, if that was what he wanted. There might have been even more, if Boy Greville had not insisted on altering at least some of the more ludicrous 'underwater' costumes, where it could be done cheaply.

Thus Emily as Nina was no longer dressed as a mermaid and Vic Marcovich as Trigorin had thankfully got rid of his Neptune's trident, as well as adding extra garments of a rather more conventional nature to the brief golden loincloth required by Nat. No one had ever discovered why Trigorin was to be played as a sea-god: and now it was too late to find out. Ollie Summertown, however, still wore Konstantin's original white sailor-suit, although with the short trousers lengthened (he rather fancied himself in it, he told Cherry, what with his new Bridset tan, and was sorry that his knees were not after all to make their début on television). And Tobs clung to his sou'wester and oilskins which he had decided lent to Dr Dorn what he described as 'an old tar's dignity — I'm a kind of ship's doctor I think'.

Christabel too still wore her original costume. Since this was made of becoming white muslin, over a large hoop skirt, it did give her a suitably nineteenth-century air, especially once the festoons of dark-green sea-weed were ripped off the skirt and bodice. Christabel therefore looked appropriately Chekhovian and even elegant, at a distance: the special grace which she brought to every stage movement was underlined by the sway of her huge skirt.

In herself, however, Christabel was not nearly so poised.

Her face, seen close-up through the camera lens, looked drawn. She was more nervous than usual on stage and inclined to dry. In such an experienced actress — at any rate in terms of the past — it was difficult to believe that this was the effect of the television cameras. Besides it was odd that Christabel should falter now: Megalith had already filmed two other rehearsals, and Jemima had noticed that Christabel had been one of the few to be virtually word-perfect from the start — 'off the book already', Nat had said proudly, as though he had learnt Christabel's part for her.

It was more plausible to seek the cause of Christabel's strain in the renewed police questioning of Mr Blagge, under way at the present time. It was true that if Mr Blagge had indeed been the hidden element of fear in Christabel's household, she should by rights have been relieved at his disappearance, at any rate as far as Beauport Police Station. Perhaps it was the uncertainty which was responsible for her anxiety: when they broke for lunch, Jemima was among those who wandered over to the Royal Stag with Christabel, and among those — not a few — who noticed the alarming amount of vodka she consumed. It was left to Old Nicola, who had managed to wander along too, to make some loaded remarks about actresses who drank during rehearsal in her young days and what had become of them — 'Not still acting in their eightieth year like Old Nicola, dear, that I can tell you; they lost their looks first of course . . .'

The Blagge developments had been outlined to Jemima the day before by Detective Inspector Harwood, over the tea-cups in her tiny chintzy hotel sitting-room. There he told her that Jim Blagge was well known locally to have conceived a violent hatred of the theatre, and of all things theatrical, as a result of the career of his son Barry. That this career had actually ended with Barry's death in a road accident was hardly the fault of the theatre; and Iron Boy had been a pop star not an actor. However this was not a distinction that had bothered

Mr Blagge among his Bridset cronies. Neither of the Blagge parents had had any real contact with Iron Boy after his elopement with (or abduction by) Christabel; she belonged unarguably to the theatre — so it was the theatre which had led to Barry's death. If not logic, there was a certain natural justice in his resentment.

Mr Blagge's paranoid dislike of the theatre had found a new focus in the person of Nat Fitzwilliam. Had not Nat been a school friend of Barry's? Nat had gone to university and with his superior education should have somehow saved Barry from his fate instead of corrupting him (this was Mr Blagge's version of events). Worse still was the emergence of Nat as Director of the Larminster Festival — the local boy made good when their own Barry was lying in his California grave. Worst of all was the return of Christabel to the stage, directed by Nat himself. Mr Blagge had ascribed the actual responsibility for that return to Nat. He had told his friends, with a knowledge born of his intimate position in the Cartwright family, that without Nat, 'she'd never have had the cheek to do it — not even Her'.

All of this, as Detective Inspector Harwood judiciously acknowledged, added up to no more than current Larminster gossip. He had not come to tea, he assured Jemima, merely to regale her with a lot of old tabbies' talk. The threats of violence made by Blagge against Fitzwilliam were more serious, the evidence of Blagge's second visit to the Watchtower Theatre more serious still. The visit had been witnessed by two strangers to Larminster with no personal knowledge of Blagge or his situation. Their timing was also unshakeable, based on a particular news bulletin on the car radio: so there was no question of their confusing Blagge's innocent first visit with this alleged second sortie.

'Threats of violence?' Jemima queried. She cast her mind back to the only two occasions when she had been aware of Mr Blagge and Nat being in close proximity. One was the original Easter Sunday lunch at Lark when the Blagges had handed round the food: the other was the occasion of the fatal picnic at Larmouth beach. In both cases Mr Blagge had, as far as she was concerned, concentrated entirely on serving food and drink. She had certainly noticed nothing untoward or threatening in his attitude to Nat Fitzwilliam.

But then, thought Jemima wrily, did one ever notice very much about the reactions of the various serving figures at a party, if one was a guest oneself? It was as though one expected their function somehow to dehumanize them, rob them of natural feelings of disgust and envy. Whereas the exact reverse was much more psychologically probable. Her mind went back to Gregory's recent revelations of Julian Cartwright's insensitivity. Mr Blagge no doubt felt even more violently towards Nat Fitzwilliam for having to hand him dishes, and pour him wine at Sunday lunch at Lark Manor. While Nat had sat there, his eager cherub's face pressed forward, utterly unconcerned about the emotions of his erstwhile friend's father dispensing claret over his left shoulder.

Detective Inspector Harwood was able to confirm these vague suppositions in a surprisingly accurate way. By instructing Jim Blagge to get the key of the theatre to fetch Christabel's shawl, Julian Cartwright had obliged Blagge to seek out Nat at the table where he was dining in Flora's Kitchen. This mission had turned into a highly unpleasant encounter when Nat had refused, apparently wilfully, to interrupt his conversation with Anna Maria and find out what Mr Blagge wanted. The older man's pale face had flushed visibly.

'Mr Marcovich who was the third party present was very particular about this detail,' Detective Inspector Harwood told Jemima. 'No mere figure of speech, he assured me. The colour of fine old port was how Mr Marcovich expressed it. And he gobbled like a turkey. After that it became a case of What The Butler Shouted. Mr Blagge actually threatened to thrash Nat, adding for good measure, "if not something worse".'

'We have several witnesses to the fact that he lost all control,' pursued the Detective Inspector. 'But then he does have these fits of sudden explosive rage, they tell me; has done, ever since the war. Terrible thing, uncontrollable rage. Rage and strength. Jim Blagge had both.'

At this moment, as the Megalith cameras focused on the Watchtower stage, Mr Blagge was being questioned at Beauport Police Station. Jemima knew that in the first place he would merely be asked for a further explanation of his movements. Matt Harwood and his team of detectives would be bearing in mind that famous police catchphrase: 'Method: Opportunity: Motive'. So far Mr Blagge had proved to have both Opportunity and Motive. The Method by which Nat had been killed was also obvious — strangulation by his own scarf. It remained to connect Mr Blagge, with his Opportunity and Motive, to the Method. Matt Harwood had assured her that the Bridset police would be quite as rigorous as those in London in applying the Locard exchange principle:

'I daresay that our friend Pompey has made you familiar with it,' he conceded kindly. 'And I hope young Gary bears it in mind as well. A criminal always leaves something at the scene that was not there before —'

'And carries away something that was not there when he arrived,' finished Jemima. Pompey had indeed made her familiar with the phrase. He was particularly fond of it. So, according to the aforesaid exchange principle, Mr Blagge's clothing on the night of the murder would be tested by a kind of giant hoover — for particles from Nat's clothing, and particularly Nat's long white silk scarf. While fibres of Nat's scarf and other clothes would be similarly 'hoovered' for tiny but tell-tale traces of Mr Blagge's garments.

The quiet remorseless police process going on at Beauport was certainly in marked contrast to the furore which had by now developed inside the Watchtower. Jim Blagge too was doubtless meeting with the traditional guarded politeness of

the police, whereas there was precious little politeness left
inside the cinnamon-coloured auditorium of the theatre.

The costume parade which had begun the morning gave
way to a short rehearsal of the last act and then a run-through
of the play. In the third act of *The Seagull* Christabel dried
twice. Boy Greville ran his hands through his long greying
hair in despair, like some ageing wizard whose spell was failing
to work. Emily Jones's voice, when it was not trembling, rose
higher and higher. Tobs's impersonation of a hunchback Dr
Dorn failed to please despite his protests: 'But I spent the day
at an old folks' home *studying* them,' he exclaimed indignantly.
Finally Vic Marcovich decided off his own bat to deliver all
his lines in a completely new manner reminiscent of George
Sanders in *All About Eve*. It gave a very odd twist to Trigorin's
famous speech about the creative process of a writer and made
it sound as if he was talking about a gossip column.

The last phenomenon reduced Boy to the verge of collapse,
and he had to be helped from his seat to take some special
herbal remedy for when things went really wrong.

Megalith, in the shape of Guthrie as director and Jemima
as presenter, had agreed in advance that at least one day would
be spent in filming 'work in progress' — in order to contrast
the unfinished rehearsal with the final achievement of the
First Night. The trouble was, as Guthrie groaned to Jemima,
there was altogether too much work and too little progress
about this particular rehearsal. Boy's official attitude to the
run-through of the last act was that since the first three had
gone so abysmally, by the law of averages, the fourth act must
go better.

It went much worse. The famous scene between Emily Jones
as the fallen Nina and Ollie Summertown as the despairing
Konstantin shortly preceding his suicide had about as much
tension in it — as Vic Marcovich whispered to Anna Maria
— as the reunion of a rice pudding and a treacle tart. Vic was
still smarting at the rejection of his George Sanders turn and

in no mood for generosity; all the same the comment elicited an embarrassed snigger from those members of the company who overheard it.

'All this should make a wonderful contrast with the First Night,' Cherry observed brightly to Jemima, who wondered not for the first time whether Cherry's gift for stating the obvious was all good.

Just as Vic Marcovich was getting into his stride, his George Sanders manner forgotten or at any rate held over, Boy Greville got a sudden frightful new kind of headache — possibly the onset of his first migraine, but who could be sure? Anyway, he said it was quite different from the nagging low-grade headache he generally endured. His anguished cry and the startling way in which he clapped his hands to his head was, Guthrie and Jemima decided, the most effective bit of acting they had seen all day. They had it on camera, of course. They might even decide to leave it in. Anna Maria cut an interesting figure too, tripping over Old Nicola's knitting as she rushed wildly into the auditorium with a sachet and a glass of water.

The television crew, who had elected to behave angelically all day — even the sound engineer ceased to hear both buses and seagulls through his head-set — suddenly chose the last act to turn into the proverbial work-to-rule demons. Guthrie had been contrasting their behaviour most favourably with that of his disaffected Greek crew: now this fit of patriotic fervour gave way to something more like nostalgia for the vanished glories of the Parthenon programme. The crew would not agree, for example, to run over their supper break by even one minute. Thus it was by no means sure that Megalith would be able to complete the filming of the final scene, the vital moment at which Christabel would react to the noise of Konstantin shooting himself off-stage. For this a dramatic close-up was planned.

It was a case of the whole crew agreeing to this extension or none. Spike raised Mephistophelean black eyebrows to Jemima across the auditorium, smiled ruefully, and put his thumbs down. Jemima suspected the lighting-men of obduracy, as part of their enjoyable guerrilla warfare with the Watchtower stagehands. However there was never any point in suffering additional frustration over these matters; it was all part of the interesting tapestry of English television and had to be accepted as such, along with weather which washed out summer harvest filming in Constable country or played gentle sunshine on the Brontës' moors just when you wanted a Heathcliffian thunderstorm. The actors, most of whom had worked in television and were used to the phenomenon, were equally philosophic.

'We'll just have to take a chance.' Whatever his private thoughts, Guthrie sounded equally resigned.

Emily successfully — well, more or less — declaimed Nina's last speech: 'When you see Trigorin don't tell him anything . . . I love him. I love him even more than before . . .' Her voice did evince its unfortunate little wailing note from time to time, but at least she looked suitably wan and very pretty, still wearing the navy-blue dress with a sailor collar which Boy Greville had substituted for her mermaid's outfit.

Now Christabel was seated on her plastic rock; she had changed from her white muslin into her own clothes — a pale-blue shirt and navy-blue pleated skirt which showed her excellent legs in their narrow-thonged white sandals. Jemima thought that she had the legs at least of a young girl (although Emily Jones, who was a young girl, had rather thick legs, not entirely hidden by her long skirt).

Trigorin gazed at the stuffed seagull before him. Just as planned, a loud noise was heard off-stage. Jemima just had time to think that it did not sound very like a shot, when two things happened.

The supper break was officially reached, so the plugs were pulled and the crew stopped filming. And Blanche Cartwright rushed on to the stage. It was, in its way, a splendidly timed entrance, except for the fact that the camera was no longer turning.

Otherwise Blanche had everyone's fullest attention, from her mother, who gave the most perfectly startled look of any Madame Arkadina reacting to her son's shot off-stage, right down to Old Nicola, who awoke very startled from a little snooze in her seat and started to scrabble frenziedly for her knitting.

Blanche was crying: 'They've got him, they've arrested him. The police have arrested Mr Blagge. Mummy, they're saying it was Mr Blagge killed Nat. Mummy, you've got to do something, it's all your fault, Mummy, you should never have come back.'

TWELVE

Weak Flesh

The arrest of James Roy Blagge, 63, chauffeur, of Stable Cottage, Lark Manor, Bridset, for murder created a major sensation in Larminster. In a way it was an even more shattering — and thus exciting — event for the local inhabitants than the crime itself. Something about Nat's shady theatrical career, it had been vaguely felt as the weeks passed, must have contributed to his fate: his departure from Larminster to university had already marked him out as different and, on his return as Festival Director, he had made no effort to ingratiate himself with Larminster society other than that section of it represented by the Festival Committee.

Jim Blagge was different. They all knew Jim, and they all knew Rose Blagge too, as they had known Rose Kettering, and still claimed to know Katherine Kettering, for all her grand airs up at the Manor. Father O'Brien, the Larminster parish priest, went up to Stable Cottage to comfort Rose Blagge. He reported that she had collapsed totally when the police arrived with a warrant for Jim's arrest. It had been in one way fortunate that Rose's sister had been visiting her at the time, and could succour her, although less fortunate that Ketty was accompanied by Blanche Cartwright, so highly strung at the best of times; before anyone could stop her, Blanche had run screaming from Stable Cottage, grabbed her father's Land-Rover and driven to Larminster and the theatre, where she had broken the news of the arrest in dramatic terms now known to the whole of Larminster.

Ketty was praying with her sister when Father O'Brien arrived; he had subsequently asked to see Mrs Cartwright but had been told by Mr Julian Cartwright that she was unavailable. Father O'Brien added that Mr Julian Cartwright himself had been extremely kind and promised to do everything in his power to help the unfortunate Jim Blagge: give support in the magistrate's court, stand bail if there was any chance of that, and all the rest of it.

'Of course I know Blagge's innocent, Father,' Julian exclaimed testily in his loud voice which penetrated, had he but known it, the darkened bedroom upstairs where Christabel lay resting and thus rather removed the point of his next remark: 'All the same, my wife mustn't be disturbed: we don't want to bring her into this, any more than is absolutely necessary. She's got her performance to think of, two of them. It's not as if she was involved personally in any way in this ghastly business.' Julian Cartwright glared at Father O'Brien as if defying him to contradict this assumption, and for one moment looked remarkably like his uncle the Major.

Father O'Brien tried to conceal his disappointment. He had much looked forward to a good talk with Christabel Cartwright, consoling or at least condoling. But for Jim Blagge's sake, and because he was a tactful man, at any rate where Protestants were concerned, he murmured something noncommittally soft and Irish.

Secretly, Father O'Brien cherished a very different attitude to Christabel from that of the Blagges and Ketty. In theory, of course, he deplored the flagrant adultery which had led to her disappearance with the Blagges' son — although he had never actually met young Barry, having arrived in the parish a few months after their departure. But Father O'Brien was also a dedicated admirer of television, a medium which he was convinced was directly guided by the Holy Ghost in view of the vast benevolent influence it exercised in the world. Old people comforted, the lonely solaced — but these were minor benefits. Above all, in Father O'Brien's opinion, high moral values were upheld on television: look how the evil were punished nightly for their sins on the television news, while at the same time you could learn to recognize the devil and all his works, with a choice of channels, in the safety of your own home. Even Cy Fredericks, in his wildest fit of euphoria, would not have advanced for Megalith Television alone some of the claims which Father O'Brien, in his study at St Bede's presbytery, took for granted about the whole medium.

Christabel Cartwright was the nearest that Father O'Brien had ever come to the baleful world of the enchanter. He had greeted the news of her return to Lark Manor, broken to him in accents of horror by Rose Blagge, with public gravity but private excitement. Father O'Brien was one of those who dropped by the Watchtower Theatre box office at an early stage and enquired after a seat on the night that the television cameras would be present. Poll, encased in the darkened glass booth, had been quite shocked by a priest wanting to come to the theatre in the first place, let alone on the First Night: she assuaged her feelings by making him pay for his own seat, and the top price too. This in turn rather shocked Father O'Brien who thought that the performance of his parish duties — in this case witnessing the public penitence of Christabel Cartwright — should come free.

The advent of Megalith Television to Larminster, followed by Christabel's resumption of the stage, he regarded in general as a striking example of the power of prayer; Father O'Brien having offered up Mass for Christabel and her family and in the course of it mentioned something of the sort to the Almighty: 'For her own good, and the good of her darling girls, and the good of the whole community. Let the sinner be seen to repent in public, preferably not on BBC2, which Thou knowest O Lord is not too clearly received in the presbytery . . . Acknowledge her sin like the publican in the Bible,' added Father O'Brien hastily, lest God, at the sound of his familiar complaint about the presbytery television set, should lose interest in Christabel Cartwright's artistic future.

Julian Cartwright, unaware of the maelstrom of yearnings in the priest's breast, simply repeated to Father O'Brien that he would do his best for Blagge. As for Mrs Blagge, she was of course excused any further duties in the house until she saw fit to return. Ketty too might stay with her as long as she liked.

'Though God knows the girls need her too,' he concluded wearily. Father O'Brien, in a rush of sympathy quite at odds with his usual romantic appreciation of the situation at Lark Manor, realized that Julian Cartwright had come to look quite a lot older and sadder since his wife's return to the stage.

'All the same, Mrs Blagge comes first, I insist on that,' Julian finished. Father O'Brien then wondered whether perhaps Blanche . . . perhaps a word or two from him . . . he was not of course her parish priest, no wish to poach on the Vicar's preserves, but if he could be of any help, since he was right here at Lark . . .

'There's nothing for a priest to do. Of any persuasion.' Julian Cartwright sounded crisp. Soon Father O'Brien found himself being escorted out of the beautiful light drawing-room where Julian had received him, with its blues and greens, and its view of the sea, in the direction of the front door. But as they passed the open door of Julian's study — a glimpse of manly dark reds and browns was to be seen through it — Julian appeared to think better of his decision.

'A quick whisky, Father, before you go?' His tone, if forced, was suddenly much more friendly.

The priest and Julian had actually just had tea, which had been brought them by Regina Cartwright, in the absence of Mrs Blagge, Ketty, and of course Christabel. Father O'Brien said that the pretty curly-handled Rockingham cups reminded him of the china his mother had had when he was a boy in Ireland; diplomatically, he ignored the stained cloth where Regina, carrying the tray and looking rather magnificent as she did so, like some kind of dark-haired caryatid, had nevertheless managed to slop tea everywhere.

'The cups that cheer but not inebriate, wait on each . . .' Regina had murmured as she deposited the tray. Father O'Brien, unaware that she was quoting Cowper, was nonetheless quite willing to follow the cheering cup with an inebriating glass. Julian ushered him into the study and splashed a good deal of whisky into the heavy-bottomed Waterford glasses.

At Julian's request Father O'Brien then dutifully admired an enormous portrait of Julian's mother, Lady May, as a young girl, in riding-costume, whip at the ready, dog at her feet, some enormous louring white stately home in the background, painted by Sir John Lavery. But as an Irishman, Father O'Brien had never been able to see the British aristocracy as part of the divine plan: he was busy looking round for portraits of Julian's wife, not his mother. He was rewarded immediately by one glamorous photograph and one family group including the girls as well as Christabel (if Father O'Brien had been on calling terms with Gregory Rowan, he might have been surprised to discover exactly the same photographs abutting Gregory's own desk, in the rather less grandly decorated surroundings of Old Keeper's Lodge).

Julian Cartwright leant back easily in his large tobacco-brown leather chair: the heavy velvet curtains of the study, their colour matching the whisky in his hand, partly shrouded the view and ensured that very little of the summer light filtered through into the handsomely sombre room. What Julian Cartwright wanted to explain to Father O'Brien was this: when Blanche had burst out in her dramatic denunciation of her mother at the end of the Watchtower rehearsal, she was above all not to be taken seriously. Julian supposed that Blanche's words might have caused some shock and alarm in Larminster — Father O'Brien, he was sure, never gossiped nor did he, Julian, but it had to be faced that there were many 'less heavily employed people than us, shall we say, Father', who did little else.

The fact was, Blanche was absolutely devoted to her mother, Julian continued in the kind of voice he used for reading the lesson in church (not Father O'Brien's church). But it happened that she was just at the age when she took things very much to heart, and Blanche had this silly childish habit of speaking her mind, or what appeared to be her mind. The arrest of Mr Blagge, whom she had known and loved since babyhood, more or less in front of her eyes, had quite upset her balance. Whereas her sister had many more resources with which to deal with the situation.

'Rina is more the dreamy type, you know, reads a book and rides her horse, has even been known to do both at the same time, read a book *on* a horse —' Julian laughed rather more loudly perhaps than the joke warranted, but Father O'Brien hastened to add his own polite soft chuckle. 'The trouble with Blanche is that she has not yet found her own niche. With Rina being so much more bookish, intelligent one might even say, Blanche needs to develop her own interests —'

'The theatre maybe, I believe she has talent, like her mother? Television —' The moment he had spoken, Father O'Brien realized that he had made an error. It was too late. Julian Cartwright had already drained his whisky and ignoring the fact that Father O'Brien had barely begun his, was jumping to his feet.

'Hardly the theatre, I think, Father.' He sounded both cold and furious at the same time. 'It was somebody's mischievous suggestion that poor little Blanche should read for a part at the Watchtower which upset her balance in the first place. Sheer trouble making. My wife was very upset about it too. We were united on the subject. Neither of us feels that Blanche is suited in any way to a life in the theatre.'

Julian was now walking so fast on his long legs, out of the front door in the direction of the priest's old black Rover, that Father O'Brien, much shorter and quite a bit stouter, could hardly keep up with him.

'Oh, I hardly think Miss Kettering meant to make trouble,' Father O'Brien managed to pant out, just as they were reaching the car. 'She only wanted her dear little girl to have her own chance — just as her mother had done. So she sent a little message. That nice old Miss Nicola Wain helped her. All *quite* harmless.'

Once again Julian stopped. His resemblance to Major Cart-wright this time as he fixed Father O'Brien with a ferocious look was so marked as to cause the priest to take a nervous step back. He had never cared for Major Cartwright, ever since it had come to his ears — via the intelligence service of Mrs Blagge handing round the food — that the Major had described him over lunch as 'that confounded Holy Roman busybody.' The Major's daunting expression persisted in Julian as he repeated several times:

'I see. So that was it, was it? I see. So that was it. Ketty set that one up. Ketty thought of that little plan.'

Father O'Brien was at last free to bustle into his car and drive away — rather too fast, under the circumstances, rattling over the cattle grid on the drive. Julian watched for a moment and then turned on his heel and walked back through the front door.

'Ketty,' he roared. 'Ketty. Come here, will you! I want to have a word with you. Ketty!'

But Ketty did not answer. Perhaps she was still over at Stable Cottage with her sister Rose, or perhaps she was at the top of the next flight of stairs where years ago she had set up a little sewing-room to make or alter the girls' clothes, with the sound of the sewing-machine drowning that of Julian's voice. Or perhaps she was in her bedroom, along the landing, between those of Regina and Blanche, and managing to sleep through his calls. At any rate she did not answer.

Everything was very still inside Lark Manor. The early evening air hung heavy and silent in the beautiful tidy rooms. Where was everyone? There was no sign of Regina, for example — but she had probably ridden Lancelot down to the sea. Blanche had spent the morning sobbing loudly in her room after the previous day's outburst; either she was asleep, or she had gone out — at any rate no sound came from her room. Gregory sometimes came over from his cottage in the woods at this time of day to collect his milk and have an early drink with Julian. Today there was no sign of him.

Finally Julian Cartwright's voice too fell silent. His last words had been a raucous cry of 'Ketty'. Any chance Christabel had of enjoying a peaceful nap in the tranquillity of the manor would surely have vanished altogether at the sound of that stentorian voice. But in fact Christabel Cartwright was lying awake.

She was awake and frightened. She wished that Boy Greville had not decided to rehearse the other scenes which did not include Madam Arkadina, in order to give Christabel a rest from her ordeal. She wished she was at the Watchtower Theatre, in her little modern dressing-room, gazing at her face in the harsh light of the electric bulbs round the mirror, dragging at the grease-paint on her face with cold cream.

She wished she were anywhere except alone in her bedroom at Lark Manor.

The person who had thought all along that Christabel could not just come back like that and expect to get away with it knew that she was alone. The person knew too that Christabel was frightened. The person decided that the right moment had at last come to put an end to Christabel. Extinguish her. Above all put an end to her soft pampered body, that body which had betrayed her and everybody else close to her, because it was the desires of Christabel's warm greedy body which had taken her away from Lark Manor, caused her to fly away with Barry Blagge about whom nothing good could be said except that he had thick red hair and an enormous —

The person stopped short at the next word, because even to use it in the person's thought, such a coarse, such a rough crude physical word, aroused bad feelings in the person, feelings from the past which the person did not wish to experience again. It was better to concentrate on purely helpful thoughts of how to obliterate Christabel's body, the body which had entertained Barry — the person felt calmer now: there was no temptation to dwell on exactly how Christabel's body had entertained Barry Blagge.

The person began to croon the old familiar litany of hate: if only Christabel's soft skin had not betrayed her like that when she could have spent all her life so happily in the luxury of Lark Manor, with her nice husband and the nicest most convenient lover in the world in the shape of Gregory Rowan — for that's what he had been, had he not? Then there were her loving daughters, oh such loving little girls, worshipping the ground — and the stage — their mother trod on. All thrown away, thought the person, for who could pretend that Blanche and Regina would ever worship their mother again? Who could expect them to?

Christabel's career too — all thrown away. Younger actresses had come to take her place, or actresses who were never half so good like Anna Maria Packe — that failure, the failure of her career too could be blamed on Christabel's weakness. Certainly it was quite ridiculous, the way that Christabel thought that by repenting, she could simply resume her stage career just like that . . .

If only Christabel's body had not grown greedier with the years. If only that spoilt soft flesh could have tolerated, just once in a while, the embraces of her own husband — instead of which Christabel's treacherous body, Christabel's *weak flesh*, had caused her to shrink and turn and turn away, and lie passive and reluctant in her husband's arms. While all the time in the arms of Barry Blagge —

But here the person checked the dangerous thoughts again.

Moving very quietly in the empty house — for the person knew every board, exactly where every stair creaked, and how to listen for every door that might open, the person began to lay plans for the death of Christabel. Once Christabel had had a perfect life. She had thrown it all away. Now she should have a perfect death.

No one would ever know that it had not been an accident, the way the person planned it. After all, the person had drowned Filly Lennox — a mistake, admittedly, and everyone had believed that to be an accident. As for Nat Fitzwilliam, who had got altogether too close to the truth about the girl's death with his prying binoculars, that rather unpleasant death was being blamed on Mr Blagge.

The person, now in a room upstairs, quietly rummaging for something essential to the person's plan, paused for a moment to consider the whole question of Mr Blagge. He was now in police custody. If Christabel's death was made to seem like a proper accident, he might still be blamed for the murder of Nat. The police were such idiots: Jemima Shore Investigator was not quite such an idiot, but, even so, the real truth was unlikely to strike her. For one particular reason. The person smiled. The idea of fooling Jemima Shore was by no means displeasing to the person.

So how did the person feel about Mr Blagge being blamed?

It was important to decide before these preparations went much further. The house was empty now but you could not expect a house the size of Lark Manor to remain empty forever, on a late summer's afternoon. Oh, it would be terrible, the most dreadful pity, for the person's plan to kill Christabel to be ruined at the very last moment!

On the whole therefore it was best to proceed and let Mr Blagge take his chance . . . after all this time, the person had no particular feelings about Mr Blagge either way. The person merely hungered for the end of it all: the resolution of the tragedy. So the person proceeded with quiet and deadly preparations for the death of Christabel.

Julian Cartwright, rushing from the back of the house, collided with Gregory, coming from the front. Gregory was breathing hard and looked alarmed. There was no sign of his large car in the drive.

'It's Christabel, it sounds like Christabel,' he said. Julian said nothing, but pushed past him and started to run again, through the wide open french windows of the kitchen, towards the hall. After a moment, Gregory, his tall figure towering over Julian's, ran after him. Both men stopped at once when they got to the hall. The first person they saw was not Christabel but Ketty.

Finely dressed as ever in a dark patterned crêpe dress, and wearing her usual jangling earings, Ketty was standing in the middle of the hall, looking up the well of the stairs. It was remarkable, in view of the formality of her frock, that she was wearing no shoes; her feet were large and well formed: the toe-nails, painted dark red, showed incongruously through the stockings. Christabel, above them, was wearing a pale-blue silk peignoir, the material so light you could see the shape of her soft ample body, her breasts, quite clearly. Her pale hair was in disarray; it looked as if she had just got out of bed. She was leaning on the balustrade. She looked both startled and frightened.

'My darling! You screamed! Are you all right? I heard you scream,' Julian ignored Ketty and rushed on up the stairs.

'I did scream,' said Christabel slowly; her low voice was not quite steady. She too like Gregory was breathing very fast. Julian put his arms round her. The slight involuntary check with which she met his embrace was painfully noticeable to the two watching below. 'I heard a noise in the house. I thought I was alone. It was only Ketty. She gave me a fright, that's all.'

'I'm sure it wasn't me that made any noise,' Ketty spoke in her usual grimly self-righteous voice; alone of those present she seemed quite unperturbed by Christabel's distress. 'I took my shoes off when I came back into the house from my sister's, so as not to cause a disturbance when certain people were resting.' Ketty stared defiantly, first at Gregory, then back up at Julian. Then she added in an even more emphatic voice: 'I'm sure there is nothing about *me* that should frighten Mrs Cartwright.'

THIRTEEN

Simply Guilty

At the remand hearing in Beauport Magistrates' Court the police — in the shape of Detective Inspector Matthew Harwood — opposed bail for James Roy Blagge. This, coupled with the very serious nature of the offence with which he was charged, was sufficient to convince the magistrate that the accused should be kept in custody.

'And a good thing too!' Matt Harwood commented to Jemima Shore, when Jim Blagge, neatly dressed and impassive, had been taken back to the prison at Bridchester on a seven-day remand. 'Bail-for-murderers indeed, which my little brother Gary tells me is becoming quite the fashion in London's fair city these days. Here in Bridset we think there is just one place for a man suspected of a violent crime, and that is a nice cosy prison cell. Just in case.'

'Just in case he does it again? Or just in case he decides to do a bunk on a boat from Lar Bay?'

'Just in case,' repeated Matt Harwood, sounding rather

pompous. Then he softened. 'There are a good many things a man on a grave charge can do if he's left at liberty, you know, apart from the above. Not only tampering with witnesses. He can do away with himself, for one thing. It's been known to happen.'

Jemima, remembering the erect silver-haired figure of Mr Blagge in the court, appreciated the policeman's point. Self-destruction must be a real possibility — if he had indeed murdered Nat Fitzwilliam as the police contended; murdered him in a fit of spontaneous and uncontrollable rage, brought on by the younger man's casual contempt on the night of the murder, his long-term insolence — or worse still insolent indifference — in the months preceding it. And all rooted in Mr Blagge's paranoid hatred of the theatre itself, of which he had made no secret since his son's departure. Such a man might well wish to put an end to an existence irredeemably wrecked by his own violent impulse.

Mr Blagge was certainly not likely to vanish abroad — for where would he go? What would become of Mrs Blagge? His whole life was here in Larminster and up at Lark Manor, as Gregory had explained. Nor was there any possibility of Mr Blagge tampering with witnesses: the strangers who had witnessed his second visit to the theatre had already given their written statements. Anyway the case against him rested strongly on the forensic evidence.

It was a classic case of the Locard exchange principle at work, Matt Harwood told Jemima happily: he suggested that she should let Pompey of the Yard know all about it when she was next in touch with him. 'We're not so dim in Bridset, you know, not dim at all.'

Minute fibres of Nat's white scarf had been discovered on Mr Blagge's jacket, and Nat's own clothing had revealed similar tiny traces of Mr Blagge's dark jacket. Faced with this unassailable evidence, Mr Blagge had broken down at his second questioning and admitted to paying a second visit to the Watchtower, while the Cartwright family was still celebrating in a private room at the Royal Stag.

When he had presented himself in the foyer of the hotel, Julian had told him to cut along, the car would not be needed for at least an hour or so. So he had been unable to resist returning to the theatre — knowing where he had deposited the key — and 'giving that young man a piece of my mind'.

Mr Blagge even went so far as to admit that in the course of this process, he might have come close to plucking at Nat's scarf, might actually have given it a tug, especially when the young man in question waved him away, refused to speak to him, talked about Mr Blagge interrupting his precious meditations . . .

'His precious meditations!' snorted Mr Blagge, indignation once again overcoming him at the memory; with his face flushed, he looked altogether a more dangerous animal than the impeccable butler-figure he generally presented to the world; the detective questioning him noted how quickly his anger could erupt. 'As if he was in church, as if he was some kind of holy being. When he was only sitting in the theatre, wasn't he? I told him, I told young Master Nat —'

But Mr Blagge still maintained firmly and steadfastly that he was not responsible for Nat's death. Had not in fact strangled him with the white scarf, despite the evidence of his handling it.

'They often do that, murderers,' said Matt Harwood comfortably to Jemima Shore afterwards. 'Admit everything but the deed itself.'

Mr Blagge had then added that he had been vaguely conscious of someone else outside the theatre, a man, waiting, lurking in the shadows. A man who would have noticed him put back the key under the stone trough, and would then have been able to enter the theatre unobserved.

'That's the man you should go for,' Mr Blagge told the

police, still truculent. 'The person who was watching me. That's the person who did for Nat Fitzwilliam, that's who. I put the key back, second time as well, and now it's missing. The murderer took it. That's who.'

In desperation he went even further: swore that Nat himself had left the theatre again shortly after Blagge for a breath of fresh air — 'Told me I'd interrupted his thoughts! *His* thoughts! And what about *my* thoughts? What was I supposed to think when young Nat Fitzwilliam cheeked me in front of the whole of Larminster inside that restaurant? Fresh air indeed! Yes, he needed fresh air all right, I'll grant him that. And I heard him come out of the front door of the theatre too. Heard those great doors opening as I was crossing the square back to the hotel. Anybody could have used the Stage Door then. Anyone who knew where the key was. What about that man then, the other fellow?' Mr Blagge concluded truculently.

But: 'They often say that too.' Matt Harwood told Jemima. 'Someone else was around at the same time, someone unknown with exactly the same opportunity, who actually committed the crime.' And he pointed out how easy it would have been for Blagge to dispose of the key somewhere where it would never be found. There were also no witnesses to confirm the presence of a third party lurking in the shrubberies, nor had anyone else seen Nat Fitzwilliam leave the theatre for a breath of air, if indeed he had.

Jemima Shore, for her part, wished she could feel so totally convinced about the guilt of James Roy Blagge. It would have made life so much simpler. Instead, her instinct was troubling her; that famous instinct, merrily castigated by both Cy Fredericks ('Your lady's instinct, my dear Jem, always so expensive, what is it asking for this time?') and Pompey of the Yard ('My wife suffers from the feminine instinct too; you could say we both suffer from it.'). But Jemima knew by experience that this instinct was not to be derided.

The single word 'instinct', drawing the fire of such quizzical males as Cy Fredericks and Pompey, was in fact not quite accurate. It was more that Jemima possessed a very strong instinct for order. This would not let her rest so long as the smallest detail was out of place in the well-regulated pattern of her mind. On this occasion the small detail which was troubling her, and would continue to do so naggingly until she resolved it, was Christabel's distress at the televised rehearsal and her continued nervous state since Mr Blagge's arrest. Jemima had suggested rather flippantly to Matt Harwood that Mr Blagge might be being held in custody 'just in case he does it again'. But there could be no question of Mr Blagge attacking anyone while he was in the cells at Beauport. What then was frightening Christabel Cartwright?

The best way to find that out was to ask the lady in question. Jemima would use as an excuse for a meeting the need to discuss the new shape of the programme. She found that television provided an excellent cover for investigations of a very different nature, because the victims themselves were so eager to submit themselves to interrogation; the demands of the medium apparently vindicated in their eyes inquisitive approaches which Jemima herself would never have tolerated from a comparative stranger.

So Jemima invited Christabel to lunch at Flora's Kitchen. Inflamed by Cherry's descriptions of her gastronomic adventures with the Major, Jemima did for a moment flirt with the idea of roaming further afield, tasting the delights of Giovanni e Giovanna at Deep Larkin, for example, or even voyaging as far as The French Lieutenant just across the county border. In the end she rejected both plans: Giovanni's Special Bridset Spaghetti (Lar Bay mussels) and The French Lieutenant's Coupe Sarah, about both of which Cherry had waxed lyrical, would have to wait for another occasion for Jemima's seal of approval.

There was the complication of rehearsals as the First Night of The Seagull approached (and Widow Capet was billed to open the following week). More than that, Jemima wanted

Christabel to be exceptionally relaxed and confidential at this particular meal. Such an insecure woman — Jemima was increasingly inclined to take Gregory's estimate seriously — would be at her least guarded on familiar Larminster ground. Elsewhere, she might be tempted to give a performance, as it were, to Giovanni if not to Jemima Shore.

But as she faced Christabel across the Botticelli-printed tablecloth at Flora's Kitchen, Jemima did not find her noticeably relaxed. She could not help contrasting this jumpy nervous woman with the confident charming Christabel who had first introduced her to the restaurant. Her clothes were still perfectly chosen in their feminine way; full skirt of a very pale pink, echoed by the deeper pink rose on her jacket lapel, cream-coloured silk blouse tied in a floppy bow at the neck, and pearls. The great aquamarine ring still flashed on her finger, as though to remind anyone in danger of forgetting that Christabel's unblinking eyes were the same translucent tropical-sea colour. So was her eyeshadow, for that matter, and one noticed that fact too.

Critically, Jemima wondered whether Christabel wasn't wearing too much make-up for that time of day — and that particular restaurant. Her cheekbones were prominently highlighted with rather harsh blush-on powder; frequent dabs from her gold basket-weave compact, with its diamond and lapis lazuli catch, did not serve to soften the picture. Her overheavy mascara made her lashes look rather spiky. Next to Christabel, Poll's scrubbed powderless face, as she swept on her silent way producing the Florentine — or pseudo-Florentine — food, had a welcome freshness.

It would not be long before Blanche Cartwright would represent a prettier, as well as a younger version of her mother. This reflection was inspired in Jemima by Blanche's sudden eruption into the restaurant in the middle of lunch. She demanded some cash from her mother. She sounded jolly rather than hysterical and it suited her; her cheeks were pink, and a new short layered haircut drew attention to the heart shape of her face. Evidently Blanche was reconciled with her mother, at least to the extent of taking her money; her outburst at the Watchtower Theatre appeared to have had some kind of purgative effect. Even in her man's — or rather boy's — clothes of shirt and white knee-length shorts she looked rather pretty, now she had lost weight.

It was Regina Cartwright in her father's Land-Rover who dropped her mother at the restaurant — she had recently passed her driving test and Jemima had a feeling that the days of Rina's teenage passion for the horse Lancelot might be numbered. Striding away from her mother, black hair swinging on her shoulders, Rina looked both beautiful and confident. In the three or four months Jemima had known her, she too had changed out of all recognition. The girls had both emerged from the summer's ordeal strengthened and rather improved; it was the mother who languished.

One memorable aspect of Jemima's first meeting with Christabel was however still present. She continued to dip into the vodka bottle concealed in her expensive handbag. Guiltily, Jemima was rather glad, she presumed that drink had loosened Christabel's tongue on that previous occasion and hoped it would produce the same effect on her today.

Jemima insisted that this was her lunch — 'Megalith's lunch', she said with her sweet wide television smile, the one that made people who watched her on the box, men and women, fall deeply in love with her and decide she was really a very sweet person. She ordered a carafe of red wine for Christabel and a glass of white wine for herself.

But as it turned out, Christabel was not to be drawn. All the wiles of Jemima Shore Investigator, the practised tricks of the professional interviewer, failed to secure any form of personal revelation from her. In particular she declined to respond to references to their original conversation. Had Christabel felt 'safe' back on stage, as she had hoped to do?

'Oh darling, it's no good asking me that. Safe! I'm always so terribly terribly nervous before a First Night. A bundle of nerves. Not safe at all. Ask anyone. I'm on the verge of quitting the profession. Again!' Christabel added with a ghost of her old humour. It was really the only light moment in what was otherwise purely a defensive operation.

'But something was frightening you —' pursued Jemima. 'You told me.' Christabel looked at her quite steadily for a moment, her huge eyes appeared to glisten with tears.

'Oh it's too late to talk about all that now, darling', was all she said. She hesitated. 'Maybe I should have talked to you about it more then. It all seems so long ago. If I had, darling, well, all sorts of things might have been different. But now — well, it's too late, isn't it?'

'Too late for what, Christabel?' In her desperation, feeling the brief moment of confidentiality passing away, Jemima became bolder. But at this Christabel merely opened her blue eyes even wider in a parody of surprise.

'Too late to go back, darling. That's all. That's all I meant. One can never go back in life, can one?'

You did! Jemima longed to cry in frustration, seeing Christabel's face settling itself into a mask of polite non-cooperation. She still looked infinitely sad, but at the same time remote. In a moment she would be waving the dreaded powder compact again, powdering her nose for the third time, as one who shakes dust in her pursuer's face. You came back! But the words died on her lips. She could not risk antagonizing her at this stage. The question of Filly Lennox's death was crucial.

Afterwards Jemima was to regret bitterly not pressing Christabel Cartwright further on those few melancholy words, so much at variance with her public air of cool — and maddeningly successful — repentance. If Jemima had done so, might not Christabel have broken out from behind the pathetic painted mask? And if so, would Christabel have been 'safe'? — what she declared she so much wanted to be at their first meeting. Or was it already, as Christabel now so sadly said, 'Too late'?

At the time Jemima was too concerned to satisfy herself on the subject of Jim Blagge's guilt or innocence to turn aside.

'Christabel,' she said urgently. 'There's one question I must ask you. Do *you* think Mr Blagge murdered Nat? Is he quite simply guilty? Should I accept that fact? Supposing he did, and I must admit that the police evidence against him is very strong, is it possible — wait for it — that poor Filly Lennox was murdered too? Deliberately drowned: murdered in mistake for you? Mr Blagge went out in the boat on the day of the picnic. Does Mr Blagge hate *you* too? For the sake of —' now she had to come out with it 'for the sake of his son?'

At this point Jemima fully intended to shock. She did not intend to let Christabel drift back into her gracious reticence. And there was something deeply shocking about voicing her theory — to the woman whom Mr Blagge had perhaps intended to drown in Filly's place. Even so Jemima was quite unprepared for Christabel's reaction.

She fainted.

When Jemima told Spike Thompson about it late that night, as they lay together in the four-poster bed conveniently provided by the Royal Stag, it suddenly struck her that the faint — a dead faint, off the chair to the floor, carrying glasses and cutlery with it — might have been a protective measure. After all Christabel never had answered Jemima's question about Filly's death. Nor for that matter about Jim Blagge's guilt. Yet if it was a protective measure, who was Christabel so concerned to protect?

At the time Christabel's startling physical collapse made it easy for her to escape from Jemima's inquisition: 'I'll go back to the theatre and rest,' she murmured. 'Terribly silly of me, darling. I've been overdoing it. Two productions. Poor little Filly's death. Then Nat. And the strain of the arrest.'

Christabel would not let Jemima summon Regina to drive

her home and reacted even more strongly to the idea of Jemima's telephoning Julian at Lark. Blanche, who could be seen inside a bow-windowed Larminster boutique opposite, trying on a pair of velvet knickerbockers, was the only person Christabel agreed to have contacted and sent after her to her dressing-room. So Jemima had to let her go.

Spike, prepared to take a lazy interest in the subject of Christabel's faint during a temporary lull in the night's proceedings, encouraged Jemima in her suspicions. 'These actresses are up to any old trick. I could tell you a thing or two about actresses. But then you, my lovely, are also up to any old trick, aren't you?' But the thought of Jemima and her tricks turned Spike's thoughts away from Christabel Cartwright and once more to that activity with which the gallant Spike always liked to fill as many as possible of his off-duty hours when on location.

He did spare one Parthian chauvinist shot for Julian Cartwright: 'I can't get over her old man taking her back like that. Screwed all over the press by a pop star — and then it's welcome-home time when he ditches her, and-did-you-have-a-good-time, darling? I wouldn't stand for it in my missis, I can tell you,' said Spike virtuously. 'I'd give her a proper going over.'

'Not all men are the same. And not all women either. If I was Christabel Cartwright, it would drive me quite mad to have to come back to Lark as penitent Magdalen.' The conversation might have gone further — for Spike's Parthian shot had started an interesting train of thought in her mind. But by now Spike had succeeded in turning Jemima's attention too from Christabel Cartwright; for the rest of the night, Jemima was entirely possessed by Spike, the touch and taste and feel of him.

What with one thing and another, it was not until the next day that Jemima fully analysed her conversation with Christabel. She was now in renewed conclave with Matt Harwood.

It was time, she decided — the time was really overdue — to confide to him her suspicions about the death of Filly Lennox and her instinct that Christabel, while still fearful, was nonetheless protecting some person close to her.

But Detective Inspector Harwood, in his most reasonable voice, merely asked for proof of all these female fancies. He freely admitted that a good many people had had the opportunity to kill Nat Fitzwilliam, including, if she wished to consider them, the entire large Cartwright family party installed at the Royal Stag on the night of Blanche's birthday. Gregory, Ketty, the Cartwrights in force, they had all been there milling about in the hotel: Mrs Tennant, the manageress, had given them an empty suite on the first floor — Jemima's suite was the only other one in the hotel — out of local loyalty.

Up there however the party had rather fizzled out. The suite was stuffy because it was not in use. At Christabel's request Gregory had then gone downstairs to rout out the champagne which Flora's Kitchen had not been able to produce before leaving for his late-night swim. Christabel had been overcome with exhaustion — 'or maybe something stronger' said the Detective Inspector — and during Gregory's absence, which had been quite prolonged, had at Julian's suggestion retired to the bedroom to lie down. Blanche, removing a few of her hotter garments and unbuttoning her shirt as she went, had then taken the opportunity to flit off to find Ollie Summertown. She had ignored Ketty's protests — 'It's my *birthday*, Ketty, and anyway it's *not* indecent — some people think it looks pretty' — and after a bit Ketty had gone to look for her. Julian agreeing that it *was* very hot had gone out for a breath of air. Regina went down to the lounge to look for a book . . . the Detective Inspector was happy to give Jemima as detailed an account as she liked of their various movements.

It all amounted to this, said Matt Harwood: many people had had Opportunity and Method to kill Nat Fitzwilliam. Only Jim Blagge had had Motive. Only Jim Blagge had had close physical contact with Nat Fitzwilliam on the night concerned. Only Jim Blagge admitted paying Nat Fitzwilliam a late-night threatening call. Jemima was really the only person in Larminster who had any doubts about Jim Blagge's guilt.

Curiously enough, this was not actually true. There was another keen-eyed observer in Larminster who was not quite satisfied that Jim Blagge had murdered Nat Fitzwilliam. This was seventy-nine-year-old Nicola Wain. The old actress, with only her role in *Widow Capet* to consider, was left with a good deal of liberty on her hands as rehearsals of *The Seagull* grew more intense. Knitting, as Old Nicola often remarked, gave her plenty of time for thinking 'and also watching all you naughty boys and girls'. It also gave her plenty of time to figure things out, movements, noises, statements which did not add up.

The room to which she had moved at the Royal Stag, a room about which she constantly complained to anyone who would listen ('No bathroom *en suite*, well, dear, at my age . . .') lay at the top of the service staircase on the first floor. Admittedly the room's single window overlooked the back of the hotel instead of the pretty square which was Larminster's chief beauty and contained the Watchtower Theatre, set among mature trees, in one corner of it. Even Mrs Tennant, the manageress of the Royal Stag, who was an optimist, had had to agree that the view from Old Nicola's room — over the back entrance of the hotel and the courtyard which served as a car-park — was not inspiring. On the other hand she had firmly rebutted the notion that the service stairs, adjoining Old Nicola's room, would prove to be an unpleasant source of nocturnal disturbance.

'No one uses them at night,' Mrs Tennant had assured her querulous guest, at the time of her arrival. 'But we just can't lock them, dear, because of the Fire Regulations. You never know when someone might not need access. In an emergency, that is.'

'Exactly,' Old Nicola had grumbled at the time, as though

an emergency was just the kind of needless disturbance she gloomily predicted. Yet in its own way, Old Nicola's sojourn in her little first-floor room had not been unrewarding. Either Mrs Tennant's reassuring remarks about the service stairs not being used except in an emergency had turned out to be inaccurate or perhaps the occasion when they had been used recently had been considered an emergency by the person concerned. Either way, Old Nicola was really quite pleased with the new piece of information which had come her way as a result of her room's geographical location.

As the dress rehearsal of The Seagull approached and everyone else grew more and more frantic, Old Nicola began to reach a certain rather interesting conclusion. For, as she told herself, there was really nothing wrong with 'these poor old wits' — wits which had certainly kept her afloat in her own profession, by fair means or foul, for over sixty years.

It remained for Old Nicola to decide exactly what use she should make of this discovery. After a period of thought, spent by the old woman knitting ostentatiously in the lounge at the Royal Stag — the sight of the battered plastic bag from which the knitting emanated began to madden even the good-natured Mrs Tennant — Old Nicola went upstairs to her room. Once there, she locked the door, and placed her knitting, bag and all, in the solitary armchair as carefully as if it had been a child. Then Old Nicola sat down at the tiny writing-desk and began to write a letter.

Although Old Nicola had frequently complained to Mrs Tennant about the size of the desk and the inadequate light above it, on this occasion she looked positively happy as she penned the words in handwriting which, as she often told herself, was really quite remarkable for her age. She did not however think that the person to whom she was addressing the letter would feel quite so happy at receiving it — despite the care with which it was written, and the clarity of the handwriting.

FOURTEEN

Happy Ending

The dress rehearsal of *The Seagull* was not going to be filmed for television. Too like the real thing the next night to be dramatically interesting, Guthrie decided.

'Unless there's a disaster,' contributed Cherry brightly. 'We don't want to miss that, do we?'

'Don't we?' Jemima sounded cold. It was now impossible to enter Cherry's bedroom at the Royal Stag for the reek of fruit — nectarines and peaches — and flowers — mainly fat richly-scented crimson roses sent down from Major Cartwright's greenhouse and garden at Larksgrange. The Major had also started to quote poetry to Cherry over the dinner-table although otherwise his conversation remained strictly gastronomic. In the cosy depths of Giovanni e Giovanna the previous evening, he had recited Tennyson's Song from *The Princess*: 'Now sleeps the crimson petal, now the white . . .'

At the end: 'I wrote that', said the Major sternly. Cherry, despite months spent working on 'Tennyson: The Tortured Years' had not contradicted him, which Jemima told her was very disloyal. Jemima feared the worst: was Flowering Cherry's long quest for the Substantial Older Man in danger of coming to a happy ending?

'We haven't missed many disasters yet,' was Guthrie's gloomy comment. He had just learned from London that the first of his non-controversial programmes about 'The Elgin Marbles — Ours or Theirs?' was held to be such political dynamite by the Greek government that they had locked up an entire Megalith crew (coincidentally out in Greece at the time the programme was shown, harmlessly filming 'Sappho: A Woman for Our Time'). Most unfairly, he felt, Cy Fredericks blamed the entire expense of bailing this crew out of prison on Guthrie. As a punishment he was threatening to pare down Guthrie's editing time for 'In a Festival Mood: Part IV: A Seagull-by-the-Sea'.

Only Spike was blithe. This was because in the absence of any filming, he had a free evening which meant he could get over at last to The French Lieutenant for dinner. Its prices sounded promising — if not from Megalith's point of view. He took Jemima's refusal to accompany him (conscientiously she felt she must attend the dress rehearsal) in good part. Spike took food almost as seriously as Major Cartwright: in a way it was a pity they could not eat together as their tastes in this matter at least were very similar.

Guthrie, Cherry and Jemima sat together centrally, but towards the back of the wide amphitheatre, which fanned out from four sides of the pentagonal stage. Gregory came and sat beside Jemima. A good many rows nearer the front sat Julian Cartwright, Blanche and Regina. Ketty was with them.

Gregory whispered to Jemima that he was most surprised to see Julian. 'He never used to come anywhere near a dress rehearsal in the old days. Not invited for one thing. Didn't want to come either, I dare say. Made a polite supporting appearance at the first preview, if there was one, and then a

gracious supporting appearance at the First Night. Otherwise
he left it at that — apart from picking up a good many bills
for large dinners at expensive restaurants when required. As
a matter of fact I never thought even in those days Julian was
really all that much in love with the theatre as a whole. It
was Christabel he loved. When he secured her by marriage,
that patient courtship paid off, the *raison d'être* for all that
theatre-going had vanished.'

Gregory smiled. He added, still in a low voice: 'Ironically
enough, I always thought that made Julian rather a good sort
of husband for a leading actress. Certainly better than an actor
would have been — no competition, no rival First-Night
nerves in the home. Until events proved me wrong.'

But Julian *was* a good husband, thought Jemima: it was
Christabel who had not been a good wife. What was more,
she guessed that Julian's presence tonight was due to a laudable
desire to support Christabel yet again on the eve of her come-
back to the stage.

The lights dimmed, to a sharp cry from Boy Greville — he
had warned Jemima earlier that dress rehearsals had an extraordinary effect on the nerves in his spinal cord and he often
found himself going into spasms just as they started. His production of *The Seagull* was clearly to be no exception to this
painful rule.

Apart from the physical agonies suffered by the director,
the first act of the dress rehearsal really went remarkably well.
Boy Greville had to lie flat on the thick soft pile carpet of the
auditorium. Gallantly, he observed that it was one of the great
consolations of his affliction that theatre floors, especially
modern ones like the Watchtower, provided an ideal arena
for recuperation. He spoke warmly of the Olivier at the National in this context as though recommending an expensive
private nursing-home.

'Like dock leaves growing near nettles,' Cherry piped up:

her new passion for imparting pieces of country lore, where previously she had concentrated on literature was, Jemima thought, another bad sign.

The company advised Boy to think of himself, and not worry about the production. 'Lie back and enjoy it, like rape,' added Vic Marcovich. In view of what was known about Boy's general passivity, and in view of Vic's special relationship to Boy's wife Anna Maria, this jocular remark if well meant, was felt to be in rather poor taste.

Still, the play went on. In their efforts to atone to Boy for this latest blow of fate, the actors did as well, even better perhaps, than if their director had attended the rehearsal in the more conventional upright position. As a result, the performance was singularly free from those petty theatrical disasters of the sort to be expected and even welcomed at a dress rehearsal because they seemed to promise a trouble-free First Night. 'Dangerously smooth,' Vic Marcovich described it. 'Hope it's not a bad omen for tomorrow.'

In particular Christabel shone. In view of what happened later, the few people who had been present would remember this last shimmering of her talent with agonized regret for what might have been. Guthrie announced in the first break that Christabel was using her voice as if it were a musical instrument whose range was being explored for the first time at the hands of a master. 'A clarinet perhaps,' he suggested enthusiastically, the image clearly taking hold. Jemima, trusting that he would not expect her to incorporate any such sentiment in her commentary, did not speak. She was still deeply moved by what had happened on stage, and wanted to collect her wits before joining the unofficial Critics' Forum.

'Violin!' cried Cherry.

'Bassoon maybe? Christabel's voice is quite deep.' This was Gregory. Cherry shot him a reproachful look. Jemima felt grateful.

All the same, Christabel's voice was peculiarly sonorous

and varied that evening. Her performance radiated exactly the kind of automatic careless charm, followed by sudden vulnerability and frightened hungry reclaiming of the wandering Trigorin, which the part of Arkadina, the actress playing the actress, had always seemed to Jemima to require. Gone were all the hesitations and nerves of previous rehearsals. Christabel Herrick was back. Christabel Cartwright was forgotten.

Even Old Nicola, never one to shower a fellow-actor with compliments, acknowledged that. But then Old Nicola was in an unwontedly seraphic humour that evening. Her knitting too was less maliciously orientated, less audacious in its attacks on the ankles and elbows of passersby. It remained incarcerated in the old grey plastic bag at her feet most of the time. Old Nicola did not even attempt to knit during the first three acts of *The Seagull*.

'Just as well. I would have murdered her if she had,' muttered Guthrie.

'You keep threatening that kind of thing,' complained Jemima. 'You know Cy's strong views about a director's individual responsibility. If anyone does in Old Nicola we shall have our programme cancelled and it will be all your fault.'

Guthrie snorted. But really, it had to be admitted that Old Nicola was not in a tiresome mood at all, and as a result no one had any proper excuse for wanting to murder her. If she was not, all the same, an absolutely ideal member of a small audience, this was because Old Nicola had a habit of chuckling audibly whenever she herself perceived one of the jokes. These perceptions of Old Nicola's concerning the humorous side of Chekhov had not by any means been shared by the late Nat Fitzwilliam nor by Boy Greville subsequently.

Old Nicola had nevertheless proved quite remorseless in her note-giving after rehearsals: 'You naughty boy, you should really listen to Old Nicola, you know. I've known them all in my day, Stanislavsky, Komisarjevsky, all the Russians. I even went to Moscow. Have I ever told you about the time I was in the audience when Stalin came to the theatre? Now when Stalin laughed, you see, everyone had to laugh . . .'

But neither Nat Fitzwilliam nor Boy Greville, disappointingly, was prepared to show undue interest in Stalin's contribution to Russian humour. Besides, Old Nicola's reminiscences were growing more daringly fantastic every day. Since she even claimed to have been bandaged by Chekhov's own hands ('He was a perfect duck, Chekhov, he was a doctor you know, and when I accidentally tripped over at a rehearsal and fell . . .'), perhaps too much credence was not to be given to her memories.

Now her chuckles punctuated the performance like a persistent low cough, irritating when the performance flagged, unnoticeable when it was at its height. During the second break, on the eve of the last act, Old Nicola first went and exchanged some remarks with Blanche, then sidled up to Jemima. Gregory had moved and was chatting to Julian and the girls.

'Isn't she quite perfect tonight?' Old Nicola put her face with its bright bird's eyes and bird's sharp beak very close to Jemima's. 'Christabel, I mean. I've just been telling that sweet little Blanche; never mind about Nina, her chance will come, I'm so pleased for Mummy. I do hope everything will go right for tomorrow. After so long, you can't help being worried for her, can you? Wouldn't it be just tragic if anything went wrong? Just when everything's coming to a happy ending for her?'

'What could go wrong?' Jemima was afraid she sounded irritable but she found Old Nicola oozing sympathy even more intolerable than she was grumbling. 'Other than a bad performance. And I don't think Christabel is likely to turn in one of those, do you? Or are you suggesting she can't do it twice?'

'Oh no, dear, no, no, no. Please don't misunderstand Old Nicola. My, some of you clever ladies from television can be

sharp sometimes, can't you? Not all of you, though. My friend
Susan Merlin was interviewed by a young lady, a *very* pretty
young lady, the other day on her memories of the theatre —
though Susan is really quite a newcomer to the stage compared
to me, and you didn't want *my* memories, but we'll let that
pass. Be that as it may — we'll talk about it later, dear —
Susan said that this young lady was really terribly sweet and
gentle and helpful to her, in spite of being so pretty. Still I
suppose it takes all sorts in television, doesn't it, as well as in
life?'

Jemima had not survived the repeated fruitless attempts of
the press to stir up rivalry between her and her female contemporaries on television in order to succumb to the poisoned
darts of Old Nicola.

'I think that's so very true,' she said in her warmest television voice. 'It certainly does take all sorts. And not only in
television. The theatre too. Now tell me all about *Widow
Capet* and your part in that. I'm sorry that in the end we went
for filming just the one production —'

Normally, any mention of this appalling dereliction of duty
by Megalith was enough to set Old Nicola off on a tirade. An
interview with Gregory was being included, but no clips of
the play itself (which might have shown the old woman in
her famous role as the jailer's mother). It had turned out to
be too expensive to film both productions and do them justice.
But on this occasion, Old Nicola's own version of a high good-
humour was not to be shaken.

'Well, dear, there's not much to tell, is there? Otherwise
I suppose we'd find ourselves telling it to all you clever girls
and boys on the box, wouldn't we? To tell you the truth, I'm
not quite as thrilled with the part as I was. I've done it many
many times, you know, really created the role for that nice
Gregory, at his own personal request. But that was a long time
ago. The stage is not like television, dear: here today, gone
tomorrow. It's a very hard life. So you may be interested in

hearing, dear, *on or off the box*, that Old Nicola is going to retire.'

In its way, it was a startling declaration. And Old Nicola made it not with regret or complaint, but with an air of triumph. What, no more Old Nicola besieging young directors with her irresistible demands for parts? No more Old Nicola giving those same unwary directors endless notes after rehearsal on the proper way to get the production right — which meant listening to her tales of bygone triumphs? And what about her flat in Fulham, hers for so many years, whose ever-increasing rent was one of Old Nicola's most persistent laments? What about the cost of living, another personal affront to Old Nicola's survival, especially since she was blessed with an equally ancient companion, in the shape of an enormously fat grey cat called Thomas. Jemima had seen his photograph: from his girth and insolent expression, it came as no surprise to her to learn that Thomas could only exist on a diet of minced best steak and fresh fish, salmon being a particular favourite. Jemima, who had always thought she liked all cats, wondered if she might find herself making an exception in the case of Thomas.

'Oh no, dear, it won't be a disaster financially, not at all,' Old Nicola hastened to reassure her, her complacency even more marked. 'You see, someone is going to look after Old Nicola in future. Someone who can *well* afford to do so, plenty of money, when you think how Old Nicola herself has to live. But how good of you all the same to think of my Thomas, my dear, and his special diet; I shall tell Susan Merlin that you have a heart of gold under your' — Old Nicola paused — 'up-to-date exterior. Yes, Thomas and I will be able to afford lobster in future — something he has never yet tried, but I have a hunch he may take to it.'

'A gift?' enquired Jemima delicately. From the bustle on stage, the next and last act was going to proceed at any moment.

Old Nicola looked immensely sly and at the same time very pleased with herself. 'A gift? Not quite, dear. A reward, you could say. A reward to Old Nicola for having sharp eyes, and a clear mind in her eightieth year, and being able to put two and two together and still make more of it than most of you young people. Yes, you may not believe it, but I shall be eighty on December the sixteenth. Jane Austen's birthday and people have often pointed out that I have exactly the same talent for observation.' Old Nicola clearly awaited some comment from Jemima on this coincidence.

But Jemima's instinct as an investigator was at war with her respect for Jane Austen. The latter won. She said nothing.

'Of course I also know all about the theatre and its little ways,' went on Old Nicola, sounding disappointed. 'After all these years. It was really most fortunate I moved my room to the Royal Stag when I did, in spite of the manageress making such difficulties about giving me a proper light. It even turned out lucky in a way that my room overlooked the back entrance to the hotel although I trust you will not mention the fact to Mrs Tennant.' The old woman, in her newly bonhomous mood, gave a conspiratorial chuckle. 'Fortunate too that I kept my eyes open at that picnic, no naps for Old Nicola in the afternoon, even though she is in her eightieth year. Eyes open and mouth shut, that's the way to get rich, dear.'

For a moment Jemima had the strongest possible feeling that Old Nicola was going to confide in her exactly what it was that she had seen. She held her breath. The Stage Manager appeared at the edge of the stage.

'Right, Boy?' he called. From his prone position, Boy Greville raised his arm on high in assent, in a gesture of the dying Siegfried, and the house lights were dimmed.

'Miss Wain,' whispered Jemima urgently, 'what was it you saw? Who is it who is making you this handsome gift?'

But Old Nicola merely put up her thin gnarled finger to her lips, and went 'SSSh' in a self-righteous way. Then she scuttled away to one of the side rows of the theatre, away from the central block, taking her plastic bag with her. She was still smiling. She looked both greedy and cheerful, like a gourmet cat who expected to be fed on lobster for the rest of his life.

After the theatre, Old Nicola was not to be seen. She must have gone straight back to her room at the Royal Stag, across the square. Jemima looked for her for as long as decency allowed, but that was not for very long. There were the actors to be congratulated and encouraged, and even more to the point Boy Greville to be brought back from the verge of despair. Although everyone else agreed that the dress rehearsal had gone wonderfully well, even worryingly so, Boy Greville declined on the one hand to believe this, and on the other hand prophesied woe on the morrow.

It was not until he reached Flora's Kitchen where a special late dinner had been arranged for the Cartwright family that Boy became remotely content. Jemima walked across the square to the restaurant, with Christabel's expression at the very end of the last act haunting her.

'What's that?' she had exclaimed, at the sound of the shot off-stage. Tobs, as Dr Dorn, had made a very passable stab at comforting her: 'That's nothing. It must be something in my medicine chest that's gone off. Don't worry.' Christabel had then sat down and pretended to be comforted. But all the while Christabel's expression, her over-wide eyes, had remained stamped with some terrible premonitory fear. When Dr Dorn confided to Trigorin at the end of the play: 'Take Irena Nikolayevna away from here somehow. The fact is, Konstantin Gavrilovich has shot himself', you knew that she already experienced the tragedy within her.

It was as well that dinner at Flora's Kitchen was rather demanding with Boy needing not only spiritual reassurance but medical remedies. (Moll coped with the latter, sending

Poll out from the kitchen with some strange vegetable concoction of her own, her raucous voice shouting, 'See if that will shut the bugger up.') Otherwise Jemima might have had to live with that image of Christabel's expression throughout the evening. As it was, everyone was relieved when dinner, begun late, broke up early, with the prospect of a First Night ahead. Julian Cartwright it was who masterfully tore Christabel away, and announced in his loud voice that he and Christabel had booked rooms at the Royal Stag for themselves and the girls: 'Christabel certainly needs a proper sleep, as she says, and Lark is not very comfortable at the moment, in view of poor Mrs Blagge's condition.'

'Can't I drive back by myself, Daddy?' began Regina. Ketty silenced her.

'This is much nicer, Rina,' she said firmly. 'Please say thank you nicely. Daddy has been his usual thoughtful self.'

'I'm thinking of Mummy as well,' Blanche contributed in a virtuous voice. 'I'd like to stay, if it makes things easier for Mummy.'

It transpired that the suite in which the Cartwrights had been allowed to continue their party on the night of Blanche's birthday — and Nat's death — was still empty. Christabel was to sleep in the inner bedroom, Julian on a bed in the sitting-room, 'to give her maximum rest' as he put it. The girls and Ketty had been found rooms on an upper floor.

All these domestic arrangements appeared to have a warming effect on Gregory. He offered to buy Jemima a drink at the bar — champagne, why not? — and when the bar was closed, suggested jovially that they should adjourn to her suite and order it there. This suggestion, in view of the possibility that Gregory might find Spike Thompson already installed in her sitting-room, black leather jacket and all, or worse still in her bed, black leather jacket and everything else discarded, Jemima was obliged to turn down. She found herself feeling distinctly regretful about this, which both annoyed and un-settled her. And when she did get upstairs, there was no sign of Spike, which annoyed and unsettled her still further.

Old Nicola, when she had first reached her bedroom some hours earlier, had been in an altogether more contented frame of mind. So she was fast asleep when the person who was supposed to reward Old Nicola for her sharp eyes and ears entered her room by means of Mrs Tennant's pass-key. Certainly the last night of Old Nicola's life had been a very happy one. As the person placed the dark-grey plastic bag over Old Nicola's head and fastened it tight with the flex of her despised table-lamp, perhaps she was dreaming of lobster, of proud Thomas tasting the first consignment with his fastidious pink tongue.

At any rate Old Nicola made no noise as she died, in the small room at the top of the service stairs in the Royal Stag Hotel.

FIFTEEN

Your Lady's Instinct

In all the terrible furore which followed the discovery of Old Nicola's body — by Marie, the hotel chambermaid, bringing her morning tea — nothing was more painfully vivid to Jemima Shore in retrospect than her conversation with the Chairman of Megalith Television. Somehow breaking the news to Cy Fredericks was an even more traumatic experience for Jemima than Marie's prolonged if natural hysterics (she was only sixteen) and Mrs Tennant's equally natural hotelier's agitation.

At first Mrs Tennant showed herself a model of calm; but her nerves grew progressively more ragged with the inevitable influx of a large work force of policemen and their associates. The doctor on call to the police, who arrived at the same time as a Detective Constable from Beauport, was actually well known to her, because he happened to be the hotel doctor too. Mrs Tennant thought this only made his behaviour in using the front staircase more outrageous.

'Doctor Lamb ought to know how dreadful all this is for us!' she exclaimed to the nearest sympathetic audience, which happened to be Jemima Shore. 'What will the guests think? What will the Cartwrights think? Mr Cartwright was so upset to hear the news: he said he'd break it to his wife personally when she awoke. I'm afraid Miss Kettering had already got it from Marie before I made her lie down upstairs, the noise when she dropped the tea tray woke her, and then it was too late to stop the young Cartwright girls finding out. Regina went terribly quiet, but Blanche was quite hysterical, I always say she's the feeling one —' Then, in her nervous state, Mrs Tennant concentrated on the essential difference between the front staircase and the service stairs, as though by upholding this distinction, she could avoid further dire troubles for the Royal Stag Hotel.

The cause of death — asphyxiation — was not too difficult for Dr Lamb to suggest, especially as neither Marie nor Mrs Tennant had removed the plastic bag. Marie, after one horrified look, had fled screaming for Mrs Tennant. The manageress, rushing up the stairs — 'Hush, Marie, for goodness' sake, you'll wake Mrs Cartwright; and Marie, what *have* you done with that tray?' — had fallen back at the grim quiet sight on the pillow. No wonder poor Marie had backed away. It looked as if some lumpish grey cuckoo had entered Miss Wain's bed.

Mrs Tennant had the presence of mind to touch her hand, and on finding it cold, she felt for her pulse. Finding none, she felt next, for a heart beat — equally in vain. She did not however attempt to remove the plastic bag — something Mrs Tennant could not explain to herself afterwards, but for which, since nothing could have been done for the old woman anyway, the police were duly grateful.

At least it was some consolation to Mrs Tennant that Old Nicola's body was taken away down these back stairs when Detective Inspector Harwood finally authorized its removal. Her corpse was now encased in a protective black plastic covering — so much cleaner and newer-looking than her own grey knitting-bag had been, but equally a shroud; it looked shrunken by death into a very small size indeed. The room itself, after being subject to the most thorough scrutiny that the wit of Matt Harwood could devise for fingerprints and other clues, was then locked up. Now all the patient investigations, takings of statements, siftings, collations of evidence which had taken place after the death of Nat Fitzwilliam would begin all over again.

All of this was still not more testing to Jemima — perhaps because the routine of police work had become familiar to her — than the ravings of Cy Fredericks.

'You were quite right. He actually blames me for the old bird's unfortunate demise.' Thus Guthrie Carlyle, reeling away from his own call. 'The man is out of his mind. He seems to hold me personally responsible for what he calls "an extraordinarily high death-rate — even by your standards" of the population of Larminster. Naturally, he's cancelling the programme. I expected that. But what the hell does he mean — an extraordinarily high death-rate by *my* standards?' Guthrie ended angrily.

'I'm sorry about the programme. After all your work. Our work.' Jemima herself was more weary than angry after her own forty-five minutes of telephonic hysteria. 'I think he's referring to the fact that one of your Greek crew, you know, the one you nicknamed Two-and-Twenty Misfortunes after the character in *The Cherry Orchard*, had died in a car crash. His widow has just worked out a way of suing Megalith —'

Guthrie groaned. 'Stop, stop. Just do me a favour and never mention any aspect of Hellenic civilization whatsoever, alive or dead, to me again. I want to lead the rest of my life as far removed from the Glory that was Greece as possible.' Jemima wondered whether this was a tactful moment to break it to Guthrie that Cy Fredericks proposed to substitute for Larminster, as Part IV of 'In a Festival Mood', an eight-day Gaelic song contest on a remote island off the west coast of Scotland. In spite of his last bold words, she decided against it.

In the course of the conversation Jemima herself had had with Cy, almost the only serious charge which he did not hurl down the telephone was that of high treason. She could only suppose this was because Cy had yet to discover political overtones to Old Nicola's death — no doubt he soon would. Words like 'betrayal' and 'conspiracy', always high on his list of expletives, tripped off his tongue. After 'conspiracy', 'lack of all consideration for Megalith Television' sounded rather tame, but was clearly intended to be an equally lethal insult on Cy's lips.

Jemima, who had seen out these storms before, waited till there was a pause, because Cy was recovering his breath and then struck back: 'Cy,' she began in an ominously quiet voice, 'an old woman, a very old woman, as it happens, has died — been murdered, I gather from my friends the police. She was also a singularly unpleasant old woman and was probably blackmailing her killer. This old woman also happened to be an actress and she happened to have a part in one of the two productions in a Festival programme being televised by Megalith. All of this is most unfortunate. I agree with you. It's most unfortunate for Megalith because we've wasted a lot of money — and time and trouble, incidentally — on this programme and now I agree with you — *I do agree with you*, Cy, it has to be scrapped.'

Jemima gathered momentum: 'It's also unfortunate for the Larminster Festival because they've now suffered two fairly macabre murders on the eve of opening, and yet they can hardly just cancel the whole affair, just like that, with all the tickets sold out, mainly to see Christabel Herrick, and suffer financial ruin. It's even more unfortunate for the King Charles Theatre Company — think of what they've been through. Their director dying on them and now a member of the company stricken down, even if she was only in one production and replaceable: at this moment the wretched Boy Greville is trying to get hold of Susan Merlin who's played the part before, and who he wanted to cast originally anyway. Most of all, you could reasonably say it's unfortunate for Nicola Wain who died on the eve of what she fancied would be an affluent retirement and will probably be mourned by nobody but her cat.

'But none of this, Cy,' Jemima slowed down as she delivered her peroration and raised her voice a couple of decibels (she also did not think Cy's silence would last much longer for she could hear strange snortings and pantings down the line as of a great beast seeking to free itself from control), 'none of this, not one single element of this, amounts to a conspiracy against Megalith Television. I did not kill Nicola Wain. I did not kill Nat Fitzwilliam. Nor, I would dare swear, did Guthrie Carlyle. Nor did Cherry Bronson. I would even hazard a view that Spike Thompson, whatever his expense sheets, is not a murderer and,' she threw in inspirationally, 'I am quite prepared to be his alibi if necessary. In view of all these manifest facts, Cy, and in view of your attitude to me and my colleagues this morning on this distressing occasion, I must ask you to accept my immediate resignation.'

There was a long horrified silence, with no snortings or pantings at all. Then Cy said, in what for him was a whisper: 'Jem, Jem, you haven't — you haven't got another job? Breakfast Television? The BBC? No, Jem, you couldn't have done that to me, not you, Jem. The BBC? My God, what are they paying you? It's an outrage. Public money . . . I shall raise questions . . .' His voice rose, 'Listen, do nothing, Jem, do nothing at all until I have seen you. I am coming down this afternoon in the Rolls, straightaway. Miss Lewis,' he was by now shouting, 'tell Leonard I shall be going down to — to — well, wherever it is, find out where the festival film unit is, Miss Lewis, well, where is it? Find out, woman! Don't ask me *which* festival film unit, all right, *all right*, yes, of course, I know there are several, I commissioned this series, didn't I? The one lucky enough to have the company of Miss Jemima Shore. Tell Leonard I shall be leaving at two o'clock for it, wherever it is, and yes, yes, I will be back for dinner. Dinner at Mark's Club, but please telephone Lady Manfred and ask her to make it nine o'clock instead of eight-thirty —

'My poor child,' he then crooned loudly but tenderly down the telephone, 'my poor Jem, of course you've had a terrible time —'

It was with the greatest difficulty that Jemima convinced Cy that not only had she no other job in view, but also that his presence in Larminster, even with the incomparable Leonard at the wheel of the Rolls, would only make matters worse than they were already. The conversation thus ended amiably but sharply with the news of Guthrie's exile to the Western Isles ('You will know how to break it to him, Jem, your lady's instinct') which showed that Cy was once more quite himself.

As Jemima predicted, the Festival Committee were in no position to cancel their programme, even if they were so inclined. The tickets were mainly sold, and the Festival had thus to pursue its course, unassisted by the presence of Megalith Television — and of course Miss Nicola Wain. The latter was easier to replace as an attraction than the former. Susan Merlin did indeed respond most sweetly to Boy Greville's appeal, and promised to arrive 'word-perfect' within a few days: 'Which is an advantage I think I can say I have over poor Nicola. She was always a slow study, but then of course she was really quite a few years older than me, even if she didn't like to admit it . . .'

The news of the departure of Megalith Television spread rapidly through a Larminster already appalled by Old Nicola's decease — but more by its locale than anything else. Like the arrest of Jim Blagge, anything concerning the Royal Stag and its manageress struck straight at local sympathies.

'Poor Ivy Tennant, when she's worked so hard to build the place up . . .' These words were heard far more frequently than: 'Poor Miss Wain'. Old Nicola was chiefly known as an actress for her appearances in Dickens serials in which she generally played some appropriately witch-like character: the impression of malice she conveyed had not been contradicted in real life by her behaviour at the Spring Guest House and the Royal Stag itself. Even the kind-hearted Mrs Tennant found it difficult to say many nice things about her guest, while Marie was a good deal more explicit: ' "Late again, dear," she would say, sitting up in bed like an old bat. I often wanted to throw the tea things at her head. And in the end that's just what I did, except that her head —' At this point Marie collapsed in loud howls.

The retreat of Megalith from filming the First Night was quite another matter. Father O'Brien for example found it very difficult to reconcile himself to this working of the divine will. His Christian resignation was further tested when Poll, doing a heroic stint at the theatre box office, absolutely refused to refund him for his ticket, an exchange which he requested on the grounds that the television cameras would not now be present.

'The rules say that I have to tell ticket-holders in advance that the programme will be filmed. But they don't say I have to compensate them if it won't be filmed,' she maintained firmly, her long hair swishing the seat plan in front of her like a soft broom. 'You'll just have to grin and bear it, Father, won't you,' said Poll, all unaware that she was advocating Major Cartwright's own recipe for getting through a night at the theatre.

Compared to Cy Fredericks, Major Cartwright was really a model of reason and good sense.

'Much of this sort of thing go on in the West End theatre?' the Major enquired of Gregory. Taking his silence for assent, he went on: 'Humph. Thought so. Wonder how you ever got a show on at all.'

'It is fair to say our disasters generally occur on the First Night itself,' Gregory replied diplomatically. 'Rather than shortly before it.'

'Bit quicker off the mark here, eh? Not quite the backward provinces, are we?' And the Major gave a ferocious chuckle.

So far as the Festival was concerned, that was that. The Major's mixture of taciturnity and authoritarianism enabled him to deal with such potentially recalcitrant bodies as the press and his own committee with admirable despatch. His address to the actors of the King Charles Company was certainly a model of its kind:

'Bad show,' pronounced the Major from the stage of the Watchtower to the assembled company: 'See that you give a good one tonight. Damn sure you will. Like the war. Ensa. The Windmill. We never closed.' The mention of the Windmill seemed to recall to the Major some more urgent appointment, and shortly afterwards he was seen whirling away in his Bentley, with Cherry's dark head in the passenger seat. It was left to Boy Greville to calm the understandable nerves of his actors along more orthodox lines, a task made easier by the fact that a real slap-up disaster, as Anna Maria observed, always brought out the best in him. It was noticeable that throughout the day and the night which followed it, Boy never once referred to his own physical condition nor sought any remedy for it.

Jemima Shore was still in her suite at the Royal Stag by the late afternoon, although most of the clearing-up of the abortive television proceedings had already been done. Spike Thompson generously offered to stop over — 'We could have a real evening, dinner together, sea-food spaghetti at Don Giovanni's, or whatever it's called. Steak maison — £2 supplement, the best claret, champagne to round it all off, my place of yours. I'll pay, no, honest, my love. It would be my pleasure, I can't say fairer than that, can I?'

He could not. Jemima still rejected the offer. She bid an affectionate farewell to Spike and watched his jaunty departure, black head held high, thumbs stuck into the pockets of his black leather jacket, with genuine regret; she would miss them both — the man and the jacket. But Jemima needed solitude, a pause for vital recollection. She needed desperately to think back over all that had taken place in Larminster and around it, if she was not to betray her famous 'lady's instinct' as Cy termed it. In short, the abandoned pagan nymph of Spike Thompson's nightly revels had to take second place to that sterner character Jemima Shore Investigator.

Jemima sighed. And put her mind firmly to work on the whole vast problem of the Larminster murders: she knew she would not think about Spike again until her 'lady's instinct' had come up with at least some kind of interim solution.

No solution was for the time being offered by Detective Inspector Harwood. Jemima managed to snatch a few minutes of his beleaguered time over a cup of tea at the Royal Stag. He looked tired, lifting his tea-cup automatically, as though it was the twentieth cup he had drunk that day — which was possibly true. The murder of the old woman following so closely that of Nat Fitzwilliam, and the arrest of Jim Blagge had obviously come as a shock to the police. It was likely that Mr Blagge's solicitor would now make representations for him to get bail, which under the circumstances the police would probably not oppose.

'A maniac loose? That's what they're saying in Larminster, Jemima. Yes, only a maniac would kill a young man and an old woman, and for what? That's what we don't know, Jemima, assuming the two killings are linked. But what is a maniac? You tell me that. Mad or sane, these murderers never much want to be caught by the police, do they? Take X who killed Fitzwilliam, for we'll rule out the chauffeur for the moment. He took good care to cover up, didn't he? Maniac or no maniac. Take X who killed the old lady — the same X as we now think, this X wore gloves and was very careful indeed to leave no traces behind. No clues. Not altogether mad, you see. Not mad enough to be caught. Not so far. Whatever the do-gooders will say when he or she comes to trial.'

Jemima who had no intention of arguing about the definitions of criminal insanity with Detective Inspector Harwood, if she could help it, asked instead: 'So what now? The police never give up. That I do know.'

'They do not.' Matt Harwood sounded quite shocked. 'Hard work, that's what happens next. Hard work. Routine questions. Taking all the statements of the residents in the hotel on the night in question — a good number of them members of the Cartwright family, I understand. Funny — or not so funny — the way they keep recurring, isn't it? They were all here the night Fitzwilliam was killed too. Oh we shall plod on all right. We may be slow, but we are very very sure. We'll get him — or her — in the end.'

'And suppose there is another murder in the meanwhile?' suggested Jemima. 'My instinct tells me . . .' she realized she had gone too far.

Detective Inspector Harwood shot her a look which somehow reminded her of Cy Fredericks — Cy in one of his more chauvinist moods. Matt Harwood's next words also reminded her of Cy Fredericks.

'If your feminine instinct tells you there's going to be another murder, maybe the same useful instinct will tell you who's going to do it and to whom. Then you can go ahead and prevent it.' On which note of jocularity the Detective Inspector departed.

Jemima decided not to attend the First Night of *The Seagull* now that there was no television work to be done. She had seen a superlative performance from Christabel the night before: she doubted it could be matched tonight, especially under the traumatic circumstances of another death striking at the company. She was not sufficiently thrilled by any of the other actors to see them twice outside the line of duty — not even Vic Marcovich whose Trigorin had been very impressive or Anna Maria Packe who had turned in an appealing Masha. It was a pleasure not to have to gaze on the rocks and fisherman's netting further. Besides the First Night at the Watchtower would be a morbid occasion, she suspected. She was not surprised to learn that Julian had taken his daughters back to Lark Manor. He himself planned to return later, 'But if not, well, Christabel has Gregory to support her, doesn't she?' he observed to Jemima on his way out of the hotel. Christabel herself had returned to Lark for a short rest, fleeing the confusion of the Royal Stag. Then Gregory had driven her back to the theatre.

But Jemima's famous instinct was letting her down in allowing her to stay in her suite at the Royal Stag, instead of attending the First Night at the Watchtower. For the person who had long sought to destroy Christabel, killing three people in the process, had just chosen that particular occasion to put an end to her once and for all. After some heart searching, the person decided that Christabel should die as she had lived — in the full public eye. So that everyone should see and understand that there was no real forgiveness possible: that no one could ever come back if they had done the things that Christabel had done.

Jemima Shore, as yet unknowing of this decision, sat in her suite and pondered on all the murky circumstances surrounding the cool repentance of Christabel Cartwright. She had just, dazedly, reached a solution — a horrifying solution — when there was an imperative rap on her door.

Jemima came with a jolt out of the dream, nightmare really, into which her own reasonings had plunged her. Automatically she looked at her watch and was further startled to find it was very late. The Seagull must be well on its way by now. The door was locked — Mrs Tennant had insisted on that after the murder.

'Who is it?' she called, looking round for the key.

'Miss Shore, I must speak to you. It's desperately urgent. Please let me come in.'

Jemima recognized the voice of Miss Kettering.

SIXTEEN

Death of a Seagull

Ketty's sharp tapping interrupted a very long train of thought in Jemima. It had been punctuated — unpleasantly — by bursts of music from a radio played much too loudly in the room above. Pop music. Somewhat against her will Jemima recognized the tunes because they had once been so colossally popular that it had been impossible to avoid contact with their demanding monotonous beat. One of these tunes which she recognized was 'Cool Repentance'.

Was it the Iron Boy record being played? She could pick up — could not really fail to pick up whether she liked it or not — the repeated long-drawn-out first syllable 'coo-oo-ool, oh so cool repentance', but she could not recognize the voice of the singer. Some of the other Iron Boy hits were played, including 'Daring Darling' and 'Iron Boy' itself, but then she could also hear some of the Rolling Stones' numbers. During the brief pauses, however, when she could hear the disc jockey talking, Jemima found it was 'Cool Repentance' which stayed beating in her head and would not go away.

It was not a soothing experience. Lying back on the chintz-covered chaise-longue in the sitting-room, Jemima contemplated asking Mrs Tennant to have the offending radio turned down: on reflection she decided that the unfortunate manageress had endured enough for one day. Then it occurred to her that the chambermaid Marie had been installed in the empty room above her to recuperate. Marie too had had an unpleasant experience. If pop music on the hotel-room radio contributed to her recovery, then perhaps she should be allowed to play it. Even loud.

Feeling virtuously fair-minded — and also rather cross — Jemima set her mind back to work, to the tune of the loud beats coming from above.

It was a question of the past, and of things in their proper order. Where had it all begun? It had begun, properly, with the moment when Christabel had confided her fears to Jemima: how she would only be safe again back on stage, 'with the eyes of the world upon me . . . Oh, Jemima, I've been so terribly, terribly frightened . . . Locked away at Lark. It's so dangerous . . .' Then Gregory had arrived with Ketty and the girls. So Jemima had never really discovered where the mysterious danger lay, beyond the fact that it was clearly somewhere close at hand — connected with Lark Manor itself.

After that there had been the picnic. She passed certain images back through her mind, as though replaying the key moments of a television programme. Christabel, with Nat Fitzwilliam at her feet, the young man talking away, the older woman's attention wandering. Jemima had spotted an oddly upset glance in the direction of Gregory, himself chatting cheerfully away to Filumena Lennox.

Gregory, who had tried to warn Jemima off originally at their first bizarre encounter on the sea-shore: 'Why don't you just chuck this programme . . . Have you thought of its effect on people with something to hide?' He had pretended that he had been trying to protect Christabel's privacy. Had it after all been Gregory himself who had something to hide? Was it possible that it was Gregory whom Christabel had feared all along?

Gregory had been in Larminster on the night of Nat's death — had no subsequent alibi beyond swimming as Matt Harwood had scornfully told her — and it was certainly feasible for Gregory to have entered the Royal Stag last night, since security, under Mrs Tennant's easy-going eye, was lax to non-existent. In many ways Gregory fitted the bill very well — all too well for Jemima, since she discovered in herself considerable reluctance to postulate Gregory's guilt (she hoped that this reluctance could be attributed to instinct — the right kind of instinct).

Gregory had disliked Nat Fitzwilliam: he had made no secret of the fact. Gregory was a successful playwright, with no visible dependants, who had plenty of money to spare to support Old Nicola in her chosen retirement. So far, so good. Or rather, so bad.

But all of this had to be based on a foundation-stone of hatred — hatred not of Nat, nor yet of Nicola, but of Christabel. Was it really possible for Gregory Rowan to hate Christabel Cartwright? Hate her so much that he had planned to drown her? And in so doing had tragically and mistakenly put an end to the life of a young girl — a girl with whom he had been openly flirting only an hour before?

'Come with me and see pre-revolutionary Paris.' Jemima had overheard his offer. Most of the rest of the picnic must have heard it too. Gregory of all people had not expected Filly — rather than Christabel — to be wearing the magpie hat. For it was Gregory who had tried to persuade Filly to swim and, as he thought, failed. He had strode away towards the west cliff to swim by himself — wearing nothing but a pair of tennis shoes, no doubt. Or had he? Was this what Nat had seen through his binoculars? At one point it had seemed that Nat must have focused on something connected with Mr

Blagge and his boat; now Mr Blagge's boating expedition had turned out to be quite innocent — just what it purported to be, a rescue expedition in choppy waters, at his wife's suggestion. So what had Nat seen — not seen — through his binoculars? 'I saw nothing where I should have seen something.' Gregory not under the west cliff at all . . . for Gregory was by now cutting through the waters to the east like a black shark . . . Was this — 'just a little discrepancy between text and sub-text' — what Nat had tried to discuss 'several times with the person concerned' receiving an answer, which 'wasn't satisfactory either'. Old Nicola too, she had glimpsed something as she sat on the beach — an unknown 'helper' or 'cuddler' there in the water close to Filly; she had never referred to the incident again — was it Gregory Old Nicola had observed?

Another image flashed on to her personal screen: Gregory in his cottage, telling her with perfect good-humour: 'It sounds ridiculous but at first I felt quite violent . . . She only showed one pang of emotion and that was when we had to tell her her dog Mango had died . . . For one terrible moment, I wanted to do her some frightful physical injury. I almost wanted to kill her for all the suffering she had caused . . .'

'Coo-oo-ool, oh so cool repentance' beat and wailed and rocked above her for the second time: that really must be Iron Boy singing it. She thought: was it really possible for anyone to come back as Christabel had done, abandoned first by Iron Boy, then by the world, and not arouse devastating murderous passions in the injured?

Jemima began to list them to herself. First of all, her children, but was Regina really for all her literary allusions to be classed as a potential matricide? A modern version of Electra, perhaps, with Christabel as Clytemnestra? She decided to hold on to that one and passed on to Regina's sister. Blanche had evidently been most resentful of her mother when Jemima first visited Lark and theoretically the Nina incident should not have helped their relationship; yet she had the impression that mother and daughter had seemed much closer lately. Jemima thought of Blanche, over-heated in her Annie Hall outfit on the night of her birthday, and in any case physically most ill-suited to such a parody of masculine clothing: she had certainly improved since then.

Jemima decided to hold on Regina and Blanche and pass on to the rest of the Lark Manor circle. Jemima was patiently reviewing the various characters involved: the Blagges . . . after all, no. Ketty — in love with Julian Cartwright, said Gregory, hating Christabel's return which had demoted her in the household . . . yes, perhaps . . . All of a sudden the music above her head came to an abrupt halt.

Footsteps were heard instead. Then voices. Then a door banged. Evidently Mrs Tennant had come to claim Marie, or at any rate restore peace to her hotel.

The shock of the sudden silence, for one instant quite as shocking as the endlessly reverberating noise had been, had a most surprising effect on Jemima. It was as though she had suddenly seen everything exactly reversed: silence was shocking, noise the norm . . . She began, with rising excitement, to look at all her own images from exactly the opposite point of view, to ask herself a whole new set of questions, questions which she knew at last were getting close to the heart of the mystery.

Cool repentance . . . but was it really possible in any couple for a wife to be quite so bad, a husband quite so good, as Christabel and Julian Cartwright seemed respectively to the outside world? Was Christabel really so complacently composed, Julian really so doggedly adoring as they appeared in public? Had she really felt no shame at what she had done to him, her loving husband of so many years, the younger man who had married her when Gregory would not? More to the point, was a man, any man, really going to accept such flagrant behaviour and for so many years. She thought — nostalgically, as she lay on the chintz chaise-longue — of Spike. Chauvinist Spike who had not been able to understand Julian's husbandly meekness: 'I'd give her a proper going-over.' In vain Jemima had responded: 'It would drive me quite mad to have to come back to Lark as penitent Magdalen.' Suppose that secretly . . .

Following this train of thought proved very interesting indeed to Jemima Shore.

She conjured up a whole new set of images. She remembered the Sunday lunch table. Julian giving the orders. Julian, the lord of the manor, very much in command of his household. She reviewed again, still patiently, the picnic on the shore. She concentrated on Julian's assiduous control of absolutely every detail of the picnic, the melancholy which seemed to underlie Christabel's attitude to him, more than melancholy, almost a feeling of shrinking from him.

She remembered Gregory's words: 'I was very surprised. She always said he was not her type: she called him her rich young man. Security, I suppose.' 'Not my type,' Christabel Herrick had said of Julian Cartwright . . .

She ran through still more of her conversation with Gregory in her mind. His surprise when Julian had agreed to fetch Christabel, the guilty woman, down to Lark immediately. Why had he rushed up to London so promptly? Why had he brought her down to secluded luxurious Lark, the house she had willingly abandoned? Gregory had given his own explanation: Christabel had been 'totally destroyed', 'scarcely sane', when Julian had fetched her — for Gregory was Julian's friend as well as Christabel's. 'Julian Cartwright,' he had loyally told Jemima, 'is much the nicest character of the Cartwright family.'

Jemima wondered about other things. The death of Nat Fitzwilliam. Nat who had intended to focus his binoculars on the sea-shore from the Watchtower to view the production 'as a whole' and to concentrate on the character of Arkadina in particular: until Christabel had jokingly suggested that there had been enough concentration on Arkadina for one production, and that focusing on Blanche and Ollie, Filly and Gregory, or even Cherry and Julian, might provide more useful insights — into the characters of Konstantin, Nina and Trigorin . . .

The death of Nat Fitzwilliam, and that figure in the shadows. That figure — a man — alluded to by Mr Blagge, who knew well where to find the key, because the topic had been discussed in Flora's Kitchen: and knew also just as well as Mr Blagge how to throw it away afterwards so it would never be found. A man who noticed when the Cartwright family and their attachments were ostensibly upstairs in the Royal Stag finishing off Blanche's birthday celebrations, but in fact proved on examination to have been widely dispersed as the evening wore on. All this at a time when beady-eyed Old Nicola, also installed on the first floor near the service stairs, could easily have witnessed an unscheduled flitting from the hotel. Aroused by the noise on the service stairs, she could have looked out of her little back window and seen *someone* — who? — leaving the hotel by the back entrance and the car-park . . . basis for blackmail later. Old Nicola: who was expecting someone 'who can well afford to do so' to provide for her for the rest of her life. 'Someone who can well afford to do so, plenty of money, when you think how Old Nicola herself has to live.'

And then at last Jemima saw it all: instinct helped her to take the last step, where first instinct, then reason, had guided her originally along her path of discovery. She saw it all in one appalled and appalling glimpse in which past and present combined.

Plenty of money. Lark Manor. The lap of luxury. Julian Cartwright. Regina Cartwright. Blanche Cartwright. It all came down to this: could Christabel be forgiven for what she had done to her husband and family? Hadn't Christabel said it herself on their second meeting in Flora's Kitchen: 'It's too late. One can never go back.'

It was at this point that Jemima heard Ketty's imperative knocks. Still startled, slightly shaking in view of the new path along which her thoughts were rapidly carrying her, Jemima undid the door. She took a step back.

Ketty was an astonishing sight: her dark-red hair, normally strained back into its thick bun, was falling round her shoulders. Her eyes were hardly touched with their usual garish eyeshadow; her quivering mouth was quite devoid of its harsh red lipstick. She was wearing a cardigan over her dark dress which was misbuttoned: everything about Ketty's outfit, in contrast to her usual style, had the air of being very hastily assumed.

'Miss Shore, let me in. It's urgent. Really urgent. Otherwise I wouldn't have come. I've driven from Lark. I took the Jaguar — he's got the Land-Rover. I've never driven it before. It's outside. Not very well parked. Oh, my God —' Ketty sat down suddenly on the chaise-longue. A glass of white wine was on the table beside her. She drained it. She did not seem to notice it was not water.

This new defenceless Ketty, looking at least ten years younger than the formidable governess of Lark Manor, was such a surprising apparition, that it took a moment for Jemima to rally her thoughts. Then she realized the full import of what Ketty had just said:

'Who's got the Land-Rover?'

'He's got the Land-Rover. Julian. Mr Julian. He's going to the theatre. I know he is, and oh, Miss Shore, you've got to help us.' Ketty was by now trembling violently as though in delayed reaction to her drive.

'How do you know he's going to the theatre?'

'Where else would he go? But to her.' Ketty looked up desperately to Jemima, her large face incongruously framed by her mass of rippling auburn hair like the hair of a forties film star: her eyes were imploring. Yes, there was no doubt about Ketty's feelings for Julian Cartwright. 'And that's not the worst of it,' she went on. 'His pistol's gone. That's the worst of it.

That's why I came to you. I know where he keeps it and it's gone. The drawer in the study was open after he left, when he rushed out of the house —' Ketty gave a sob.

'Oh, Miss Shore, he's been so patient, so terribly terribly patient through it all. I'm frightened —'

'I'm frightened too,' said Jemima grimly. 'Come on. We're going to the theatre.'

Taking Ketty's hand, she guided her down the staircase and out of the hotel, ignoring Mrs Tennant's bewildered face behind the reception desk. With Ketty's hand in hers, Jemima felt for one absurd moment like the Red Queen tugging at Alice: but she was well aware that the situation in which they were all involved was tragic not absurd.

Together they walked, half-ran and then ran across the pretty little square which separated the hotel from the theatre.

The glass of the pentagonal theatre was thoroughly illuminated. Across its central facade hung an enormous white banner. It concentrated on essentials: TONIGHT, it read, CHRISTABEL HERRICK IN 'THE SEAGULL'. There was no mention of such details as the author's name, the director, let alone the names of any of the other actors in the King Charles Theatre Company.

But when Jemima entered the theatre itself — rushing past the surprised attendant who exclaimed: 'I thought you telly people were all gone' — Christabel Herrick, the star of the occasion, was not visible on the stage. Jemima shoved Ketty down into a vacant seat on the left-hand aisle (she thought it must have been one of Megalith's unused seats, but it had in fact been vacated at the first interval by Father O'Brien, who had returned home to watch one of his favourite programmes on television). Jamie Grand, the powerful editor of *Literature*, was sitting in the same row: as usual when he was at the theatre — as opposed to reviewing a book — there was a pleased expression on his face; an unknown blonde girl was next to him. Neither of them took their eyes off the stage for a moment but Jemima saw another face look up at her with a frog-like air of injured astonishment at the disturbance. She recognized a London critic, come down to Larminster to witness the return of Christabel Herrick to the stage. There was no sign of Julian Cartwright in the crowded and darkened auditorium — but that was not where she expected to find him.

Trying to catch her breath, Jemima surveyed the stage. Emily Jones was at the beginning of Nina's last speech: 'I'm a seagull . . . No, that's not it. I'm an actress . . . I'm a seagull. No, that's not it again . . . Do you remember you shot a seagull? A man came along by chance, saw it and destroyed it . . .' She was ploughing on gamely and not unsuccessfully, if much faster than had been planned at rehearsals. Ollie Summertown as Konstantin was sitting listening to her.

There was still time, time to get round to the back of the stage.

'Slow up, Emily, slow up anyway for your sake as well as mine,' Jemima prayed desperately. 'Nina does not gabble.' And she turned and ran back out of the theatre, round to the Stage Door, in past an equally stunned door-keeper — 'Well, hello there Miss Shore, I thought —' But Jemima did not stop. She knew now exactly what had happened, what might happen. She got to the wings of the stage. Still she did not see the man she was looking for, Julian Cartwright, nor the woman, Christabel.

Emily had reached the end of her speech and ran down the steps which, for lack of a proscenium arch, stood for french windows on the set. Konstantin was still tearing up his manuscripts: ending his work preparatory to ending his life. In the absence of a desk, he had to take them out of a seaman's canvas bag. It was a long-drawn-out process. Jemima noticed that Ollie's hands were trembling.

At that moment there came a loud report from the direction of the dressing-rooms. A look of amazement followed by slight embarrassment crossed Ollie's face: as though he feared that he had somehow shot himself prematurely and would get into trouble for still being on stage tearing up manuscripts when he should be officially dead off-stage. There was a faint disconcerted rustle in the audience as though some of those who prided themselves on being Chekhovian *cognoscenti* were having the same reaction.

But Jemima had no further time to consider what was happening on stage. She looked round frantically. She still could not see any sign of Christabel, although any minute Madame Arkadina was due to make her last entrance and Trigorin and Masha were already in place.

It was Julian Cartwright who provided the solution to the mystery of Christabel's whereabouts. He came slowly towards Jemima from the direction of Christabel's dressing-room. Vic Marcovich and Anna Maria, who were waiting to enter, stared at him. The voice of Dr Dorn could be heard on-stage: 'That's strange. The door seems to be locked . . .' Without the benefit of his aged-up appearance, Tobs still sounded oddly young.

Julian Cartwright moved like a sleep-walker. But his voice when he spoke was as clear and strong as normal. So that a good many members of the audience must have heard him when he said:

'Get everyone out of here. No, don't go into the dressing-room. Christabel has shot herself.'

Inside the star's dressing-room, with all its as-yet-unopened good-luck telegrams and all its sweet-scented flowers from Lark Manor, all the flowers she loved, lay Christabel Herrick. She was still just conscious enough to be aware that she was dying at last, killed by her own hand as she had always intended, shot, immolated, ended.

Then the person who knew that Christabel could never be forgiven for what she had done, closed her eyes. The person who hated Christabel died together with her, and at the same instant and in the same body. United in death, all her voices, good and evil, ruthless and repentant, found peace at last.

SEVENTEEN

Obsession and After

They pieced it together afterwards, all of them. Christabel, the person who had killed three times, once in a sudden fit of murderous jealousy — Filly Lennox, a younger rival; twice to protect herself from the consequences of her crime — Nat Fitzwilliam who had seen something through his binoculars, and Old Nicola who had seen something else from her vantage point at the Royal Stag hotel. Christabel, the schizophrenic murderess. Christabel, the person who hated herself for what she had done, and so in the end thankfully destroyed herself.

The people who pieced it all together included Jemima Shore, who had reached the truth in a flash of illumination at the end — but too late to save Christabel from her final desperate act; Julian Cartwright, who knew only too well about his wife's unbalance but feared to face its consequences; Gregory Rowan, who had talked so convincingly to Jemima about Christabel's self-hatred — Christabel as her own worst enemy — and yet likewise feared to face the agonizing truth.

'I think we were both blinded, Julian and I, by the fact of

her leaving us,' Gregory told Jemima. 'We were obsessed by her absence, by what she had done by abandoning us. So when she did return, we were determined that everything should be just the same: it had to be. Back to normal. That was our motto. You see, it was our conspiracy to pretend that everything was back to normal, not hers. She was merely acting out what we wanted her to be. And giving a superb performance, too. That extraordinary radiant composure, which the world took for brazenness — acting, all of it. Beneath it all, she was terribly frightened, must have been frightened of going mad, frightened of what she might do if she did.'

They were once more by the sea, on the beach where Jemima had first met Gregory Rowan and he had told her harshly to go back to London — where television belonged. Behind them rose up the pale Bridset stone of Lark Manor and parallel to it the darker shape of the Watchtower Theatre, but neither Jemima nor Gregory looked back. It was one of those late summer days when you knew that autumn would not be long in coming; a cold wind raked the sea and sent iron-grey shadows scudding across its rippled surface. Jemima dug her hands into the pockets of her elegant red suede jacket and shivered. She was thankful Gregory did not suggest swimming.

Jemima had come to say goodbye to Gregory Rowan at the Old Keeper's Lodge, and found him surrounded by books and packing-cases. Some kind of move was evidently contemplated. She did not comment on the fact nor did he. He simply said: 'Come, on, let's get out of here and go down to the sea for a breath of good Bridset air. I find the woods rather claustrophobic these days.'

They were out of the cottage before Jemima remembered about the many photographs of Christabel which had surrounded Gregory's desk on her previous visit; she wondered what he had done with them. That was another thing she would not ask.

Now she spoke into the wind, in the direction of the sea, without looking at Gregory: 'She told me she was frightened, frightened of being left alone at Lark, the first time we had lunch together. Of course, at that time I thought — I imagined — so many people had good reason to wish her ill, to resent her return —'

'I can imagine what you thought, Jemima Shore Investigator. Betrayed husband, abandoned daughters, sinister servants, even perhaps menacing playwright.' But Gregory's smile, that odd smile whose sweetness had surprised her on their first meeting, robbed the words of offence.

'I never suspected you,' replied Jemima, loyally and more or less truthfully, for after all it had been Matt Harwood not her who had put his money on the playwright, and if she had suspected Gregory just for one moment towards the end, then it was only during that strange long-drawn-out process of thought, to the tune of the hotel radio, by which she had reached her ultimately correct solution. . . .

'I suppose she really had her first breakdown when I left her, or anyway didn't want to marry her. I wanted my own selfish solitary life,' Gregory continued slowly; he too preferred to look out to sea. 'Julian rescued her then. He married her and looked after her. She recovered; back to normal, you could say. He thought he could do the same thing after the departure of Iron Boy. That really did drive her mad — Julian told me so himself when he went up to London to fetch her. But he was so sure that she'd be all right when he got her back to Lark — he couldn't see, he didn't want to see that Lark, with all its memories, the daily reminder of what she'd done, cooped up with the resentful girls, condemned to be waited on daily by Barry's own parents, was the worst place for her. Even the dog she adored had been killed in her absence, without her to look after it — that must have made her feel so guilty. Her thoughts alone must have driven her mad, the voice of her own conscience.'

> The virtuous mind that ever walks attended
> By a strong siding champion Conscience —

Jemima quoted. 'Do you remember? Those lines from *Comus*. I questioned whether Christabel was altogether well cast in the part of The Lady. I was wrong. She *did* have a conscience, if not a virtuous mind.'

'Yes, why do we always assume that it's only the virtuous who have consciences? In my injured pride, I was wrong about that too.'

'That's why she was so keen to get back on the stage I suppose,' said Jemima. 'To blot it out. "I'll be safe," she said to me: she meant safe from herself, and her own terrible instinct towards self-destruction.'

'But she didn't only destroy herself!' Gregory exclaimed. 'That's the horror of it.' He swung round and looked at Jemima. His eyes were full of tears. 'She drowned that poor little girl, just because I laughed and flirted with her at a beach party and offered to take her to Paris, and because Filly was young and pretty and a good actress and the centre of attention — all the things Christabel herself had once been. Filly was going to play Paulinot in *Widow Capet*. She would have been sensational in the part too, Christabel knew that. She knew all about the theatre, never forget that, she knew that in the famous confrontation scene between Marie Antoinette and Paulinot, what the late Nat called the 'Old-France-versus-the-New Number' it was not necessarily going to be Christabel who wiped the floor with Filly.'

'Old Nicola was on to that like a flash,' commented Jemima. 'I think she must have had her suspicions about Christabel from the first and decided to keep them to herself in case they proved profitable. Sitting on the beach and "watching all you naughty boys and girls" as she used to put it, she may even have spotted Christabel taking her surreptitious swim. I suppose Christabel wore one of the other less conspicuous suits and hats unearthed by Mrs Blagge: in the general confusion after the death of Filly no one would have noticed one wet bathing-dress more or less, and of course when Christabel reappeared on the beach, she was still wearing that flowing leopard-skin printed robe: it was easy to change back into that. But she had taken off her scarf and combed her hair. I remember it stood out from her head like a golden halo —'

'Halo!' exclaimed Gregory.

'Let's get back to Old Nicola,' Jemima hastily steered the conversation away from Christabel's personal appearance. 'She made some rather odd remark, I seem to recall, about a person unknown either "having a cuddle, or else being helpful" in the sea, and then never repeated it, which was unlike her usual style. She was certainly well aware of Christabel's jealousy for Filly — "knowing about the theatre and all its little ways after all these years" — almost the last thing she ever said to me. The professional jealousy of an older woman for a younger was all too easy for her to divine, because she was eaten up with envy of Christabel herself. Christabel pretended to be resting in the inner bedroom on the night of Nat's death: Old Nicola must have spotted her slipping down the service stairs, when she was padding along to that distant bedroom she used to moan about.'

Jemima stopped. There had been enough grief and guilt. She had no wish to add to Gregory's.

'It must have been far more difficult for Nat to guess the truth,' she went on, knowing that the subject of Nat was a safer one to raise. 'At first he could have had no idea of the implications of what he'd seen through his binoculars that fatal afternoon on the beach.'

'Or not seen,' put in Gregory. 'Wasn't that the phrase he actually used?'

'Exactly. I imagine he found Christabel was missing from her resting-place, the one she said she went back to when the turquoise bathing-dress was missing. You remember the poor fellow had had one of his typical ideas for inspiration — he would gaze at her from the Watchtower and by being at a great distance derive some further insight into Arkadina's character.'

'Typical indeed,' commented Gregory.

'The thing about Nat, as we all know, is that he had this incredible persistence. Not for him to desert a plan, and watch Blanche and Ollie, you and Filly, or even Julian and Cherry as Christabel suggested. I dare say he focused on her — or where she should have been resting under the cliffs — quite relentlessly, in his dotty way expecting to understand something more about Chekhov at the end of his binoculars. And once he appreciated that Christabel's statement didn't agree with what he had seen, he would have worked on the problem. He was also — dare I say it now he's dead? — the most frightful little opportunist. He too — like Old Nicola — might even have been contemplating some superior kind of blackmail. Some kind of deal along the lines of: "You help me with my career and I'll keep quiet about what I suspect." He was awfully smug, even gloating to me about his own "investigation" as he had the impudence to call it. I had the distinct impression even then that something nasty was afoot. But Christabel had no intention of leading her professional life for the foreseeable future in the power of Nat Fitzwilliam. Besides, how could she trust him? So she deliberately worked out a way of getting rid of him.'

'It figures,' was all Gregory said.

'At least Filly's death was an impulse,' Jemima finished. 'You must never blame yourself for it. It was a murderous impulse from an unbalanced person who lost control. A maniac.'

'A maniac!' cried Gregory. 'But a maniac who knew exactly how to cover her tracks, how to put on a superb act. Between us, we had written the act for her, hadn't we, cool repentance, and she played it to perfection. I never knew her to act better in a part of mine, not even at the beginning, the time of *Lombardy Summer*, Christabel in her twenties, so fair and little, nothing to her but a pair of eyes and a pair of legs, I used to tell her, both of them beautiful. Oh God, what's the point . . . ?' It was his turn to stop. 'Those early memories are the worst of all. It's better all round to concentrate on the other side of the picture. All the damage she did, the wanton deaths she caused. She may have been mad at the end, but she was also a murderess three times over.'

Detective Inspector Matt Harwood of the Bridset Constabulary took very much the same line in his farewell interview with Jemima.

'We should have got her in the end,' he pronounced firmly. 'We always do, you know. Well, nearly always. We never give up. She wanted to be safe, you say, but she would never have been safe from us. The case would never have been closed.'

From her experience of the police, Jemima thought that was true. Nobody in the end, not even Julian Cartwright, could have saved Christabel from that thorough remorseless process of police investigation. But by then Christabel herself would surely have been dead — dead by her own hand. She would not have waited for the net of the law to close and tangle her, as the fisherman's netting on *The Seagull* set had tangled the unfortunate stagehands trying to dismantle it.

'But I could have saved her!' Jemima exclaimed. 'If only I'd trusted my instinct earlier. I knew she was a terrified woman — she nearly confided in me once, and that was long before she'd killed anyone; I realized now she was simply contemplating suicide, trying to fight down the urge. Then, as she said herself at our second lunch: "It's too late now." She'd already killed once, knew she might have to kill again. It's an awful thing to confess, Matt — but I too was put off by the apparently brazen manner of her return. The gracious hostess presiding at Lark Manor, the unhappily silent daughters, the wronged husband — it all stuck in my gullet rather. And by the time I'd worked it out correctly, trusting my instinct at last, seen that matters were exactly the other way round, well, it *was* too late, wasn't it? That ghastly night at the theatre. It was too late to save her from herself. If only —'

'Suicides,' interrupted Matt Harwood in his comforting voice. 'They'll always do it in the end, you know. If they really intend to. And we must believe that the lady in question did so intend.'

'Yes, but in that frightful way, Matt! Shooting herself with a pistol in her dressing-room, in front of her own husband's eyes.'

'Ah, but Jemima, she was an actress, wasn't she?' It was not clear whether the Detective Inspector meant by this to explain Christabel's presence in a theatrical dressing-room, or the dramatic manner of her self-inflicted death. In either case, thought Jemima, it was not an inappropriate epitaph for Christabel Herrick.

She could leave it to Detective Inspector Harwood and the Bridset police to clear up the intricacies of procedure in the wake of Christabel's death: the dropping of charges against Jim Blagge was one priority. It was probably not much satisfaction to Jim Blagge to have his story about the mysterious man in the shadows beside the Watchtower Theatre at last believed, since the police had treated it so cavalierly in the first place. But at least he could point out certain details which explained Christabel's 'Method' as well as confirming her 'Opportunity'.

The 'man' for example had been wearing a hat and some kind of jacket — hence Mr Blagge's subconscious assumption of the male gender in his reference to the glimpsed figure. The 'man' — Christabel in disguise. It was Jemima who pointed out to the police that Christabel would not have had to look very far for a rudimentary form of masculine disguise that hot night in the suite at the Royal Stag hotel. The memory of Blanche, faintly ridiculous in her man's clothes, was one of those illuminating images which had come to her when she was recapitulating the whole tragic story to herself, on the night of Christabel's suicide. Jemima recalled to the police that Blanche had been wearing her Annie Hall outfit when she left Flora's Kitchen: Ketty confirmed that Blanche had left behind the hat and jacket when she went out to search for Ollie Summertown, ostensibly because she felt too hot, actually because she considered an unbuttoned shirt more seductive. Afterwards, Christabel did not even need to dispose of the garments — she could leave them in the suite and rely on Blanche to pick them up again.

Then there was the re-examination of the forensic evidence by the Home Office laboratories which would prove — to the police's official satisfaction — what Jemima had seized upon by instinct. According to Locard's exchange principle, traces of Blanche's checked jacket found on Nat Fitzwilliam's clothes, hitherto explained by the fact that Blanche had hugged him in the restaurant when she had presented the birthday cake, would now take on a more sinister light. The examination of the evidence relating to the death of Old Nicola had only just started by the time of Christabel's suicide: that too would be thoroughly analysed. Jemima Shore Investigator could set off for London while the Bridset police were still patiently at work.

'In any case,' added Matt Harwood, at the door of Jemima's Royal Stag sitting-room, 'would you really have wanted to save her? Save her to stand trial? She was a maniac, yes, I'll grant you that, quite a lot about that is coming out too, now — now when it's too late to do anything about the deceased persons — specialists' opinions in the past, when she was in London, before her return to Bridset. But she was a triple killer too, wasn't she? Guilty but insane if you like. But Broadmoor — how would she have stood for that? Christabel Herrick. A woman like that.'

It was an unexpected view for a policeman and Matt Harwood seemed to appreciate her surprise.

'I'm speaking quite unofficially, you realize,' he said with a wry twinkle. 'Now don't you go and tell my little brother Gary what I've just said, let alone Pompey of the Yard. Whatever would he think of us in Bridset if he thought we conducted our affairs along those kind of lines? Officially in Bridset, same as anywhere else, the law is the law and murderers must be apprehended and brought to trial and the police are there to do it.'

Jemima heard his heavy footsteps going down the corridor in the direction of the stairs — the service stairs. Either Detective Inspector Harwood was a discreet man and did not wish to add to Mrs Tennant's distress further by manifestations of police presence, or else he was a busy man, who simply wanted to go about his business as fast as possible in the most convenient way. She thought how Christabel must have twice slipped along that corridor, leaving the bedroom of her suite by its unused outer door, unused, but easily and quickly unbolted. She too had wanted to go about her business as fast as possible in the most convenient way — the business of murder.

One of the people who helped to piece together what had happened was Christabel Herrick's widower, Julian Cartwright. Jemima learnt the details of his statement and some of the other macabre circumstances of the last few months from Gregory Rowan: Julian Cartwright had not wished to say goodbye to Jemima Shore. Secluded at Lark Manor with his daughters, supported by Ketty and the Blagges, Julian Cartwright presented the same face of dignified silence to the world as he had done when Christabel eloped with Barry Blagge.

Gregory Rowan told Jemima of Christabel's last note to Julian — three words only: *Darling, forgive me.* 'He showed it to me afterwards: it was on her special writing-paper, that very pale azure paper she loved, in her huge sprawling handwriting, blue ink too. Even when the police had finished with it, it still smelt of her special scent, lily of the valley . . .'

It was the discovery of this note lying in his study, with the pistol gone from its drawer, which had sent Julian on his last frantic expedition to rescue Christabel. She must have left it some time during the afternoon, when the family returned to Lark from the Royal Stag, Christabel ostensibly needing to take refuge from the loud confusion of the police *mêlée* at the hotel; she must have descended from her darkened bedroom with its thick white curtains blotting out the view of the sea, the sea where Christabel had drowned Filly Lennox not so long ago. Christabel was cunning: Christabel remembered where Julian kept the key to his private drawer. Christabel was also mad and left behind one last plea for her husband's forgiveness.

If Julian had not taken the girls over to see Gregory, so that there should be no sudden noise in the house while Christabel rested, he might have found the note earlier. And then he might have been in time to stop Christabel . . . stop Christabel putting the pistol to her head just as he entered the dressing-room . . . one last translucent unblinking sea-blue regard and then one lethal shot which instantly destroyed both Christabel and all the beauty she had once had in her husband's eyes.

Jemima asked Gregory: 'Will he ever recover, *can* he ever recover?'

'Wasn't what he'd already gone through almost worse? Because it was perpetual secret fearful anticipation. The unacknowledged dread of her suicide, or at least that she would do herself some injury. There was some odd incident with her garden scissors at Easter, just after she first came back. We don't quite know what happened. Maybe she tried to stab herself and drew back. She was in two minds — literally, I suppose — up till the very end. One afternoon, I'd come over to Lark and suddenly heard her scream. Julian heard it too and came rushing in from the courtyard garden. He thinks she may have planned to take an overdose then, she'd been rummaging in the various bathroom drawers upstairs, thinking she was alone, and at the last minute somebody disturbed her. Ketty. Pussy-footing about with no shoes on — and seething with jealous resentment — because Julian had said there was to be no noise in the house while Christabel was resting.'

'But the murders?' cried Jemima. 'Did he have no inkling that Christabel was responsible — because if so . . .' She left the sentence ominously trailing.

Gregory considered. 'Filly — no, definitely not. True, it was Christabel who originally suggested the picnic, the picnic where she fully intended to shine with all her old sparkle, captivate everyone left, right and centre, only to find herself upstaged by Filly — but then Filly's death was not premeditated, and afterwards, in the light of the tragedy, everyone forgot who had proposed going to the beach *en masse*. It was Christabel too who suggested going back to the Royal Stag to continue Blanche's birthday celebrations upstairs — "Mrs Tennant will do anything for me, darling" — I remember it so clearly, Julian's objections, Christabel overruling them. Now *that* was premeditated.

'So was her "rest",' he went on. 'To give herself the opportunity she needed to get to the theatre and do in the wretched Nat; just as she originally asked for her shawl to get the key out of him, make sure it would be available for her. She was lucky there, of course — she could hardly have known that Mr Blagge would return to the theatre and divert all suspicion to himself; as it was, she narrowly missed running into him.'

'The man in the shadows,' quoted Jemima. 'The one in whose existence the police declined to believe.' In her mind's eye she saw Christabel that night, Christabel deftly picking up Blanche's discarded jacket and hat, maybe even suggesting herself with a casual word that Blanche would look prettier without them for Christabel was always commenting on Blanche's clothes. Christabel the professional disguising herself swiftly and effectively — if not from the prying eyes of that other professional Old Nicola. Christabel watching Nat leave the theatre by the front door for his breath of air. Christabel deftly picking up the key of the Stage Door deposited for the second time by Mr Blagge, and after the murder throwing it far away or perhaps burying it in the woods, as she buried the responsibility for what she had done. Christabel still dressed in Blanche's checked jacket and Annie Hall hat pulled down over the mauve scarf which masked her fair hair; Christabel melting back into the shrubberies and trees round the Watch-tower; Christabel who had just . . . but this time Jemima did not share her thoughts with Gregory.

'And the second night in the Royal Stag,' pursued Gregory, 'the night she needed to spend there to shut up Old Nicola once and for all — that was premeditated too. Even so, the plan might have gone wrong if she'd had to share a bedroom with Julian. But then — she knew her Julian. He was a gentle-man. He would sleep in the sitting-room on a sofa, wouldn't he, rather than disturb Christabel's precious rest on the eve of a First Night. She knew where Mrs Tennant kept the pass-keys; in fact she knew a great deal about the Royal Stag. In the old days, she and I —' Gregory coughed. 'Well, we needn't go into that now. Suffice it to say that she knew where Old Nicola was sleeping. And that everything was always easy for Christabel where Julian was concerned. She had only to ask and he granted it for her.' For the first time Gregory sounded more angry than distraught.

'So in answer to your question,' he continued, 'no, Julian had no real inkling of what Christabel had done. Julian was a man with an obsession, and his obsession was Christabel. He could see that she might destroy herself but he could not see anything or anyone beyond that.'

'So he won't recover. He can't.'

'My dear Jemima Shore Investigator!' Gregory had picked up a series of flat stones and was skidding them enthusiastically across the surface of the sea. But now the tide was going out quite rapidly across the flat sands. There was no danger today of a sudden wave engulfing Gregory's tennis shoes or Jemima's red sandals whose high heels were already slightly scuffed by the Larmouth pebbles. 'My dear Jemima, how little you know about the nature of obsession. Maybe there should be an investigative programme on the subject. You might find it interesting — "Obsession and After" — how's that for a title?'

'Compulsive viewing.'

'No, Julian will recover,' Gregory went on as if she had not spoken. 'First Christabel had to come back, then she had to be gone for good, both things being essential to his recovery. Perhaps he'll even marry Ketty one day. Stranger things have happened. Life will be easier for him that way. He's had his great love, hasn't he? He'll settle for a comfortable life and Ketty and the Blagges between them will make him very comfortable indeed.'

'And his daughters too?'

'Ah, not so. Julian will be even more comfortable because his daughters won't be anywhere near Lark. Rina's going to try for Oxbridge in the autumn, which she should have done in the first place, and — wait for it — Blanche is going to Central School!'

'Blanche — an actress!' Jemima was amazed. 'I don't believe it. Think of her disastrous audition as Nina —'

'Ah, but Christabel was alive then.' Gregory could now speak her name quite calmly. 'Christabel who was determined her daughters should not rival her by following her on to the stage. Blanche always messed up anything to do with her mother hence *The Seagull* fiasco but when Ketty and I visited her at school, she did jolly well — so long as her mother wasn't in the audience. That's why Ketty tried to get her the part of Nina secretly, without her mother knowing. No, the Cartwright girls are going to be perfectly all right.'

Major Cartwright was also going to be perfectly all right.

For it turned out that he had had the brilliant foresight to insure the Larminster Festival specifically against the collapse, illness, breakdown or any other form of non-appearance of its star, Christabel Herrick, leading to cancellation of the Festival. No one could deny that Christabel's death constituted one form of non-appearance and it was equally undeniable that the entire Larminster Festival had had to be cancelled following the tragic events of the First Night. At least the Festival would not be showing a financial loss.

'May actually make more money. May be better off than if we'd sold all the seats,' the Major told Jemima with gruff satisfaction. 'Confounded Festival generally runs at a loss. Been spared altogether this time.' It was clear that the Major felt that he had been spared more than just financial loss — several long evenings at the theatre had also been averted, when it would have been necessary, in the Major's own heroic phrase, to grin and bear it.

Jemima dared to ask him why he had taken this prescient course. 'Unstable woman, my nephew's wife,' replied the Major. 'Drank too much. Eyes far too wide apart as well. Saw a good deal of that kind of thing in the war.'

On the other hand, the Major had not exactly turned out to be the Substantial Older Man of Cherry's dreams. That is to say, on their parting, the Major had asked for Cherry's London telephone number: but he seemed to have in mind the sort of gastronomic forays which had so much enlivened Cherry's Bridset life (as well as threatening her nubile figure with dangerous new proportions) rather than installing her as the châtelaine of Larksgrange.

'Used to know a little woman just like you in the Blitz,' he told Cherry in what for him passed for a sentimental speech. 'Like to tell you about her one day. What do you think of this place near the old Berkeley Hotel — Langan's Brasserie?'

'It's very trendy,' answered Cherry cautiously.

'Oh I know that, damn it,' the Major sounded impatient.

'Have to take the rough with the smooth. But is the food any good?'

As Gregory stood beside Jemima on the beach, where the tide had now slithered out so far that he could no longer throw stones across the sea, he too, like the Major, brought up the subject of the future.

'Maybe I'll come up to London more often. Lark is over for me. I have to find another hermitage — perhaps I'll find a hermitage convenient for the capital if such a thing exists. A commuter's hermitage. I might ask you out to dinner, Jemima Shore Investigator. Would you accept?'

Jemima thought of their conversation in Gregory's cottage and gave her famous smile, the lovely wide deliberate one which made people of both sexes think she was a sweet person and fall in love with her on television. 'I warn you,' she said. 'Vulnerable I may be, but emotionally insecure I am not. Not in the slightest. And I've no intention of starting now.'

'Oh don't apologize,' Gregory gave a grand wave of the hand. 'I was thinking of changing my type anyway. Keeping up with the times. Isn't it supposed to be good for one's art? You would know about that sort of thing.'

He took her hand and found she was clutching a sea-shell. She had found it in the pocket of her red jacket. It was the souvenir cockleshell which Cherry had presented to her that first Sunday morning by the sea.

Gregory bent and kissed the hand which held the shell.

'Would you accept?' he repeated. 'I might ask you to more than that. Do you like France?'

'Pre-revolutionary Paris?' enquired Jemima. She was still smiling but by now it was the unforced smile familiar to her friends.

'Yes, if you like. Other things might follow. We could discuss that.'

'Paris anyway,' said Jemima Shore.

ABOUT THE AUTHOR

ANTONIA FRASER is the author of eight mysteries featuring Jemima Shore Investigator, *Your Royal Hostage*, *Oxford Blood*, *Cool Repentance*, *A Splash of Red*, *Quiet as a Nun*, *The Wild Island*, *Jemima Shore's First Case and Other Stories*, and most recent, *The Cavalier Case*. A television series based on the Jemima Shore mysteries was telecast nationwide in 1983. In 1986 Antonia Fraser was chairman of the Crime Writers Association.

The author of several acclaimed historical biographies, among them *Mary: Queen of Scots*, *Cromwell*, and the recent *The Warrior Queens*, she lives in London with her husband, the dramatist Harold Pinter.

If you enjoyed Jemima Shore in *Cool Repentance*, you'll want to read her next adventure, *The Wild Island*, which Bantam publishes in October 1991.

The following is an exciting preview of *The Wild Island* by ANTONIA FRASER.

A Highland Welcome

As Jemima Shore arrived at Inverness Station, it was early morning but already the sun was shining. She thought: I'm arriving in Paradise. At that moment a man's voice said in her ear:

'All this way for a funeral.' It was an intimate voice. Almost purring. Jemina felt uncomfortably startled. She looked around.

Behind her a man of a certain age, tall, cadaverous, was bending down to pick up a suitcase. A younger man of much the same ilk was standing beside him. Possibly they were related. Both were dressed with extreme formality for the place – a station – and the time – it was 8.30 a.m. Jemima had just emerged from her sleeper. She did not feel up to such a situation, at least until she had had a cup of coffee. Whichever of the two men had spoken, it was nothing to do with her. She turned her head back and concentrated on the prospect of a porter.

'It's not all that bad, Colonel Henry,' said a second voice. 'In fact, in some ways it's good. In some ways it's very good indeed.'

Jemima shivered. She was glad she did not know, and

never would know, anything more about a funeral to which it was possible to have anything but unmixed reactions of sorrow. She stepped firmly onto the platform. She had come here to get away from that sort of thing. The first sight which met her eyes was an enormous splashed scarlet graffiti on a hoarding opposite.

'Up the Red Rose!' it screamed and then something beneath in what looked like Gaelic, as well as an old separate sort of calligraph, which she couldn't make out at all. The scarlet letters were imposed wilfully on another, more formally written, white notice. To her irritation, she found herself trying to make it out instead of concentrating on the task of finding a porter, or even a barrow. Stronger men than her, with dogs and gun cases to reinforce their claim, were apparently engaging all conceivable porterage. 'A Highland Welcome', the original notice had read. That at least was friendly.

Of course the inhabitants of the Highlands could still welcome Jemima weekly on their television sets, if they were so minded. As 'Jemima Shore, Investigator' in a series put out by Megalith Television under that title, she generally found her way into the ratings. Jemima's speciality was in fact serious-minded sociological enquiry – housing, deprived families, these were the kind of topics which interested her; but the title of the series played on the notion of an amateur detective. That title had been an early inspiration of her boss, Cy Fredericks. Sometimes she felt that it had become almost too memorable, too much of a catch-phrase for journalists and cartoonists alike. But MTV, entranced by the series' prolonged success, would not dream of changing it.

Before her departure she had recorded what seemed like a monumental number of programmes in her new series.

The public would switch on. But she herself would be absent – in Paradise. The sun was still shining. In fact it had been shining all of the ten minutes since her arrival at Inverness Station and not a drop of rain in sight.

She needed a rest from curiosity. All the same, who were they welcoming? 'HRH,' those were the next letters, partly obscured by the word 'Red.' After that it was easy: 'A Highland Welcome to HRH Princess Sophie of Cumberland.' So Hurricane Sophie, as television had irreverently nicknamed the young Princess, was visiting the Highlands, was she?

That was yet another fact which need not concern Jeremima Shore. Funerals, royal visits, none of that was going to stop her enjoying a well-deserved rest away from it all. And on an island. Could anything be further away from it all than a Scottish island in the middle of a fast-flowing river, complete with cliffs and chasms to protect its privacy?

Two men watched her alight. Unlike the funeral party, this second pair were dressed in such a nondescript fashion as to rouse exactly that suspicion which they presumably intended to avoid.

'Look, Miller, that's Jemima Shore,' said the more stolid-seeming of the two. 'I fancy her.' He made his approval sound like an announcement from the pulpit.

'She was on the box last night,' the man named Miller spoke wonderingly.

'She's always on the box.'

'But she's not always at Inverness Station. And come to think of it, Tyne, nor are we. Where's HRH then?'

'HRH is putting on the finishing touches. Plenty of time.' The man named Tyne continued to look lugubriously after Jemima Shore, whose figure was vanishing down the platform. Her hair, its pure Madonna-like style made famous by television, ruffled slightly in the breeze. 'My wife fancies her too. She's somewhat the same type, my wife. Same colouring and hair style. Once in a shop, someone came up to her . . .'

A discreet cough interrupted these reminiscences, and as a glimpse of something bright and girlish, red, a coat, a hat, perhaps, was seen through the corridor window, both men proceeded to give their full attention to the interior of the train, rather than the outside world of the platform.

If Jemima Shore noticed the heads turning at all, it was in some automatic register of her brain. It meant absolutely nothing to her. The only sign of recognition she would welcome this morning would be from her future landlord, Charles Beauregard. And he was to convey her, rapidly she hoped, away from the panoply of Inverness Station *en fête* to her much-desired Highland retreat.

But twenty minutes later, sitting in the Railway Hotel, whose name belied its distinct if old-fashioned grandeur, there was still no Charles Beauregard to rescue Jemima Shore. She was now surrounded by her luggage, one of the dog-and-gun-case set having condescended to share a vast truck with her. But the effect of the multitude of suitcases distributed round her in the lounge of the hotel was to make her feel like someone who had been shipwrecked. It was expensive American luggage acquired during her last trip to the States and her enthusiastic young secretary Cherry had insisted on having it all stamped with her full name.

'Oh, Jem, you never know when it might help. Your name being so famous in every corner of the globe. In a tight corner, it might prove invaluable.' Cherry had a vivid if cliché-ridden imagination. To her, all corners were tight, and all names in television famous throughout the universe.

Now, Jemima reflected sardonically, here was a tight corner indeed. Herself sitting with her luggage in a remote corner of the world — surely the Highlands of Scotland qualified for that — with absolutely no way of getting to the holiday cottage she had rented for a month. No telephone. No directions. And an address which at the time had struck her as infinitely romantic, but now as rather ludicrously imprecise: 'Eilean Fas, Invernessshire.'

The staff of the Railway Hotel was amiability itself. Part of this amiability extended to the fact that its members had no objection to her sitting there indefinitely; they neither pressured her into partaking of breakfast, or otherwise enquired of her intentions. But it was no good pretending that this mountain of luggage proclaiming the name of Jemima Shore was cutting any ice with them whatsoever.

Jemima took out Charles Beauregard's letter which was rapidly becoming her last link with her projected holiday. 'Beauregard Estate Office,' it was headed, 'Kilbronnack.'

Dear Miss Shore,

This is to confirm the arrangement made over the telephone with your secretary. You will rent the cottage known as Tigh Fas on Eilean Fas for one month starting from . . .

Yes, right day, right month. Not that Cherry could fail, but clearly Beauregard Estates could and in a sense had done so. The letter ended:

As Eilean Fas is difficult to find, and the bridge rather tricky, it seems simplest if I meet you in Inverness with the Land-Rover. I can explain details about the cottage, heating, etc, then and hand over the keys.

I should tell you that you won't be able to get television on Eilean Fas but if there is anything special you want to see you can always come over to the Castle to watch it.

I look forward to meeting you.

The letter itself was carefully typed, and the signature: Charles Edward Beauregard, careful – even measured – in the writing. But there was a scrawled PS., where the writing was larger and not so tidy. It gave the impression of being written under some stronger impulse than the mere details of a holiday let:

PS. There is another matter concerning Eilean Fas which I should like to talk to you about personally. It can't be put in a letter.

Jemima Shore, however, was not the slightest bit interested in the personal details of the island, nor for that matter how and when to watch television in the Highlands – perish the thought! She wanted a Land-Rover and breakfast, preferably in that order. In short she wanted a Highland Welcome, such as had been promised to Princess Sophie – or any welcome. But if not, at least breakfast.

Jemima made a decision. She went to the reception desk and said in her most pleasant, brisk manner: 'My name is Jemima Shore.'

The receptionist was quite a young girl with dark hair and healthy pink cheeks. Jemima did not pause for any possible reaction. 'And I am waiting here for Mr. Charles Beauregard. If he arrives and asks for me, will you tell him I am in the dining room having breakfast?'

But the girl behind the desk continued to stare at Jemima. Her mouth was truly open, a rare phenomenon. And she said nothing at all. Jemima wasn't even quite certain she had taken in the message. As for this fan reaction, it was all that Cherry could have hoped for. So she repeated:

'Mr. Charles Beauregard. You know Mr. Beauregard?' The letter had stated the arrangement clearly enough: 'We'll meet at the Railway Hotel, where they know me and Alistair, the head porter, is an old friend of mine.'

The girl gave a strangled sound which could at least be interpreted as 'Aye,' and immediately dived through the little door at the back of the reception desk cubicle.

Jemima passed into the dining room where a series of vast pictures of steam trains rushing through Highland gorges enlivened the otherwise tomb-like room. There were a number of scattered breakfasters. Two of them, seated at a table near the door, were conspicuous in their dark suits. Jemima recognized them from the train and that snatch of rather eerie conversation. The rest wore tweeds, jeans, thick jerseys and even – on one very stout and elderly man – a kilt.

A huge dog was roaming about among the tables. A labrador? Or was it a St. Bernard? Its head came up nearly to the level of the table. Jemima was vague about dogs, the intricacies of their breeding and maintenance never having penetrated her world of television – and she herself never having led that kind of settled domestic life which would either inspire her or enable her to own one. Jemima felt an affinity for cats, cats headed by her own long-haired white-pawed tabby, with her mackerel markings, Colette.

This dog was beige, although that was probably the wrong word when applied to a dog. Jemima, however, admired the colour beige; it was in fact her favourite colour and she was wearing it at the moment. Beige, a great deal of it, including beige trousers, from a man's tailor (for free, as a discreet advertisement), beige silk shirt (Yves St. Laurent, in no way for free), beige and white pullover (ditto). Even the boots beneath the tailored trousers were dark beige.

The dog, she thought, would make an artistic addition to the ensemble. The dog seemed to think so too. He came snuffling up to the table where the waiter had installed her, wagging his tail as though he hoped to sweep the room with it, and disturbing many tablecloths round him as a result. He put his huge head in Jemima's lap and looked at her passionately.

'Jacobite – here boy.' The dog turned and bounded with instant obedience in the direction of his master. It was an impressive performance. Although Jemima could not easily imagine anyone, man or beast, or even woman, disobeying that voice.

instant obedience in the direction of his master. It was an impressive performance. Although Jemima could not easily imagine anyone, man or beast, or even woman, disobeying that voice.

Moodily, she ordered a breakfast of things Scottish, more because she thought she ought to, than because she was any longer very hungry: finnan haddock, which was delicious. The coffee was awful. She sipped it, wondering whether the next step was to ring up Cherry – a confession of failure considering how firmly she had announced: 'I'm away for a month, Cherry. No letters which aren't urgent, which means no letters. No calls – you can't telephone me anyway and I'm not going to trudge to a Scottish call box to call you. No telegrams if you can resist it.' Cherry loved telegrams, whose language satisfied the dramatic side of her nature. No, she really did not want to telephone Cherry just twelve hours after that conversation.

How maddening for the Estate Office not to give its telephone number on the writing paper. Kilbronnack itself must have telephones even if the islanders didn't.

At that point in her musings she was aware of the older man in the dark suit standing over her. For a moment, confused, she thought he had come to say something about the dog, since Jacobite had followed his master back across the room and was once more lifting his nose to the table, sniffing the elixir of the remains of Jemima's breakfast.

'Miss Shore?' he was saying. 'Good morning. I'm Henry Beauregard.'

Jemima's first reaction was enormous relief that at last a Beauregard — if not the right one, at least a member of the family — was taking an interest in her cause.

'Ailsa at the desk was telling me you were having some difficulty in getting to the funeral,' remarked this Beauregard. He really did have a most attractive voice when it was lowered. In fact, altogether Henry Beauregard was an attractive as well as a distinguished-looking man, with his bony face set off by thick hair, grey but showing streaks of what must have been the original black. Jemima thought of Hamlet's father, 'a sable silvered.' Although there was nothing particularly fatherly in the manner of Henry Beauregard. And his hair too was curiously long for a man who in other ways was so conventionally dressed. It added to the romanticism of his appearance.

However, Henry Beauregard, attractive as he might be, appeared to be under a slight misapprehension as to the reason for her presence in the Highlands.

'Oh no,' said Jemima quickly. 'There's been a mistake. I was trying to leave a message for Charles Beauregard. Your brother or cousin or something? Anyway, he's coming to fetch me. I thought the girl didn't understand at the time.'

Henry Beauregard stared at her. For such a totally poised man he looked genuinely startled.

'I'm afraid there's no mistake, Miss Shore,' he said after a pause. 'And my nephew will hardly be coming to fetch you, I fear. You see, we are on our way to his funeral. Charles Beauregard is dead.'

At Annie Laurance's Death on Demand bookstore, murder is often more than just a reading experience and the mysteries are just leaping off the shelves.

CAROLYN HART

Carolyn Hart's Annie and Max are two of mystery readers' best loved characters and in these award-winning books you'll join them on their adventures of mystery, danger and several volumes of murder most foul.